LOVE AT FIRST BIGHT

Deep Space Mission Corps 1

Tymber Dalton

D1521981

MENAGE AMOUR

Siren Publishing, Inc.
www.SirenPublishing.com

A SIREN PUBLISHING BOOK
IMPRINT: Ménage Amour

LOVE AT FIRST BIGHT
Copyright © 2009 by Tymber Dalton

ISBN-10: 1-60601-343-2
ISBN-13: 978-1-60601-343-4

First Printing: June 2009

Cover design by Jinger Heaston
All cover art and logo copyright © 2009 by Siren Publishing, Inc.

Printed in the U.S.A.

PUBLISHER
Siren Publishing, Inc.
www.SirenPublishing.com

DEDICATION

To my best buddy, Chuck, who helped make me the space geek I am today. Who told us those years of watching the original Star Trek and Doctor Who and playing RPGs would never pay off?

LOVE AT FIRST BIGHT

Deep Space Mission Corps 1

TYMBER DALTON
Copyright © 2009

Prologue

From the *Earth Almanac*, Copyright 2668:

"While similar in appearance to the primitive automobiles and trucks originally developed in the twentieth century, modern ground vehicles share a lineage with their early counterparts and little else. Today's modern, lightweight polymers mean vehicle weight is a fraction of the old metal vehicles, with a thousand times the strength and durability. And the newest generation of Solectric hybrid fission engines are clean, which drastically reduced carbon emissions in the world upon their initial introduction in the year 2284. Within fifty years, greenhouse gas levels had dropped to levels not seen before the original historic Industrial Revolution period…"

Chapter One

With the graduation ceremony over, an underwhelming sense of completion washed over her.

Done. Eight long years of classes and training and practice and...

Oh, Hades. Done.

Now what?

Emilia Hypatia's best friend, Donna, slid her hand-held reader over the coffee shop table toward her, and pointed to a highlighted advertisement.

"What about that, Emi?"

Emi took the reader and studied the ad her friend had notated.

Adventure! Training! Excellent Pay!

We're looking for a few good men—and especially women—to train for the DSM Corps. New missions leaving as soon as six weeks. Trained medical professionals earn substantial bonuses. Five year tenure required.

Emi sat back. "Five years is a long time."

"Excellent pay and substantial bonuses would buy you your own place, *Doctor* Hypatia. Set you up for life. You know the Deep Space Mission Corps makes millionaires out of people."

Emi snorted, pushing the reader back across to Donna. "Yeah, if you survive."

"They haven't lost a crew in over ten years. I saw it on the news the other night." Donna paused. "It would get you far away from Dagbert."

"Daniel."

"Whatever."

That *would* be nice. Ever since the night three weeks earlier when she caught him screwing one of her chem lab classmates, Emi had been dodging his attempts to get back together with her.

Later that night, Emi looked up the ad on her reader, noted the code, and requested an information packet. Couldn't hurt to check into it, right? Not like she had any family. Her mother and father had died ten years earlier in 2659, when a meteor slammed into their research station on the moon, near Mare Serenitatis. A totally preventable freak accident for which the government compensated her and provided a complete paid college education.

Now she was a trained healer, with holistic, medical, and surgical rankings, not to mention the empath training and minor in psych. She could probably name her price and have her pick of the juiciest job appointments.

Yet she wanted more.

* * * *

The information packet was in Emi's email the next morning. She browsed it, interested. Safety wasn't guaranteed, of course, but unless it was a hell of a lot riskier than they let on, they were honest that it wasn't a sure-fire return trip home. Those who did return home, however, would be set for over ten million bucks and a pick of future assignments within the DSMC, on or off-Earth, as desired. As an Alpha-ranked healer, she'd earn an additional five mil bonus.

They had a one o'clock interview slot available.

Why in Hades not? She took it.

* * * *

The DSMC complex sat on a wind-scoured desert plain minutes outside of New Phoenix, grouped with several other military services sharing the gigantic, sprawling dry dock facility. It was the DSMC's main compound, where ships were brought for extensive retrofits before being sent to the orbiting docking hubs to leave Earth.

The receptionist looked up Emi's appointment information and directed her to the correct building. After twenty minutes of playing twenty questions with a lab assistant, Emi was ushered into a small interview room and took a seat in front of a large desk. A few minutes later, an older man joined her.

"Sorry to keep you waiting, Dr. Hypatia." He shook her hand. "I'm Dr. Louis Graymard, the personnel acquisitions supervisor."

"Emi is fine."

"All right." He sat and consulted his hand-held console. "You're twenty-six. You just graduated?"

"Yes."

"Graduate Alpha Healer Ranking, very nice. We don't get enough of those. Psych minor, empath training. That's a bonus." He looked at her. "Why are you interested in one of our positions? You could have your pick of jobs here."

She shrugged. Why not the truth? "I have no family. I have no boyfriend. I've got a couple of degrees and a dwindling government settlement for the death of my parents. So why not?"

"You realize it's a five year contractual commitment? There's no getting out there in deep space and saying, 'Sorry, I want to go home now.'"

"I have no home to go to. I have to be out of the school dorms by the end of next month anyway."

He nodded and noted something in his console. "You went through the information packet we sent?"

She had, and that's where her questions started. "Let's cut the bullshit. What exactly is meant by crew will be expected to 'mutually care for each other?' Are we talking doing each other's laundry, or doing each other?"

Graymard laughed. "Very perceptive. The second. No force will ever be allowed, of course. Our crews are fitted with compatibility chips."

"Which tells me bubkis."

"It means they can't force you, you can't force them. Likewise, you won't find it comfortable to let them…suffer, as it were. Or them you. It also insures fidelity amongst the crew to prevent straying. They are removed upon returning from the mission."

"I don't want to spend five years stuck with some ugly-ass jerks."

"Oh, it doesn't work like that. If you don't find a compatible crew, you aren't assigned. It's no fun for anyone if it's…well, not fun."

At least they couldn't cheat on her.

"I won't sleep with a girl."

"You wouldn't be asked to do that, then."

Emi sat back in her chair. "I get to pick the crew I work with?"

"Absolutely. Of course, there are the usual precautions. Everyone is screened for health concerns, and the compatibility chips also take care of the birth control issue."

She thought about it. She'd looked through all the paperwork and contracts last night, had nothing here on Earth, wanted to get as far away from Daniel as possible. Why not try something new? Sow some wild oats. She could settle down later.

"All right, I'm game. What's the next step?"

"We'll take you first for a complete physical, including a brain scan, that takes a couple of hours. Then we'll introduce you to the crews."

"I won't commit to anything until I find a crew I like."

"You won't be signing anything unless or until you find a compatible crew. Contingent upon passing the scans and other evaluations, of course. If you didn't find a compatible crew and still wanted to be kept in consideration, we could offer you an on-Earth position until you're matched with a suitable crew."

"So I don't lose, is what you're saying?"

He laughed. "No, you're actually the one with the upper hand."

* * * *

Graymard escorted her to another building, talking as they walked. "We're assembling four-person crews right now, we call them 'four-packs.' It would be you and three men."

She hoped her knees wouldn't buckle. "*Three* men? No one else, no other women to, eh, help out?"

"No." He stopped and turned to face her. "Having second thoughts?"

She swallowed hard. "No. Let's do this."

Holy crap. Three guys. It hadn't quite slammed home until then. She'd figured one, maybe two. *Three* guys?

Well, at least it wasn't more. And she *had* wanted something different.

The converse was three guys who depended on her, and who wouldn't be cheating on her.

Couldn't cheat on her.

Maybe not such a bad deal after all.

The scanning center was filled with rows of dozens of units that looked like old-fashioned tanning beds without the lights, some of which were already occupied. After Emi gave blood and urine specimens and went through a physical, a technician hooked her up and made sure she was comfortable.

"This takes about two hours, feel free to doze off. We can adjust the temperature, any of that, just tell us." He handed her a small cup of clear liquid. "Take this, it helps with the results."

She sniffed it, but it was odorless and colorless and tasted like water. "Doze off, huh?"

He smiled. "People usually do."

Chapter Two

Emi looked up as someone shined a bright light into her eyes. It felt like she'd closed them for only a minute.

The brain scan technician smiled. "Did you have a nice nap?" He helped Emi sit up.

"I guess. How long have I been asleep?"

"A couple of hours. It's better when you sleep, because the results are more accurate."

"Oh. Okay." He helped her stand and led her to a recovery room to make sure the sedative had completely worn off. Dr. Graymard walked in a few minutes later, smiling.

"Very good, Emi. Everything looks fine, the lab work came back with no issues. You're eligible to move on to the next stage."

"What's that?"

"Well, if you're still willing, we'll introduce you to three crews. If any of them interest you, we'll match you with them for further training."

"Introduce how? I don't want to get into space and realize they all stink in bed." Somehow it didn't feel real, talking about her future sex life like that. In fact, she still felt a little fuzzy, disconnected. Must be a residual effect of the sedative they gave her.

"Crew pairing is the toughest part of the process. You take as much time as you need—within reason, of course—with each crew. The usual procedure is to go to their ship in dry dock and visit them, talk with them, and see if there's any initial chemistry. A first meeting, then make an appointment to go back later for another visit if you wish to get to know them better. Feel free to do whatever you need to do to get to know them before making a decision."

"By that you mean…"

He smiled. "It's usually helpful for crew who have initial attraction to have a test run, as it were, in an intimate setting, to see if they are a match. It's better to find that out sooner rather than later."

"What if they don't like me?"

"I sincerely doubt *that* will be an issue."

* * * *

Actually, the first step was inserting a compatibility chip. "The crews already have them," Graymard explained. "This will make sure there is no force allowed. If you're not assigned to a crew this time, yours will be deactivated until the next round of introductions."

"Once I'm paired with a crew, what, we're synced or something?"

"Correct."

It was completely painless, the needle inserting the small capsule under the skin in the back of her neck. She never even felt the needle prick. "Sort of like microchipping an animal?"

"Similar theory. We can also track the crew, but only if the ship's emergency beacon is activated. You'll be synced to the ship and other crew members in that way, so there are no privacy concerns to worry about."

* * * *

It was already late afternoon as Graymard led her across the compound to the dry dock facility. The first ship was the Kendall Kant. Graymard gave her a small hand-held console.

"Here's their information. Feel free to take notes, whatever. The other crews and their dry dock locations are also there."

There were approximately two dozen ships docked in the hangar, maybe a dozen of those with DSMC markings, the others from

Merchant Marines and the ISNC. He pointed to two other large ships. "The Braynow Gaston and the Tamora Bight."

"How long should I talk to these guys today?"

"As long or as little as you wish. Depends on whether any of them strike your fancy. If you don't like any of these crews, we start over with a new set for you to consider. They're all on board right now, just send them a notice requesting permission to board—"

"Permission?" She arched her eyebrow.

"It's an old holdover from the maritime days. Just a formality. The Kendall Kant is already expecting you. I sent them a message before we left the building. So whenever you want to go…"

It was a hundred-yard walk to the main gangway leading to the hatch. Where they now stood, a short distance away was a construction table with chairs loosely gathered around.

"Can I sit for a minute and look through the info?"

"Of course. Did you want me to stay?"

She shook her head. She was nervous enough. "No, that's okay."

He handed her a small cell phone. "If you need me, my number's programmed into it. Feel free to contact me twenty-four/seven. You can also message me through the hand-held. Good luck."

Emi watched him walk away before she sat and consulted the console.

According to the records, the Kendall Kant was a ship of a type called a medium-heavy, a mid-sized, deep space freight transport being converted for exploration work. Built for cargo, not speed. The crew were transfers from the ISNC—Interstellar Naval Corps.

Ugh, military.

She called up the crew bios. *Ooh, pictures.*

Not bad looking, each of them with close-cropped hair, muscles, and unsmiling in their ID photos. The captain was a lifer, apparently, over fifteen years in the ISNC before switching to exploration. The crew had been together three years, with the first officer in the ISNC for seven years, and the mate in for six. Highly decorated with many military honors amongst them.

The Braynow Gaston's crew came from the other end of the spectrum—geeks. All three crew members transferred over from the NSI—National Science Institute. Not much in the way of deep space experience, with the captain just off a three-year training stint in the ISNC. The ship was also a medium-heavy, but of a slightly different configuration.

The three officers were also not bad-looking despite their serious expressions. Highly recommended in terms of their professional achievements and commendations.

So far, no ugly grunts.

The Tamora Bight's crew looked to be an odd choice. The ship was called a full heavy, over a third larger than the other two and being retrofitted from military outpost cargo duties. The crew were Merchant Marine transfers but had worked together for twenty years, all of that spent on space duty and with quite a few commendations between them. Ironically the most experienced of the three crews, and the oldest crew in the running.

The crew pictures…The captain, Aaron Lucio, forty-two. He'd be handsome if he smiled. He looked like a brooding man, with deep brown eyes she couldn't fathom, but his serious stare wasn't the hard, professional glare of the first two crews. First Officer Caphis Bates, forty, had shaggy blond hair, not long but definitely overdue for a haircut, playful green eyes, and an infectious smile. She found his appearance to be an interesting contradiction when she studied his impressive service record. From his picture, he didn't appear to fit the role of experienced officer. Mate Ford Caliban was forty-one, and his blue eyes and teasing, sly grin stirred something inside her.

In the spirit of disclosure it was noted that while the Tamora Bight's crew was experienced and highly decorated, they had so far in their six months at the dry dock facility wracked up more demerits than any other crew in DSMC history.

Ever.

Because the DSMC wasn't military, crews didn't get disciplinary action beyond pay cuts and mission assignment withdrawals, but apparently they were the bad boys of the dry docks.

Fantastic.

She switched back to the Kendall Kant's crew file and took a deep breath before making her way to the main hatch. A low tone sounded when she stepped up to the closed hatchway, and then the intercom crackled to life.

A male voice spoke. "Dr. Hypatia?"

"Yes."

The hatchway slid open. "Permission to come aboard, ma'am."

"Um, thank you."

She nervously stepped through the hatch and looked around. She'd never been inside a spaceship before, even though she'd seen pictures her parents had sent home from their journeys. A sterile-looking corridor stretched out into the distance before her. She hesitated, unsure what to do.

The man spoke again. "Wait there, please. The mate is on his way to meet you."

She wished they called the second officer something else, considering what her duties would entail, but that wasn't her decision. "Okay. Thank you."

A few minutes later, a man turned the corner down the hallway and strode toward her. Big, beefy, broad-shouldered, he apparently grew taller the closer he got.

Whoa.

Exactly how tall he was became apparent when he stopped in front of her. "Dr. Hypatia?"

He was a good foot taller than her, and she was a respectable five-seven. "Uh, yeah. That's me." His tight T-shirt stretched across his huge chest, defining every sculpted muscle. And he had quite a few.

She might not mind playing doctor with him.

While his face wasn't cold, it was…appraising would work. His eyes unapologetically traveled up and down her body and—was that a slight frown?

"Nice to meet you, Doctor." He held out his hand. She shook it but got the distinct impression he wasn't thrilled. "Follow me, please." She knew his name was Gregor Davis from his crew file, but he didn't introduce himself.

With that he turned, and she had to rush to keep up with his long strides. She wasn't a natural empath, but she'd had extensive training, enough to earn a class two ranking. If she wasn't mistaken, this guy wasn't totally happy. Not hostile, but he was certainly chilly.

They wound through corridors and passageways and walked deep into the ship. Hades, she'd get lost in this damn place. They ended up in a common area, where two other men waited at a dining table. Both men stood at their arrival. Emi noticed all three men were physically stacked, dressed in identical T-shirts and work pants. Apparently the military was turning out tough guys in more ways than one.

They also wore stern looks nearly identical to Davis'.

The captain stepped forward. "Dr. Hypatia, I'm Captain Elloy. This is First Officer Johnson and Mate Davis."

Each man nodded, as did she.

"You can call me Emi, that's fine."

"No offense, Dr. Hypatia, but we tend to stick to regulations about addressing crew."

"Oh. Um, okay."

He indicated a seat at the head of the table. They waited to sit until after she did. *Well, they got points for that, at least.*

Captain Elloy sat at the far end of the table. "Did you have any questions?"

The other two crew members flanked him. While handsome and certainly with great bodies to match, they didn't fill her with lust.

They barely filled her with like.

"Yeah. Why are you going into exploration when you were military?"

She tuned out after three minutes. Twenty minutes later, he finished droning and the other two men nodded.

"Okay," she said. "That was…detailed."

"I run a tight ship, Doctor. It's how I've managed to stay alive all these years."

"That's always a plus. I'm rather fond of living." They didn't even crack a smile.

Greeeeeat.

The men stood, and the captain spoke. "Davis will show you around the crew quarters."

"Don't you have any questions for me?" she asked.

He shook his head. "We already reviewed your file and found that your qualifications are adequate."

Adequate? She'd graduated at the top of her class as an Alpha-ranked healer. And his eyes didn't look very pleased. "But?"

He frowned. "I don't understand."

"There's more to your statement." That much she *could* sense.

The men exchanged another glance. "Well, we'll have quite a bit of time ahead of us before we ship out. I'm sure it won't be difficult, with our help, to get you into a training regimen to improve your physical condition."

She swallowed, hard, to keep the acerbic retort in her mouth. She instead opted for, "Improve my physical condition?"

The captain nodded. "Not that you're not attractive, because you are, we all agree on that. For a mission like this, every crew member's life depends on the others. Each member must be in top physical condition."

"So, you think I'm fat?"

Apparently he wasn't much in the relationship department because he didn't even flinch at the question. "No, but your musculature isn't as developed as it should be for endurance and strength. I mean, for an on-Earth assignment, that's fine. In a mission such as ours, however, there are certain expectations. All crew members must be in top physical condition. I'm sure a few months of physical training would bring your BMI and other stats within regulations.

Regulations?

Oh, she and this dude would be butting heads if she picked them. Still, they were all good-looking. No reason to discount them—yet.

"Let's get the tour out of the way," she said.

Davis showed her around the crew quarters. The men each had their own small cabin with a standard single bunk. The only way she could tell whose was whose was the nameplate on the door. There were no signs of personality in any of the rooms.

"This would be your quarters." He opened a door, and the room looked…identical.

"Those are pretty small beds."

"Space is tight. It's not like everyone will be sleeping together. They're adequate for what they'll be used for."

That was about as romantic as a root canal. "Anything else I should know about you guys?"

"Feel free to ask whatever you want, ma'am."

"No Emi, huh?"

Not even a hint of a smile. "Doctor, we're preparing for a deep-space mission. Our focus must be on our jobs. Surely a professional with your academic qualifications can understand that?"

She felt something else. "Tell me about your captain. He makes the calls around here, doesn't he?"

"Of course he does. He's the captain."

"I think I want to talk to him again."

He led her without further comment through the ship to the bridge. Captain Elloy looked annoyed at the intrusion. "Yes, Doctor?"

"I have a few more questions."

"All right."

Might as well grab the bull by the balls. "How would the scheduling be set up?"

He frowned. "The crew duty roster?"

"Uh, yeah. You know, sleeping arrangements."

"All crew sleeps in their own quarters."

Stupid man. "Okay, the sexual arrangements." *Might as well get used to saying it.*

"You'll have duties other than that, obviously. You'll be trained to take watches, maintenance, other duties. Cross-trained in some of the systems monitoring, light weaponry as well, I'm sure."

"You didn't answer the question."

"I'm sure that's negotiable when we first set it up, but the easiest way would be to schedule you off one day a week in terms of sex, and with three male crew, that gives everyone two times a week, and then we'd work around your…monthly issue."

Apparently he wasn't comfortable talking about that. *No midnight tampon runs for this dude.*

"So what happens if the mood strikes someone and it's not their scheduled night?"

"We wouldn't deviate from the set duty roster unless someone is ill or injured, or there are circumstances preventing us from maintaining it, such as mission duties. That's the best way to avoid any unpleasant personal situations."

"Okay then." She stuck out her hand and shook with all three men. "Thank you for your time. I'll let you know. I have two other crews to interview before I make any decisions." She consulted the hand-held. "The Braynow Gaston and the Tamora Bight."

At the mention of the third ship, the men broke out into their version of hysterical laughter, which was amused smirks. Elloy might have snorted.

"The Tamora Bight? Really. I didn't think they were seriously sending *them* out."

Emi immediately felt defensive for the crew she hadn't even met yet. "Why?"

Elloy's professional mask slipped back into place. "Dr. Hypatia, I would prefer not to get into that discussion. I don't want to be accused by other crews of trying to scuttle their chances with you. Let it suffice to say it's not braggadocio on our part that we think you'll find us the most qualified crew of the three you are evaluating."

"Right. Thanks." Without further comment, Davis led her back to the hatch.

She stepped down the gangway and sent Graymard a message from the hand-held.

Kendall Kant—No. Fucking. Way. Not enough money in the world.

Send.

Chapter Three

On her walk to the Braynow Gaston, Emi figured out how to send a request. Within a minute they replied, welcoming her.

First Officer Alex Parisi waited for her at the hatch and greeted her with a smile.

"Permission to come aboard?" She hoped she didn't sound too snarky, but her experience with the Kendall Kant's crew had left a bad taste in her mouth.

He actually laughed. "Permission granted, Doctor. Please follow me."

She relaxed a little. Parisi talked with her on the walk to the common area.

And talked.

And talked.

If she'd been paying attention, she would have known his detailed life history by the time they finished their walk through the ship. Emi, however, tuned him out after two minutes, and was relieved to see the other two men waiting. Both stood when she walked through the door. They were all handsome, better looking in real life without the totally serious mugshot expressions they wore in their ID pictures.

Okay, that's another plus. They're cute and polite. While not as stacked with rock-hard muscles as the military guys, they were all in great shape.

"How formal will we be in terms of titles?" Emi asked.

The men shrugged and exchanged slightly puzzled looks. "What do you mean?" Captain John Tarrence asked.

"Any problem calling me Emi?"

"Whatever you want us to call you. You can call us by our first names, if you want," he said.

Apparently her "physical condition" wasn't an issue because they never brought it up. After a few minutes of pleasantries and getting acquainted, their questions started. It was obvious the three men had backgrounds in science and research, because they were the ones doing all the asking. After ten minutes, Emi held up her hands.

"Time out, boys. My turn."

The three men actually blushed and sat back. "Sorry," the captain apologized. "We get carried away sometimes."

They were nice, if not geeky. That wasn't a bad thing. Maybe they were wild boys inside. At least they had more personality than the other crew. "Where's my quarters? Well, if I choose your ship."

They exchanged a nervous look. The captain spoke. "*Your* quarters?"

"I'd like to see what my quarters would look like."

They didn't respond. She'd finally managed to shut them up. *Wow.*

"Um, there are only three crew cabins," the captain eventually admitted.

"Then you're one short, aren't you?"

Now the men were uncomfortable, shifting in their seats, their collective anxious energy almost overwhelming her.

"Well," Captain John said, "we assumed you'd sleep with someone every night—your choice who, of course," he quickly added. "And not even for sex if you weren't in the mood. We thought if you needed to be alone you could use the cabin of whoever was on watch that night."

"No cabin of my own?" They were losing points quick.

"I can talk to the retrofit crew about it if it's an issue, but we had another lab installed on the crew level for additional research capabilities. I'm sure we can accommodate you, if that's what you really need."

The way he said it made her think he thought she wouldn't really need it. More points taken away.

"Well, let's see the crew quarters anyway."

All three men walked with her, trying to make increasingly nervous small talk along the way. While neat and organized, each cabin looked and felt distinctive, with personal effects visible and displayed, and the beds slightly larger than those on the other ship.

Time to get this out of the way. She turned to the men. "You said it'd be my choice of where to sleep every night."

All three men nodded, but that's all they were offering.

"What about the duty roster? Any 'regulations?'" She used finger quotes around the word.

The men exchanged a confused look. The captain spoke. "Well, we all have normal crew duties, and so would you. Maintenance, systems checks, that kind of stuff. And of course you'd be the medical officer. But…um…the extracurricular stuff, that's all up to you. As long as you're…you know…fair."

She softened her voice "Look, I'm as uncomfortable about this as you guys obviously are, so let's just cut to the chase. Is there anything I need to know about ahead of time? Any special…predilections?"

The men frowned in confusion. She closed her eyes and pinched the bridge of her nose. "I'm not a wild and crazy girl. None of you will want me to dress like a dominatrix or swing from the ceiling or anything?"

They quickly shook their heads, their collective blush deepening. The captain appeared to be the group spokesman. "No, we're all pretty boring. I mean, we're not sex fiends or anything." He forced a nervous smile. "I think the term is 'vanilla.'"

Let's push the envelope. "So, like, guy on top? Blow jobs? Hand jobs?" She wasn't excessively experienced. Daniel had been her second lover, and she considered herself an open-minded, but fairly conventional girl. She wasn't adverse to the idea of experimenting a little if she trusted someone, although she hadn't had any opportunity to experiment. She did want to know up front if they had any expectations she wouldn't be able or willing to meet.

She didn't know men were capable of blushing that deeply. They didn't reply.

"I'm not a sex fiend either, guys, don't worry. I just need to know these things up front so I can make an informed decision. I'm assuming you'll all be willing to not leave me hanging, right?"

The men nodded, relieved not to have to say anything.

They made their way back to the common area. While she wasn't sure she wanted to pick them, she would definitely pick them over the first crew of personality-deprived macho men.

She shook hands with them. "Thank you, gentlemen. I appreciate your time. I still have another crew I need to talk to. I wanted to talk to all three crews before I make my preliminary decision about spending more time with any of them."

Tarrence cleared his throat. "Mind if I ask who?"

"I've already interviewed the crew of the Kendall Kant."

At that their faces fell as if anticipating defeat. "Oh."

She felt bad. While she knew it wasn't professional, she added, "I'm pretty confident they are off my list. Personality conflicts."

The men looked hopeful again. "Oh," Tarrence said. "Who's the other crew?"

"The Tamora Bight."

All three men looked shocked, then burst out laughing.

"What?" she asked.

Tarrence's confident grin pissed her off, but she hoped she hid it. Their sudden, smirky self-confidence rubbed her the wrong way.

"I thought we had some *real* competition. I didn't know it was the TB." The men laughed again, as if enjoying an inside joke. Then it hit her they were making fun of the ship's initials, comparing it to a long-eradicated communicable disease.

"What's wrong with the Tamora Bight's crew?"

This was the first wide grin Tarrence and the others had displayed, expressing genuine amusement and relief. "Well," Tarrence said, "they're experienced, to say the least." All three men snickered in an impressively irritating way.

"How about saying more than the least?"

The men exchanged a knowing look. "They're pretty much the polar opposite of the Kendall Kant's crew. Captain Lucio and his *boys*—" how he said that also pissed her off, "—have a lot of service duty…under their belts." The men snickered again, and Captain Tarrence personally escorted her to the main hatch.

He took her hands and held them for a moment. There was no doubt he was good-looking. "Thank you, Emi. It was a pleasure to meet you, and I can safely speak for my *men*—" how he emphasized that managed to piss her off again, "—when I say I hope we'll be spending more time with you soon." He gently squeezed her hands in a tenderly seductive way. For a second, she forgot his arrogant and assumptive attitude.

Five years with these three wouldn't be so bad. Not bad at all.

"Thank you." She returned to the gangway after the hatch slid shut behind her. She sent Graymard another message.

Braynow Gaston, maybe. I'm not taking them off the list yet, need more time with them.

Send.

* * * *

Emi looked up the Tamora Bight and sent them a message. A moment later she received their welcoming reply.

What was it about this crew the others didn't like, other than their apparent bad-boy image? She slowed her pace as she walked down the gangway and studied their personnel files again. There weren't many long-past details on them, just recent history. No details on how they obtained their demerits. Technically, she supposed they could be for anything from murder and mayhem to not docking straight.

Couldn't be too serious or they wouldn't have been assigned a larger ship than the other two crews, right? They weren't in jail or the brig or whatever the frak they called it in the DSMC, so most likely they hadn't broken any laws either.

She hoped.

When Emi arrived at the Tamora Bight's hatch, she waited for an intercom greeting and didn't receive one. She found the recessed panel in the hatchway and pushed a glowing button. A long, irritating moment later, she received a reply.

"Yeah?"

Okay, they lose points for not being prepared. "Hi, I'm Dr. Hypatia—"

"Oh, shit! You're *here*?" There was a moment of desperate, garbled whispers, and the man came back on. "Sorry! Uh, I didn't realize you meant right now. Hold on."

She tried to hold on to her irritation and couldn't. There was something desperately sweet about the man's voice. She wondered which crewman it belonged to.

The intercom crackled again, as if someone had accidentally hit the button. "…I freaking told him to clean that mess up, goddammit! She's here! *Now!*"

"Caph, you're leaning on the intercom," another, deeper male voice calmly said.

"Crap—" It went silent again.

The second voice bore a totally different timbre and demeanor than the first. Calm, steady, in charge. Something about it immediately stirred her.

*Caph must be…*she consulted her hand-held. First Officer Caphis Bates.

She wondered if the other voice belonged to Captain Aaron Lucio.

Emi couldn't help but smile. She was never one for great formalities, despite her training. There was no doubt in her mind that she'd be miserable on the Kendall Kant. The Braynow Gaston's crew…maybe they just came off a little wrong on first impression.

These guys, however, were already living down to their reputation.

After another moment, the intercom crackled to life and the second voice spoke again. The man's smooth, calm tone not only soothed her, but touched someplace deep inside her. She'd like to get to know the owner of that voice.

"Sorry about that, Doctor. I'll let you in. Just follow the main corridor all the way to the very end and take the last doorway on the right. That will put you in the secondary corridor. One of us will catch up with you there."

"Okay." The hatch slid open. She immediately realized this ship was of a different breed than the two medium-heavies she'd been on. Its larger size translated into a more complex layout.

I hope they have a freaking map for this monster.

The corridor stretched nearly two hundred yards by her best guess. From the external size of the vessel, she knew that it wasn't extending the ship's full length. She took the last doorway on the right, and another fifty yards down a running man emerged from a doorway and jogged to meet her. As he drew closer in the dim light she realized he was the mate, Ford Caliban.

When he caught up with her, he held up one finger, leaned over with his hands on his knees, and caught his breath. When he could speak he straightened and apologized. "Sorry, Doc. I was down in cargo. We're not very well organized right now. We're in the middle of inventory."

"Is this a bad time? I could come back—"

"No, no. As long as you don't hold the mess against us." His infectious smile couldn't be denied a reply, and his blue eyes looked even bluer in real life. He wasn't the second voice she'd heard. That must mean it had been Captain Lucio.

"No problem. I understand you're working…" She knew who he was, but she wanted him to introduce himself.

He correctly interpreted her hesitation. "Oh! Sorry. Ford Caliban. Mate." He stuck out a hand and shook, hesitating before letting go of hers. "Do you prefer Doctor Hypatia, or is Doc okay?"

"Emi's fine."

She loved his smile. "Great. Emi. Just call me Ford, we're pretty casual around here. Come on—this way." He stood a few inches taller than her, on the slim side of the spectrum but athletic, naturally muscled, and he moved like a cat. She couldn't help but watch his tight ass as he walked in front of her, leading the way.

Ford led the way through the vast ship. She was surprised at how easy he was to talk to despite his obvious nerves. It took them over five minutes to reach the crew common area. While it didn't look like a bomb had gone off in the past five minutes, it did look like one had exploded within the past few days. It was a mess. Arranged chaos the men apparently understood, not a random disaster like they couldn't pick up after themselves.

Ford looked nervous. "Seriously, I mean, we're not neat freaks or anything, but this is *so* not normally us. Aar decided to go all captain on our asses last week when we lost his stupid spare razors. Now me and Caph have to do a full inventory and get it all tagged and logged. This is one of the neat areas right now. The rest is worse."

Nervous energy washed off him. He was terrified she would refuse them on this basis.

She offered him a kind smile. "It's okay, seriously. I understand. Hey, this is what dry dock is for, right?"

He relaxed a little, and was about to speak when another man bolted into the room, hanging onto the door frame as he rounded the corner. Caphis Bates.

"Holy crap, Caph. Show a little dignity," Ford scolded.

"Sorry, man." Caphis blushed, something that looked incredibly sweet and endearing on the large man's face. "Hiya." He walked forward, hand extended. "Caphis Bates, call me Caph. First officer."

His green eyes dazzled her. *How could they be real?* He was cute, taller and beefier than Ford, but while a large man, he still wasn't a muscle-bound maniac like the grunts had been.

She shook his gigantic hand. While his practically swallowed hers he was gentle, as if afraid to hurt her.

"Call me Emi."

He smiled. She felt a little thump in her chest in response. *Definitely a cutie.*

"Cool. That's pretty." He looked at Ford. "Have you seen Aaron? He said he'd meet us down here."

Ford shook his head. "No, haven't seen him yet."

Caph scooped an armful of supplies off the table and moved them to the floor. "I hope Ford told you we're not normally like this."

Emi laughed. "Yes, he did. It's okay, please don't worry."

Caph also relaxed, reassured by her tone. The three of them sat. Ford and Caph nervously looked at each other.

The men spoke together. "Well." They looked at each other. "Go ahead," they parroted, then both grimaced.

She laughed. "That's interesting."

Ford glared at Caph as if daring him to speak. "That happens a lot. I hope it doesn't freak you out. Aaron calls us the twins."

Caph agreed. "When Aar's in a foul mood, there's been days he's made us take turns speaking so it doesn't happen. If it's not our 'day,' we can't talk around him."

Emi tried to hold back her amused giggle. "Really?"

"Yeah."

The men stared at each other for a moment as if deciding who should speak. Ford looked at her. "Any questions?"

"Don't you think we should wait for the captain?"

Both men looked nervous again. "Yeah," Caph said. "Let me see if I can track him down. He should have been here by now." He stood and walked to an intercom on the wall and paged him. Caph also had a smooth, fluid gait, a natural motion. His broad chest tapered into a narrow waist and tight ass she wouldn't mind...

Yum.

"Hey, Aaron," he paged. "We're in the commons. Mind dropping what you're doing? You're keeping the doc waiting." He winked at her. She knew she didn't imagine the heat flare deep in her belly.

She hadn't had any reaction even remotely like this with the other two crews.

After a long moment, the captain replied. "I'll be there in a few minutes. Go ahead and start without me." The deep-timbred voice of before.

Caph shrugged. "Okay, Cap." He rejoined them at the table. "He's the boss."

Maybe asking them some questions would help put them at ease. "How did you go from Merchant Marines to exploration?"

The men exchanged a glance. Apparently Ford got to do the honors. "We crew together, been together for years. We won't split up. We decided we wanted to do something different, and the DSMC's been after us for a while to transfer over. We've been hauling for a lot of years now. We thought maybe one last big run like this, before we settle down for short hops, it wouldn't be bad. Put some money in the bank, you know?"

"Short hops?"

The men exchanged another glance, but Caph answered. "Yeah, moon runs are minis, day trips. Short hops are anything in this sol-sys. Medium hops are to the range two sol-sys regions. Long hops are any sol-sys beyond that, and anything outside the galaxy."

"What did you do a lot of in the Merchant Marines?"

Ford's turn. "Mostly long hops. Lot of military outposts, frontier stations. Some mediums doing larger transport loads."

They talked for several minutes, the men parroting each other a few more times before Lucio entered the room. She felt him before she saw him, his brooding, unwelcoming glare throwing a nearly visible pall before him.

Ford and Caph fell silent when he entered. He walked to Emi and extended his hand. "Dr. Hypatia, I'm Captain Aaron Lucio." He spoke quietly, the same voice as before, but softer.

She couldn't quite figure him out, was having trouble reading him. They shook hands. "Call me Emi."

He nodded. Instead of sitting with them he leaned against the wall, his arms crossed in front of him. He was handsome, taller than Ford but shorter than Caph, his cautious brown eyes not giving much away. His brown hair with just a sprinkle of grey at the temples lent itself to the overall "leave me alone" air he exuded.

Wow. How could a guy who looks that good come off so chilly?

Ford and Caph exchanged glances, and then Caph spoke. "Um, so. What else?" he asked her.

She looked at Lucio. "You don't want to join us, Captain?"

"I'm okay. I can hear just fine." That was it.

All righty then. She focused on Ford and Caph. As of now, if it was just these two, she'd say yes in a heartbeat. They were sweet and funny and definitely welcoming, albeit apparently very nervous. "You're the third crew I've interviewed today. As I told the other two crews, I wanted to talk to all three if or before I make any tentative decisions."

Lucio spoke up. "Which other crews?"

He wouldn't join them but wanted to speak up? *Annoying.* He made no apologies for asking about the others.

"The Kendall Kant and the Braynow Gaston," she replied.

She watched immediate disappointment paint Ford and Caph's faces. Before she could reassure them, Lucio spoke again. "Doctor, come with me, please."

"What—"

"Please." He pushed off from the wall and walked to the doorway he'd entered, waiting for her.

Casting a look at Ford and Caph, Emi set off after Lucio.

* * * *

Emi had to hurry to catch up with him as his long legs quickly carried him down the corridor.

"Listen, Captain, I don't know what's going on, but—"

He stopped and turned so fast she nearly ran into him. He kept his voice low, probably so it wouldn't carry down to the other men, who hadn't followed. "Those two guys are my crew. I'm responsible for them," he said. "We've been together a lot of years, and I make no apologies."

That confused the hell out of her. "I didn't ask for any apologies—"

"Let's get this over with before they fall any harder for you than they already have."

"What?" But he'd turned and strode away again. She raced to catch up.

"I'm sick of people coming in here and getting those two guys' damn hopes up and then turning us down. I'm tired of the other fucking crews laughing behind our backs because they're not men enough to say it to our faces, and I'm tired of a bunch of pissant wannabes who don't have a fraction of our experience thinking we're some sort of goddamn joke."

Now she stopped, frustrated in addition to being totally confused. "Will you *please* tell me what the fuck you're talking about, Captain Lucio?"

Her tone must have taken him by surprise. He stopped and turned, walking back to her. "You're the tenth one they've sent to us. Another five rejects after you, they'll deny us a mission and we're stuck on short hops for the rest of our careers. Let's get this over with, quit wasting your time and mine."

"Why are you so sure I'll reject you?" He'd started walking again. She caught up, trying to match his strides.

She was the tenth? *What the hell* was *wrong with them?* She still had difficulty reading him, whether it was his anger or her confusion, she didn't know.

He stopped short in front of a door. "Because so far we haven't found anyone with an open mind, that's why."

"Uh, yeah, like that clears things up. Just say what you mean, Captain."

"You want to see the crew quarters?"

She mirrored his aggressive tone, hoping that might distract him. "Sure. Show me."

He opened the door and she followed him inside. The cabin was much larger than quarters in the other two ships. In the middle of the room lay a very large bed—more like a pallet—on the floor, large enough for several people to comfortably stretch out with room to spare. Four cabinets and sets of drawers lined the walls. She didn't know whose cabin this was, but there were some personal effects placed here and there. It was neat and tidy overall.

"So what's the problem, Captain?" she asked. "I don't see a problem with this."

Lucio smirked, crossed his arms and leaned against one of the cabinets. "This is the crew quarters."

She studied his face, then looked around again. When her eyes fell on his he still wore the same smirk. He nodded. "Yes. The *only* crew cabin."

Now speechless, she looked around again. It took her a moment to decide what to say. "The *only* crew cabin?"

He nodded. "Ready to leave, Doctor? I can escort you out the back way so you don't have to face the twins again. I'm getting good at making excuses for you people."

Emi hated being pushed around, and she'd be damned if she'd let handsome Lucio make her decision for her. She leaned against the opposite wall and crossed her arms, mirroring his chilly pose. "Why?"

His eyebrow arched. "Why?"

"Did you not hear me, or did you not understand me, Captain?"

He studied her, perhaps re-evaluating her "Maybe you're the one not understanding. This is it. We all share a bed."

She forced herself to maintain her chilly composure. "I get that. I'm not stupid."

Impasse. They silently stared at each other for several minutes. She waited for him to speak.

"That doesn't bother you?" he finally asked, genuinely curious. Maybe a breakthrough in his chilly wall.

"Considering I'm supposed to sleep with all three of you, should it? I'm a doctor. It's not like I'm freaked out over a naked body." *Especially not three hunky guys...*

One corner of Lucio's mouth curled up in the slightest of smiles. Emi fought the urge to walk over and kiss him. He was handsome, and combined with that voice, it was a downright dangerous combination to her reserve.

"My crew and I are very close, Doctor. We always have been."

She played dirty and tried to read him again, this time succeeding as he'd relaxed a little.

"So you're all bisexual. The problem is what, exactly?" The problem was she was surprisingly and uncomfortably damp between her legs at the thought of seeing all three of these guys—even obnoxious Lucio—naked in the same bed.

He slowly walked over and braced his arms against the wall on either side of her, leaning close, his face inches from hers. She couldn't say she didn't want this. Something about him drew her in.

"The other women ran, calling us a bunch of perverts." His low voice stirred her. She really wanted to grab his shirt and pull him to her, feel his mouth crush hers. "You sure you wouldn't want the brainy boys or the brawny boys instead of the bi-boys?"

Emi refused to back down. "I get the feeling you're trying to keep me off this ship, Captain."

His mouth hovered inches from hers, his eyes piercing her. "I won't see my men get hurt because of whatever games you want to play."

She hoped her tone sounded as serious as his. "I don't play games, *Captain* Lucio. I also don't believe in pre-judging people, a lesson you could learn. I was having a great time talking to Caph and Ford. If anyone scuttles my assignment to this vessel, it would be your attitude, not them. I don't have a problem sharing a bed with those two guys. You, however, have the personality of a fucking porcupine, asshole."

His breath caught—she heard it. She'd finally knocked him off-balance mentally.

She pursued the advantage. "Maybe you're used to dealing with some less than average women, Captain Lucio, but I graduated first in my class. Frankly, I don't take too kindly to someone telling me *I* should run away just because *he's* scared of getting a little too emotionally close to someone."

Both his eyebrows shot up. That told her something. He was worried for his men, but a part of him felt scared, too. He'd been hurt before.

One more shot across his bow, to see if it was really worth spending more time with them. She liked Ford and Caph, but if this guy didn't do an about-face on attitude, she'd walk no matter how cute he was.

She leaned forward, challenging his close personal space, and whispered, "If you want to quit dealing with girls and deal with a woman for a change, let me know." It was soooo tempting to kiss him, but she needed to see if he would trust her a little.

Thank the gods for her psychology degree.

He did. Lucio leaned in the rest of the way and kissed her. She enjoyed every second of it. There was something…off…about it, like he wasn't quite real, like her sense of taste and smell was messed up or something, but his lips on hers distracted her. She pushed away from the wall into his body, wrapping her arms around him.

Wow! Daniel *never* kissed her like that.

When he stepped back a moment later, a shocked expression on his face, she knew she'd won the first battle with him.

"You ready to start over with me, Captain Lucio?"

Stunned, he nodded.

She stuck out her hand. "Dr. Emilia Hypatia. Please feel free to call me Emi."

He took her hand and didn't let go. "Captain Aaron Lucio. Please call me Aaron."

They stood there like that for several minutes, their eyes locked. She softly asked, "Why are you afraid to let me in?"

"I told you. I don't want my men to get their hopes up again just to get shit on."

"Do you honestly think I'm like that?" She wouldn't let go of his hand. The extra contact helped give her a little edge in reading him.

"No."

"You don't have to tell me today why you're afraid."

"I am devoted to my crew. If you join us, you'll be part of my crew, and I'll be responsible for your life."

"That's very admirable."

"It's my job."

"It's bullshit. There's more."

"Do you have to know that right now?"

"I told you, you don't have to tell me today. But if I'm trusting my life to you, then you'd better give a little trust in return." Then she felt it, his pain. How he carefully concealed it she'd never know, but it was there, and deep. Grief. He'd lost someone. That meant she would need to do some digging.

"Not today, Emi. Please. One day, but not today."

"Fair enough." Emi wanted to test the lesson he'd just learned. "You don't want to fall in love with someone just to have them leave in a few years."

"I don't want my men hurt."

"You feel responsible for them."

"I *am* responsible for them."

"And if I join your crew? Or will you decide to refuse my assignment?"

His hand tightened a little around hers. "I would be responsible for your life, too."

"You didn't answer my other question."

He studied her, apparently not used to dealing with someone who didn't give a rat's ass about their crew sleeping arrangements. "I wouldn't refuse your assignment. Not right now, anyway."

He pulled her to him and kissed her again. This time she relaxed her body into his and enjoyed it. When he lifted his lips from hers, he didn't release her. "I'm sorry," he apologized.

She nodded. "It's okay. I understand this has been rough on you guys. Just don't lump me in with everyone else."

"Okay." He let her go and started to lead her from the room.

"Oh, sorry, was I supposed to ask for permission to come aboard or to kiss you or something?" she snarked.

When he turned and saw her smile, he finally smiled. It changed his brooding face into a very handsome sight. "Permission granted, Doc."

Chapter Four

Caph and Ford had frantically struggled to tidy the common room. It looked marginally better, but the sheer amount of stuff all over the place meant it was simply neater piles, not necessarily neat.

Both men looked up, anxious, when Emi followed Aaron into the room.

Aaron pointed at the table. "Let's all sit down and talk," he suggested.

"She's staying?" the twins parroted. Aaron grimaced, and the men said, "Sorry, Cap."

Emi laughed as she sat. "That's funny."

"Tell me that after twenty years," Aaron said. "You might have a different opinion then."

When they were seated, Aaron across the table from Emi, he took over. "Do you have questions for us?"

She studied their faces. "Yeah. Do any of you snore?"

All three men looked startled. Ford finally laughed. "Did she just ask what I think she asked?"

"Yeah, I asked it. Anyone going to answer?"

Aaron, relaxed and smiling, leaned back in his chair. "Caph sometimes talks in his sleep. They don't snore and haven't complained about me snoring, so I guess that's a no."

"Good. Before we go too much further, I wanted to tell you all I already know I'm not picking the Kendall Kant. Since your sleeping arrangements—albeit unusual—don't shock me, I'd like to spend some time with you guys and get to know you better." She met and held Aaron's gaze.

Ford and Caph looked at each other. "Cool!"

Aaron rolled his eyes.

"But I've got a few things of my own to get out there. The Kendall Kant guys seem to think I needed some physical conditioning."

All three men immediately glared.

"Those assholes called you fat?" Ford asked.

They were mad for her, she felt it, their protectiveness washing off them. That was a good sign. "They didn't call me fat, they said I am attractive but indicated I'm not their idea of prime physical shape."

"They're blind assholes," Caph said, glaring. "Remind me to fucking punch their goddamn lights out next time I see them."

"You're beautiful, Emi," Ford said, reaching for her hand. "No shit, you are."

Emi had never considered herself beautiful, even though she knew she wasn't ugly or fat. She didn't like to exercise, and was a little more rounded in her hips and thighs than she'd like. She usually kept her dark brown hair pulled up in a twist on the back of her head. Otherwise it fell just below her shoulders. She'd inherited her mother's grey eyes and fair skin, and her father's long hands and graceful, elegant fingers.

"What would you expect from me as a crew member?"

Caph and Ford deferred to Aaron. He shrugged. "You'll have duties, be on watches, and you're the medical officer. We share galley and maintenance duties. Can you run a weapons system?"

She shook her head.

"No problem, we can teach you that." He paused, realized what he was saying, and his face shifted into a hard mask again. "Look, don't get our hopes up, please. If you're just fucking with us—"

"I'm not fucking with you. I thought we'd already settled this." Ford still held her hand. She tightened her grip on him. "I have to ask these questions. For all of us. Can I promise you right now I'm going to pick you guys? No, I can't. I can tell you I didn't sit down and have this kind of conversation with the Braynow Gaston crew."

Aaron relaxed. "Sorry. I shouldn't have interrupted you."

She softened her voice. "You interrupted yourself, Aaron. You'd asked me if I could run a weapons system."

He smiled again. She loved it. She had a feeling he was a man who didn't smile a lot. "You're right. I'm sorry."

Caph let out a relieved sigh. She focused on him just long enough to wink. He grinned.

She returned her gaze to Aaron. "Back to crew duties. I can't run a weapons system. But if I can treat a cranial hematoma, how hard can it be?"

Ford snickered. "It's not brain surgery."

He must be the quick wit of the crew. "Let's not beat around the bush, gentlemen." Emi looked at each man in turn, then back to Aaron. "I'm assuming from the sleeping arrangement and from our discussion that things are pretty open between the three of you, and I would fit into that dynamic."

Ford and Caph looked slightly puzzled, but Aaron nodded, not blushing, not looking away, unapologetic. "Even if we could force you, we wouldn't. It's probably safe to say if you were in the mood, at least one of us would be too. On the off chance we weren't, trust me, someone would volunteer to give you a hand, so to speak." He leaned forward, his arms crossed on the table in front of him. "It won't bother you if someone's in the mood and you're not, and they're in bed with you having sex with each other?"

She released Ford's hand and mirrored Aaron's pose. "Frankly, the idea of watching two—or three—hot guys together would probably get me in the mood if I wasn't already."

Ford's jaw dropped. "Holy shit!" he whispered.

"She called us hot!" Caph said, stunned.

"You guys have really taken a beating on the self-esteem here lately, haven't you?" she asked.

"Well, between the geeks and the grunts," Ford admitted, "it's been rough."

She remembered her irritation at how the first two ships talked about these guys. If the other crews were just as disrespectful, it was no wonder they were having a hard time finding someone to sign on with them.

Emi sat back in her chair. Time for honesty on her part. "Look, I've only ever been with two guys in my life, and not at the same time, either. I'm not exactly a wild child. I am open-minded, and I might be willing to experiment to a certain degree, but I can't promise you I'll ever be in the mood to get...crazy. That won't bore you guys?"

All three men shook their heads, not daring to speak.

"I guess if I'd be sleeping with all three of you anyway, it doesn't matter if it's with one of you at a time all together or as a group, so that's kind of moot. But what if there are times I want or need to be alone?"

The men exchanged glances, but Aaron spoke. "There's a comfortable bunk in sick bay. If it's going to be a deal-breaker though, I mean, I can talk to the retrofit crew and have them build out a cabin. There's a large storage room next to the main cabin that could be converted. There's plenty of time to have that done. You could tell them what you want."

"You have a dedicated sick bay?" She'd never even thought to ask the other crews that.

"Sure. Want to see it?"

"Yeah."

She followed the men down another corridor and was amazed at the set-up. Top-quality, state of the art machines, well-stocked drug synthesizer, a full inventory of instruments and supplies, even for extreme surgical cases.

"This is great!" she said.

The men, even Aaron, looked pleased at her response. "We can get anything else you think we'll need," Aaron said. "DSMC doesn't pinch pennies when it comes to safety."

She tried to hide her smile. He was slipping from his original distrust into hoping she'd made up her mind to join them.

"I think what I'd like to see next is the kitchen."

Caph groaned. "The galley's a mess. Inventory, I mean, not like pig sty mess. We won't make you cook all the meals, we take turns." He had a thought. "Were those grunt assholes going to make you cook all the time?"

It was getting harder to hide her amusement. "No. Is that how you got all those demerits? Getting into it with the military guys?"

The twins blushed.

The galley was disorganized, but from the lack of dirty dishes or caked-on food anywhere, it was obviously more inventory mess. Then she spotted it.

The coffee machine.

"You have a Java Max Excel 10k?" Her jaw dropped. If she had one passion in her life, it was coffee. This machine did it all and did it all well. Espresso? Cappuccino? No matter what your poison, it could make it.

Ford grinned. "Like it? That baby really took some wheeling and dealing to get. It's fantastic—"

She turned and grabbed him, kissing him, taking him by surprise, but it didn't take him long to get into it. When she stepped back he wobbled on his feet, a silly grin splashed across his face.

Aaron smiled, but Caph's jaw gaped. Not wanting to leave him out, she grabbed the large man. His stunned surprise soon changed to passion as he returned her kiss.

Then Emi turned back to the Java Max. She'd kiss it too, if she didn't think they'd think she was weird.

Aaron laughed and looked at his stunned crew. "Well, guys? Do you want to ask her, or should I?"

The twins were apparently shocked into silence, staring at Emi as if she was a goddess. She suspected if she asked, the twins would drop to their knees and bow before her.

I could get used to this.

Aaron stepped over to her. "I know you said you can't give us an answer yet, and that's fair. I would, however, like to extend the offer to join our crew. Right, guys?"

The twins nodded, speechless.

"How about we start with dinner and see where things go from there?" She turned to him. "You're right that I can't promise this minute that I'll join you, but I would like to spend at least the next day or so with you guys and get to know you better. I'm not in any rush to leave."

"Day?"

Her gaze never wavered from his. "And night."

Aaron smiled.

* * * *

The three men cooked her dinner. Not a pre-made, reconstituted, out of the box crap dinner, either. Home-cooked with fresh vegetables and meat.

"We can't eat like this all the time, obviously," Aaron said, not letting her help. "We like to cook. Whenever we can use fresh ingredients, we do."

She stole a raw carrot off his cutting board and didn't miss the smile he tried to hide from her. "What else do you guys like to do in your spare time, besides each other?"

The men froze, then laughed. Ford shook his head in disbelief. "Please don't wake me up if I'm dreaming, guys."

Caph carefully nudged past her, potholders on his hands and carrying a freshly roasted chicken in a pan right from the convection oven. "Poker."

"Is that a joke?" she asked.

He looked startled, caught her playful smile, and laughed "Oh my gods, you are too much, girl. The card game."

"I've never played. You guys going to teach me?"

"It's sort of a requirement to be on this crew," Caph said.

"You don't play for money."

The men exchanged a glance. "No," Caph said. "Chips. Sometimes other things." Caph focused his green eyes on hers and she felt that sensual tingle again.

"What other things?"

Ford had slipped behind her. His lips lightly brushed the back of her neck, making her shiver. Hades, was she that sensitive back there? She never knew.

"Sometimes strip poker. Sometimes more than that," he murmured in her ear.

Her mouth went dry. "More?"

Aaron looked at her. "Yeah. More."

Well, this could be a good way to get better acquainted with the guys. "I'm game."

Ford pressed close behind her, his body hot against hers through her clothes. His stiff erection rubbed against her linen slacks. He felt huge even through his jeans.

"It's not nice to tease," he whispered in her ear.

She wiggled her hips against him, drawing a heated, husky moan from the man. "Then I suggest you put your money where your mouth is, Ford."

"Goddamn," he softly grunted, thrusting back, his cock even harder now.

"All right, Ford," Aaron said. "That's enough. Dinner first, then we can play a game of poker and see how anxious Emi here is to get to know us better."

Ford looked up then reluctantly stepped away.

Emi had to admit as crazy as this whole situation was, her nipples were pebbled, uncomfortably rubbing against her shirt. She wasn't wearing a bra, usually didn't unless she was exercising or something because she wasn't overly endowed in that department. Something else, she was extremely wet between her legs, a dull, constant throbbing exacerbated by Ford's seductive bump and grind. She started to reply to Aaron when her hand-held console vibrated on the counter where she'd left it.

It was also glowing. She picked it up.

A message from Graymard.

Everything okay? Haven't heard from you.

She replied.

Everything's fine. Spending more time with Tamora Bight crew. At the top of my list.

Before she had time to set the console down, it vibrated again.

Really? The Tamora Bight crew?

If Graymard was there, she would jam the fucking console down his throat.

Yes, the Tamora Bight crew. You have a problem with that?

Apparently not, because he didn't reply.

Chapter Five

Dinner was great, the guys were sweet. Clean-up was quick, and the men settled around the table with her and started teaching her the game.

"We'll play for chips first," Aaron said, shooting a warning look at the other two men. "Just so you learn the game. No pressure."

"Okay."

She realized she'd lost track of time. It had to be getting late, but she didn't care because she wasn't even tired. This was fun. The men had settled into an easier, relaxed mood now that it was obvious she wasn't running, screaming, out the main hatch. This made it a lot easier for her to read them, although Aaron was still cloudy and guarded in many ways. An enigma she wouldn't mind spending more time exploring.

Ford partnered with her first, helping her with her cards and teaching her the finer subtleties of betting and calling. Apparently they played a very standard, basic version of the game and not one of the more horribly complex ones.

Good thing, because she hated games that were more trouble to play than they were fun.

An hour later after several rounds, she started getting the hang of it, although she had trouble remembering which hands were worth more than others. She also realized she had an unfair advantage because she could tell when the men were bluffing, especially each other.

That would be cheating, right?

Or not. They had her resume, they knew she was a trained class two empath.

After another hour, Ford let her play on her own and she started wiping the men out of chips. At first she wondered if they were letting her win, then realized they were genuinely surprised a beginner could pick up the game so quickly.

When it was her turn to deal she flashed them a smile. "So what happens when you run out of chips?"

The men looked at each other, then Aaron spoke. "What do you want to happen?" he carefully asked. She tried to read him. The men had all shifted slightly back to nervous, afraid of doing something to spook her.

His eyes never wavered from hers. "So how's strip poker work?" she asked.

The twins said, "Holy shit!" She'd gotten used to their frequent unison comments and thought it was funny that two unrelated men could be so close as to talk like that.

"You want to play strip poker?" Aaron asked in disbelief.

"Well, from the looks of it, you guys would be doing the stripping." She didn't blink, holding his steady gaze, waiting until he turned to Ford to look away.

"Well?" he asked Ford.

Ford shrugged. "I'm game."

He looked at Caph. "What about you?"

The large man eagerly nodded. "Sure."

Aaron turned back to her. "We can't force you to do anything, understand? You also realize it would be fucking mean to tease us, right?"

She narrowed her gaze and imitated his amused smirk. "I've never been accused of being a tease, gentlemen. You want to talk or play? I still have chips. If you want to get me naked, you're going to have to start winning back some money."

They played. Within four hands, the three men were totally out of chips and shirtless.

And they all had very nice chests.

Emi dealt the next hand and kept raising the ante, forcing the men to give up a shoe each. Three more hands left them in their pants and underwear.

"You guys want to keep playing?" she asked.

They all nodded, their eyes on her.

The next hand saw them sacrificing their pants. Aaron wore boxers, but the other two wore briefs. All three men were stiff, and from what she could tell, large.

She smiled. "I like what I see, gentlemen. What do we play for after you lose all your clothes?"

Aaron met her gaze head-on from across the table. "What do you want to play for?"

"What do you usually play for?"

Ford and Caph silently watched them like a tennis match, their heads pivoting back and forth, their jaws slightly gaped in disbelief.

Aaron narrowed his gaze. "Once our clothes are gone, we play for favors."

"Favors as in little birthday party toys, or favors as in blow jobs?"

He smirked. "The second. Usually we play cards in bed when we get to that point."

Okay, she was definitely soaking wet now. Emi took a sip of her water and licked her lips because her throat had gone dry. "Really?"

All three men nodded.

She couldn't believe she was doing this, it didn't feel real. "How fascinating, gentlemen." She picked up the deck of cards and stood, heading toward the doorway leading to the crew quarters. The men watched her, and she turned. "Well? I thought you said you normally play in bed at this point."

After a brief moment of stunned shock, the men scrambled to follow her. Aaron took the lead. She didn't bother keeping her eyes off his ass as he opened the cabin door.

Their banter had ceased. Apparently they were too shocked by her willing acceptance of their situation to think of any pithy, snarky comments. She waited for them to get settled on the bed, then kicked off her shoes and sat with them. She removed her linen jacket, leaving her hard nipples clearly visible, pressing taut against her shirt.

From the direction of their collective gazes, they'd noticed.

Emi shuffled the cards and tried to conceal her amused smile. Five years with a crew of guys who were apparently more than satisfied with her appearance, who were pretty good-looking, who absolutely could not cheat on her, and whom she was able to stun into silence.

Not a bad deal at all. She liked the feeling of…power. Feeling desired, because frankly, her two exes never made her feel like she was beautiful, just that she was available.

"Ready, gentlemen?" she purred.

The men nodded.

She dealt the next hand and didn't have to be a full clairvoyant to know they were too distracted to play well. At the end of the hand, all three men stood and shucked their underwear without comment.

Emi stared, her throat dry. The men were well-endowed. Not porn stars, but definitely fairly proportioned and larger than either of her exes had been.

Much larger.

Holy crap!

She tried to hold onto her cool, appraising mask and knew it was slipping. She didn't know what the hell was wrong with the Braynow Gaston's crew, but these three men were all men, not a bit of boy about them.

Maybe they were jealous.

Aaron's smirk returned. "Well? Like what you see?"

She carefully moistened her lips and tried to control her voice. "Very nice, gentlemen. Next hand?"

All three grinned and resumed their previous positions, sitting cross-legged on the bed, their cocks stiff. Fortunately, none of them were extremely hairy, something that would have turned her off.

Although she suspected if any of them were, they'd probably get a full body waxing to make her happy. Caph's chest was covered with soft, downy blond hair. Ford had a light dusting of darker curls across his chest, and a dark line of hair ran from his navel down between his legs. That would keep her mind distracted if he went without a shirt, knowing where that trail led. Aaron's body hair was fine and straight, and she resisted the urge to run her fingers over his chest—and between his legs.

Now she was the one forced to concentrate. Fortunately she still had the advantage. "So what kind of favors do you usually play for?" she asked as she shuffled the deck, trying to keep her eyes on Aaron's deep brown gaze and not on his throbbing member.

His playful smirk told her more than anything that he was well aware of her rapidly disintegrating control. "Depends."

"On what?"

He shrugged. "On what mood everyone's in."

She glanced down. All three men were stiff without any indication of disinterest. "Looks like everyone's in a fairly playful mood to me."

The twins remained silent. She had a feeling if she kept this up too much longer, those two poor guys would be drooling idiots.

Aaron focused his eyes on her. "Don't get me wrong, we're men and, trust me, we get horny. But we're not a bunch of sex maniacs. It's not unusual for us to go a day or two or longer, easily, without needing to get our rocks off. Especially if we're on a mission and need to focus. We didn't survive all these years because we're a bunch of morons. Or there might be times we do it two or three times a day, depending on the mood and situation."

Between her legs, her muscles involuntarily contracted in a pleasant way. *Two or three times in a* day?

Wow.

She hoped her voice sounded as steady as she intended. "You didn't answer my question, Aaron."

"Well, one favor might be the winner of the hand gets to request something from one or more of the others." His eyes flicked down her body. "Since you're still dressed, that might be moot."

"Let me ask it this way, then—what won't you do?"

Caph found his voice. "Cap never bottoms."

The fact that he spoke surprised her as much as what he said. It took her a second to process it. "Huh?"

Ford shook his head. "Cap never bottoms," he echoed.

"And what does that mean, exactly?"

They'd found their twin voice and spoke together. "It means—" They glared at each other, then Ford spoke alone. "It means he always tops."

She admitted she wasn't as experienced in sexual lingo as they obviously were. "So you never let the girl on top?" she asked Aaron. *That would get boring.*

Aaron smiled, but Caph clarified. "Not positions. He's always the do-er, never the do-ee. Ah, intercourse, that is. Anything else, then it doesn't matter."

She felt like she'd been dropped into an alternate dimension. How long had she been here, anyway? Normally she didn't stay up very late, and she knew she'd been here for hours but didn't feel the least bit tired. "Why is that?"

The twins shrugged and replied, "Just is. Cap never bottoms."

Aaron leaned back, his hands propped behind him. "Old story." The gesture stretched his torso. While he wasn't muscle-bound like the military guys, he was naturally muscled and trim with very little extra fat on him. She wanted to run her hands down his body...

"Maybe I want to hear it."

"Maybe it's something we don't discuss outside of crew."

That stopped her in her tracks. She realized no, she wasn't technically a part of this crew yet. "I thought you wanted me to be a part of this crew."

"Freaking A we do, but you're not officially crew yet. We've extended the invitation, but you haven't accepted it."

He wasn't backing down, she sensed. "So if I officially join your crew, you'll tell me?"

He nodded, but his eyes briefly flicked away. She sensed his deep grief again. It might be an old story, but it wasn't one he enjoyed telling.

"And how about the story of how your crew arrangement came to be?"

The men nodded. "Crew story," all three parroted. Aaron briefly closed his eyes as if silently swearing. Now all three had their eyes on her.

She considered them. "I need to spend more time with you before I give you a firm yes."

The men nodded. Aaron spoke. "That's fair."

She dealt the hand and suspected this time the men lost on purpose simply to get on with their other game.

"Winner's choice," Aaron said with a smirk as the twins watched her. "What'll it be?"

Emi chewed her lip and considered it. "I think I'd like a foot rub."

Aaron's eyebrow shot up in surprise. "Foot rub?"

She nodded. "Yeah. Foot rub." She unfolded her legs and stretched them out before her. "From you. Or is that a 'bottom' thing you won't do?"

She loved his playful smirk. "No, that's not a bottom thing." He moved closer and placed her feet in his lap, his eyes never leaving hers as he carefully worked his thumbs over the soles of her right foot.

Nearly better than sex. He was very talented, taking his time and seductively caressing her as he did.

She closed her eyes and threw her head back, enjoying the sensation.

"You like that?" he asked.

"Yeah," she whispered. "That's real good."

When he switched to her left foot, she suspected he deliberately placed her right so his cock lay along the entire length of her sole. She made sure she gently rubbed him, enjoying his almost imperceptible intake of breath as she did.

When he finished with her left foot he released it and carefully lifted her feet from his lap. "How was that?"

She nodded, trying to find her voice. "Real good."

The twins were silent. In shock, apparently. Her heart ached for all of them. As deeply as she could read them, they were all sweet, good-hearted men, obviously devoted to each other as lovers, friends, and crew. She knew if she accepted this assignment—and frankly, it looked like she would—they would be just as devoted to her.

In silence and with slightly trembling fingers, she dealt the next hand. They didn't even pretend to play, all of them folding after the first round of betting, looking at her in expectation.

Waiting.

What was most fair? Well, order of rank, she supposed. "I'd like a foot rub from Caph," she said.

Could she stand it was another question entirely. While Aaron's touch had relaxed her in some ways, it also drenched her sex and left her throbbing, aching for more than just his hands on her feet.

She imagined his cock would fit inside her quite nicely, could almost imagine how pleasantly he'd stretch her…

Caph smiled and slid forward, his large hands carefully massaging her feet, his touch different than Aaron's and yet just as good. She closed her eyes and enjoyed it, surprised when she felt his lips on her toes, his tongue seductively swirling around each digit, giving her a preview of something he was obviously quite skilled at.

Oh, wow!

She gasped and knew all three men heard her.

She kept her eyes closed and somehow suppressed her disappointed groan when he finished with both feet and returned to his place on the bed.

They knew they now held the advantage. When Emi dealt the next hand they didn't even look at their cards before folding in silence and returning their gaze to her.

Emi nodded to Ford and he took his turn, yet another different set of sensations, his touch just as good as the other two, leaving her fighting the urge to plunge her hand between her legs and finger herself.

They were all sooo good.

When Ford finished and returned to his place, she realized the men were waiting. She looked at them.

"Well?" Aaron said.

"Well?" she gasped, trying to regain her composure.

"You gonna deal?" he asked.

She shook her head and crooked her finger at him. He moved across the bed and she threw her arms around him, kissing him. He laid her back on the mattress and she hooked one leg around his, keeping his body stretched beside her.

"Holy crap!" the twins breathlessly whispered, moving to lay on either side of them.

She broke her kiss with Aaron long enough to look at Caph and kiss him. Then she turned to Ford and kissed him too.

"All right, boys," she said. "Show me why I'd be making the biggest mistake of my life to turn you guys down."

Aaron slid down her body while Caph took over kissing her. She felt Aaron's strong hands working on her slacks and lifted her hips to allow him to slide them off her, leaving her bare. His lips brushed over her thighs, and she moaned as he placed his palms inside her legs and gently spread them.

Ford slipped his hand under her shirt and lifted it over her head. Caph broke their kiss only long enough to free her of her last article of clothing. Then Ford latched onto one nipple, gently running his tongue over it as he playfully tweaked her other with his fingers.

Emi moaned, not caring what they did to her if it all felt this good. She gasped when Aaron lowered his mouth to her mound. His tongue laved her swollen nub, bringing her close to release several times without granting it. After several long moments of this, she begged.

"Please!" she moaned, her need burning through her.

"Please what?" he asked.

She lifted her head and met his eyes. Caph kept himself busy by dropping his lips to her other breast, replacing Ford's fingers with his mouth.

"Do it!" she panted.

Aaron's fingers teased her wet entrance. "Do what?"

She closed her eyes and dropped her head to the bed. "Please make me come," she whispered.

All three men hungrily groaned. Aaron lowered his mouth to her sex again, slipping two thick fingers inside her. She'd never felt like this before. She'd had orgasms, most of them self-induced because, frankly, Daniel and her first ex were not that great.

Especially not when compared to these three.

Aaron's tongue and fingers set off an explosion in her lower belly. Through the waves of pleasure, she vaguely heard Caph and Ford's soft encouragements to her to let go and come for them.

She cried out, her hips grinding against Aaron's mouth, her whole body shaking. She found Ford and Caph's hands and held on as tremor after tremor raced through her. What felt like hours later, she lay gasping and spent in their arms, incapable of coherent speech.

Aaron sat up, that playful smirk on his face again. "How was that?"

She didn't even try to speak, just nodded.

He traded places with Caph, who spent a few minutes stroking her feet and legs while Ford kissed her. Aaron gently suckled one nipple while playing with the other. Then she felt Caph's tongue plunge deep into her sex. She moaned into Ford's mouth.

Ford lifted his head, his blue eyes holding hers captive. "Does that feel good, baby? You like that?"

She mewled something she hoped passed for yes, and he smiled.

"He's very skilled with his tongue. He loves using that mouth of his."

In response, Caph swirled his tongue around her sensitive nub, drawing another moan from her.

Ford smiled. "Five years of this, sweetie. Think you can handle us?"

She nodded. Oh, Hades, could she!

"Just imagine, five years of having three guys wrapped around your fingers." Ford's voice had dropped to a sultry, husky tone, seductive, enhancing what was going on between her legs with Caph's skilled tongue. He must be the talker of the group.

Damn, he was sexy.

He curled around her, his arm cradling her head, keeping her eyes focused on his. "We want to hear you moan, honey. I know how good he is with that sweet mouth he's got. Let's hear how good he is—"

With that she felt another wave rip through her, just as strong as the last one. She squeezed her eyes shut as she cried out, gasping for breath, every nerve in her body at Caph's mercy as he kept her coming.

When she didn't think she could take any more, Caph lifted his head and kissed her thigh. His rumbling chuckle stirred her heart. "That was the best sound I've heard in a long time, kiddo. Think you can deal with that for the next few years?"

She nodded, not even trying to speak, wondering how she'd ever regain the strength to walk again. She felt like she could melt into the mattress. She'd never experienced anything like this after sex—

No. Not sex. She felt it from them already.

This was making love. Their hearts were already hers. There was no way in Hades she could refuse to join their crew now, even if she wanted to back out.

Not that she wanted to back out. If she did, she'd have herself committed for a psych eval. Only a fucking moron would give up a chance to be with these three men.

They waited her out. It could have been minutes or hours, she didn't know. When she finally opened her eyes, they all smiled.

"You okay?" Ford asked.

She nodded.

"You're not falling asleep on us yet, are you?"

She shook her head and he laughed. "You've got to give us at least one more."

"One more?" she gasped. She'd never had two climaxes in one night, and never any that were as explosive as her first two had been.

Ford nodded, a sly look on his face. "Oh, yeah. Hey, you have to get a full sampling of what you'll be living with. I haven't had my turn yet."

She gave up trying to talk and he traded places with Caph. Aaron shifted position, his arm cradling her head, stroking her cheek and nuzzling her while Caph made sure her breasts were still well-tended.

Ford wrapped his arms around her thighs and let out a happy sigh. "Dammit, if that ain't a beautiful sight." She felt his possessive grip on her legs as he lightly flicked his tongue along her clit.

Aaron smiled as she made a little noise. "Feels good?"

She nodded.

"Just imagine how good it's going to feel when I slide my cock inside you."

She pulled his mouth down to hers and greedily devoured it, his tongue doing a good job of duplicating what Ford's was doing to her wet sex.

Then Ford slipped two fingers inside her and wrapped his lips around her nub, gently sucking. She exploded, screaming. Her fingers dug into the back of Aaron's neck as her entire body shuddered, completely at the mercy of the pleasure flowing through her.

Emi collapsed, limp against the bed while the men sat up and looked at her. They were waiting.

When she caught her breath again, she looked at their expectant faces. "What? What's wrong?"

Caph grinned. "You enjoy that?"

She nodded.

"Want more?"

"Uh, duh!" She remembered the chips. "You mean you can't until I say it's okay?"

Aaron smirked. "They overstack the deck in your favor until you're matched with a crew. I mean, we're guessing you don't want to stop, but—"

"Shut the hell up and fuck me!"

They pounced, Aaron sliding home first as Ford and Caph cradled her between them, murmuring to her.

She wrapped her legs around Aaron's waist. "Get busy, Cap. There's a line."

The men laughed. "Aw hell, she's a pistol!" Ford said with a grin. "You tell me this is a fucking dream and I'll shoot both your asses when I wake up."

"If she's a dream, then we're all having the same freaking dream," Caph said.

She pulled Aaron closer and kissed him, enjoying the feel of his stiff length inside her. "Do I meet crew approval?" she asked, answering his thrusts with her hips.

He moaned, his voice deep. "Gods, yes." With that he gave a final thrust, sinking deep inside her, his hips hard against hers. She pulled him down to her, stroking his back, his head resting on her shoulder.

This felt so good, it felt *right*. Despite his earlier attitude and his deep-seated worry she would back out, he wanted her as badly as she wanted them.

When he'd recovered, he pushed up and kissed her, his forehead touching hers. "That was wonderful," he whispered.

"You guys aren't so bad yourself," she said with a sexy grin. "Who's next?"

"I'm always gonna get thirds, aren't I?" Ford playfully groused.

Caph was already swapping positions with Aaron. "Not always.

We'll change it up." He winked at Emi. "I have a feeling she's gonna be leading us around by our dicks anyway, so it's not like we're gonna argue with her. Whatever the lady wants, the lady gets."

Emi knew he wasn't just saying that either. He'd meant it from the very depths of his being. It scared her that he was so immediately in love with her, but something scared her even more—that she already felt the same way.

Caph was not quite as long as Aaron, but he was a little thicker, and he felt good as he slid in, pleasantly stretching her even further than Aaron's member had. He held still for a minute, his eyes closed, his large hands firmly gripping her hips.

"Damn, you're so sweet. So goddamn tight, baby." He started a slow, sultry rhythm, thrusting in short gentle strokes with just his large head inside her, alternating with deep, powerful thrusts that rocked her to her very core. She gave up trying to match his pace. He didn't need her help anyway, taking control of her body in a pleasant way. She'd never climaxed from penetration alone, but she had a feeling if any man could give her that, it might be him.

After a few minutes, he looked into her eyes. "I can't hold it any longer, babe."

"Go ahead."

He plunged even deeper with a loud groan. She felt him inside her, throbbing and claiming her very depths. He pulled her up, wrapping his arms around her and hugging her tightly to him.

"Damn, that was fantastic," he hoarsely whispered. She suspected he might be crying but didn't want them to see. She whispered to him, holding him until he gently kissed her one last time and lowered her to the bed. He was a big man with a big heart. Emi suspected he might be the most emotionally fragile of the three despite his size and demeanor.

Ford switched places with him, smiling at her. "I get to take my time, so I guess I shouldn't complain about being last, should I?"

She grinned. "You gonna talk or fuck?"

Aaron laughed, kissing her damp forehead. "He is a talker. You pegged him right there."

Ford lifted her legs to his shoulders and stroked his cock deep inside her. He wasn't as thick as Caph but managed to hit places inside her the other two hadn't because of the angle. She could do this all night with him, with all of them.

"You like that?" he whispered, his blue eyes holding hers again.

She nodded. All three men had distinctive styles. It would never get boring, that's for sure.

Slow and steady, he took his time. She watched Ford's face as his climax built. He was more of a romantic, she sensed. He would be the one she'd need to nourish intellectually as well as emotionally and physically. She imagined nights curled at his side, talking as he slowly made love to her for hours, wanting to touch her soul as well as her body.

He leaned forward, pressing deeper. She knew beyond a doubt she couldn't let these men go. Emi reached up and touched his face, laying her palm against his cheek, and he kissed it.

"Come for me, baby," she whispered, meeting his eyes. "Show me how good it feels. Let me see how much you want it—"

"Ah!" He closed his eyes, pressed deep inside her as his release took him, his cock throbbing. After a moment, he carefully lowered her legs and let her pull him down to her. She held him, stroking his back and shoulders, grateful for the stupidity of the other women who'd turned these men down.

She looked at Aaron, who sat back, watching them intently. She nodded.

Again he was surprised, his eyebrows flicking up almost imperceptibly. He was her deeply wounded soul. She wondered how long it would take to draw him out and finally start his healing. How many years had he been in pain?

"Yes," she whispered.

Aaron kissed her, long and slow and sweet. "You sure you want to put up with us?"

Caph nuzzled close on her other side, his face tucked against her shoulder. "We're a handful."

"You're my handful," she said. "I'll send Graymard a message in the morning that you boys just picked up a medical officer. For now, let's turn off the lights and go to sleep."

And safely nestled among her men, that's what she did.

Chapter Six

Emi's eyes popped open what seemed like minutes after falling asleep. Without an outside window to gauge the sun's position it was hard for her to figure out what time it was.

A man lay tightly spooned against her, one arm around her waist, the other cradling her head. Closing her eyes again, she settled her mind, reached out, and without looking sensed it was Aaron. Eventually, she knew, she'd be able to tell each man apart from just the feel of his body or his scent. For now, her nose was stuffy or something, without clear scents or tastes.

"You awake?" he asked, his voice still gruff from sleep.

"Yeah." She rolled over and realized they were in bed alone together. He captured her hand, lacing his fingers through hers, bringing it to his lips and kissing it.

"How'd you sleep?" he asked.

She smiled. "Like a rock." Which was unusual, because normally she awoke at the slightest noise and couldn't remember the last time she'd slept through a night without waking several times. Not since before her parents died...

No. Not now. She pushed the thought back and slammed the door shut on it.

"Where's the twins?" she asked. It felt natural and right to call the two mismatched men that.

"They're scrambling to tidy up the galley. They want to cook you breakfast."

"Is that safe?"

He laughed. "Yes. They're good cooks."

"I'll send Graymard a message in a few minutes. I don't want to move right now."

"We didn't hurt you last night, did we?"

"No. Pain is not what I would think of when I try to describe last night."

She shifted position again. Actually, she should be pleasantly sore but wasn't even slightly achy. Not that she was complaining. It was yet another reason to join them.

"Even if it wasn't for the chips we'd never hurt you, you know that, right? If you ever wanted to say stop—"

She lightly touched a finger to his lips. He was especially vulnerable right now with just the two of them, a side the other men rarely saw, she suspected. "I know. I trust you."

He sucked her finger into his mouth and swirled his tongue around it, igniting a pleasant flurry of contractions in her lower belly. "How did we get so lucky?" he whispered.

"You needed the right woman who could handle you guys." She smiled, but it was wistful. "What am I going to do when the five years is up is the question. How could I ever—"

She was interrupted by the sound of Caph walking into the room. "Hey, Ford! She's awake!" His beautiful, beaming smile nearly broke her heart. These poor guys had really taken an emotional beating throughout the selection process.

He knelt on the bed next to Emi and kissed her. "How'd you sleep, beautiful?"

Ford quickly jogged in, his blue eyes gleaming. "Sleeping Beauty awakes, and Cap's hogging her. I can already see how this is going to work." But his voice was filled with amused teasing, not jealousy. He also leaned over, kissing her.

The twins were dressed in T-shirts and loose shorts, but she felt Aaron's bare flesh warm against her body. "Anyone want to show me to the shower?" she asked.

She never knew men could strip that quickly. They told her the bathroom was technically called a "head" on a ship, her first lesson of many, she sensed. They had a large combo shower unit that delivered real water or sonic-air showers as desired. They showed her how to use it, opting for the luxury of a water shower since they were in dry dock, and enjoyed helping her clean up. All three cocks were stiff and throbbing by the time they climbed out, dried by the air cycle.

"You guys are going to keep me pretty busy, aren't you?"

Aaron stepped back and let the twins press close, holding her. "You'd better believe it," Ford said.

"Yeah," Caph agreed. "I couldn't believe you were still here this morning."

"Someone help me find my phone. I'll call Graymard and give him the happy news."

The twins bolted, naked, out the door to comply.

Emi couldn't help it, she giggled. Then she looked at Aaron. "They're cute."

She couldn't read his mood as he turned to her, and didn't want to try right then. "Yeah," he agreed. "They're something else." They brought her phone. She pulled on her clothes and followed the scent of coffee to the galley.

Graymard was happily surprised to hear from her. It turned out it was just a little after eight in the morning. "Well, that is good news. They're the most experienced crew we're sending out. I'll take care of contacting the other crews for you."

She stepped away from the men, out of the galley and into the common room, and dropped her voice. "Yeah, well, tell the assholes on the Kendall Kant and Braynow Gaston that they need to quit fucking around. The jerks on those two boats were laughing about these guys."

His voice hardened. "Oh, were they?"

"Yeah. They were treating them like a joke."

"Well, they are an unconventional crew, but that's certainly no reason for the others to—"

"It's exactly why the others pick on them. I would be willing to bet all the demerits they've wracked up would be a result of being egged into something by a bunch of jerks."

Graymard was silent for a moment. Emi suspected she'd hit the nail on the head. "I'll talk to them," he assured her. "Now then, we need you all back here for crew pairing and paperwork. Preferably this morning."

Her gut twisted as reality hit home. She was really doing this. "As far as I know, I'm sticking with these guys. But…" She trailed off, not wanting to say it.

She didn't have to. "You will all get a final chance at the end of training to back out. Of course, you can always back out before then."

Relief. "Okay. Like I said, I don't foresee any problems." She hoped they wouldn't back out.

Oh, God, what if they did?

"Understood. I'll see you all here within the next two hours. The receptionist will direct you. Have fun, Emi."

Emi knew her heart had slipped as surely as the men's had. The worry that they might reject her after all this was said and done gnawed at her. Could she take that? For the first time in ten years, it felt like she had a family again.

Forcing that down, she returned to the galley to eat.

* * * *

The twins were good cooks. She felt absolutely spoiled, and they refused to let her help with clean-up. The men dressed, now in crew uniforms, and she realized she was still in her clothes from the day before. "We have to go by my place later so I can get my stuff."

Ford eyed her. "We don't have any ladies' clothes. Caph's pants should fit you, they'll be long on you. We can roll the legs up and find you a belt. Aaron's shirts will easily fit you." He waggled his eyebrows. "Unless you want to wear one of my shirts and torture us all day with how snug it'd be on you."

She grinned. "I wouldn't want to be cruel. I can save those for when we're here in the ship."

The men laughed, and she followed them to the crew quarters to change.

"Think we'll pass the other two crews when we go?" she asked as she stepped into Caph's pants. Yes, they were big, but her shape was different than the guys and there was no way she'd fit into Aaron or Ford's pants. "I'd love to flip them a bird. Assholes." She looked up at her men. "This is so surreal. In a good way."

Ford rolled the cuffs up for her and handed her one of his belts. "They look good on you, kiddo."

Aaron handed her one of his shirts, a short-sleeved, collared pullover with the ship's crest and name embroidered on the left chest. "They'll probably get you set up with uniforms today. They like us to do training as a matched set. Doesn't matter here on the ship, but we try to follow as many rules as we can."

Her shoes didn't exactly go with the ensemble, but the pants were so long they mostly hid them. Caph brought her a new toothbrush and hairbrush from storage. She brushed out her hair, pulling it back. As she did she noticed Aaron's fleeting frown.

"What?"

He shrugged. "I think it's prettier when you wear it down." She'd pulled out her hair clip the night before during their poker game and wore it loose.

"Really?"

He nodded. "You'll need to wear it up for some of the training, but…" He shrugged again.

She unclipped it, and all three men smiled. "Better?" she asked.

They nodded.

"Okay." She took a deep breath. "Let's get the paperwork over with so we can have some fun."

* * * *

Emi knew from the personnel files that none of the men were empaths, natural or trained, so she didn't have to carefully shield her thoughts or emotions from them. Good thing too, because she was nervous as hell. The morning had slipped past her, flying at light speed, it seemed. They all filled out forms—paperwork, an old holdover term from when people actually used paper—on electronic hand-helds they would use throughout training. When it came time to sync their chips they were led into a room with two dozen large reclining chairs.

A technician showed them to their seats and walked to a console as Graymard entered. They hadn't seen much of him during the day.

"This won't hurt, Emi. You won't even know anything's happened."

"What exactly does it do?"

"It syncs you all together. It also lowers a few settings and allows for more freedom of interaction during intimacy."

"That's a polite way of saying we can get rough if I'm willing?" she asked.

Ford snickered. "Damn, girl. You're gonna wear us out."

Graymard, however, nodded. "Exactly. It's an intelligent chip and can sense if no really means yes or no, so to speak. It also allows you to home in on each other while aboard the ship, and to a certain extent over limited distances when you're off-ship. You're synced to the ship so you can find your way back when you leave it. This is all limited to within the crew, and to the ship. The only time you trigger outside tracking capabilities is if you enable the distress beacon or the ship is severely damaged or destroyed, which would activate the automatic alarm."

He continued. "As the men already know, it also means none of you can willingly or voluntarily engage in intimate encounters with anyone outside of your matched crew. In the unlikely case something happens and one of you is forced, it will sense that and not activate. It is tuned to your biorhythms, as well as those of your crewmates, and it will prevent voluntary straying."

Emi smiled. "Absolutely?"

He nodded. "Without question."

"Just out of curiosity, how does the chip ensure that?"

"Well, it has a corrective pulse. The first warning pulse, if you can call it that, isn't uncomfortable. It's more like a mental tapping reminding the person to stop. If their activity continues, the discomfort continues and increases."

"What if someone didn't stop?"

He frowned. "Well, theoretically it could potentially kill someone by damaging their brain stem if they didn't stop their activity and the pulses continued for an extended period of time, but there's never been a recorded case of that. It's not possible. It would hurt too much."

She froze. "How do you know it won't misfire?"

"It can't. Only voluntary violation will trigger it. There is no way for it to malfunction, because it self-polices. Any abnormalities and it shuts off and notifies the ship, us, and you as medical officer that there's a problem. It has multiple fail-safes. We've used this model for three decades without problem. We have taken every precaution. You will also have a kit on board to remove and replace chips in case there are any issues. They're very easy to program, the kit will do it for you."

Emi relaxed a little. "What else do they do?"

"They allow you as medical officer to monitor the crew with the computers, to a certain extent. You have empath training, so you'll be able to fine-tune your senses, I'm sure, to your crew mates and sense any problems with their health. We'll go through all of this in-depth with you, and there will be a full set of records on board for your reference. And as I mentioned before, it attunes you to each other so that while it's impossible to force each other, it's also very uncomfortable to let any crew member go without release if they're in the mood and really desiring intimacy."

"An anti-blue-balls feature," Emi snarked. The men laughed again.

"Correct," Graymard said. "But that also applies to you, as well. There's no set time frame. Again, it's tapped into your particular biorhythms, whether you're in the mood once a day or once a month."

She looked at her men, who watched her, smiles on their faces. "I don't think I'll have any problem with these three taking care of my needs."

"Damn straight," the twins said. Aaron grimaced.

"You got a setting in that thing to prevent that?" he grumped.

Emi laughed.

The technician looked up. "All done."

Graymard was right—she hadn't felt a thing. Aaron took her hand when she stood, helped her to her feet.

"What's next?" he asked Graymard, not releasing her, his thumb gently stroking her hand.

"Lunch, then an orientation for Emi, which you three need to sit in on." Graymard looked at her clothes, apparently torn between amusement and disapproval at them taking the initiative to dress her in hand-me-downs. "Then you can take her by supply and get her whatever she requires there. I'll leave word with them to totally outfit and equip her as needed, no limits."

She didn't want to take off what she was wearing just yet. It was nice knowing all three of her men had contributed something to her ill-fitting couture. "I need to go by my apartment and storage locker and get my things."

"You'll have time later today. Go eat, and then the receptionist will direct you to the orientation."

* * * *

Emi wondered if she was coming down with a cold or something, because her sense of taste and smell still seemed out of whack, almost dulled. They ate together, then she snuggled, tucked comfortably between Aaron and Caph on one of the large leather sofas in the orientation room. Halfway through the first video, Caph swapped places with Ford, and Emi smiled and patted his…mmm…firm thigh.

Aaron never moved from her left side, their fingers laced together, his thumb idly stroking the back of her hand.

Usually training videos like that bored her to tears. But what seemed only minutes later it was over, and the technician was asking if she had any questions before starting the next. The videos were program overviews, how the fleet ranking hierarchy was established and her basic duties and responsibilities as medical officer—she'd be a fully commissioned, ranking fleet officer—the mission specifics to be detailed down the road. Three videos later, her men led Emi to supply to get her uniforms.

After a quick stop by the ship to drop everything off, they requisitioned a large box van from the motor pool.

"We won't need anything this big," she told Aaron as he climbed behind the wheel and indicated she should take shotgun.

Caph and Ford crammed into the back seat of the crew cab. She had a feeling, whether by silent captain decree or some mutual decision amongst the men, she would always get the shotgun seat next to Aaron.

"The pick-up trucks only seat three, might as well get everything in one trip. A car would be too small," he explained.

"True."

It took less than an hour with the men's help to empty her dorm and the storage locker. Fortunately, Daniel didn't put in one of his appearances. Donna wasn't in, so Emi sent her an email promising to get together with her in the next few days. Unloading was easy, and they cooked dinner together. She still hadn't changed her clothes, but she did switch to comfier sneakers.

"Did anyone think to get me bread crumbs, by the way?"

Ford frowned. "What are you talking about?"

"You'll have to keep sending out a search party to find me. I'll need to leave a trail of bread crumbs so I don't get lost in this place."

The men laughed. Aaron reassured her. "There are regularly spaced com pads all over the place. Find the nearest one, hit the button, it activates it and gives you a map on the screen."

"Oh. That's helpful."

"You don't think we really know this ship like the back of our hands yet, do you?" Caph asked.

She shrugged. "I assumed you did."

"We've only had her eight months. We picked her up at the Mars DSMC base and brought her here when we signed on. They wanted us to have a shakedown cruise with her old crew before we hit dry dock, and didn't want the post-refit maiden voyage to be our first on her," Caph explained

"What did you have before?"

"Med-hev. Medium-heavy," he clarified. "Larger than the geeks and grunts have now, though. Nearly as big as this girl." He smirked. "The grunts were forced to downsize from what they crewed on in the ISNC. They screamed bloody murder when they weren't given the Bight."

Which explained even more.

"Why do they use small crews on these ships?" she asked.

"The more people you have, the more resources you need to keep them alive. For what we're doing, between cargo, supplies, science equipment, and weaponry resources, a trim crew is the best. Plus we're set up with a jump engine in addition to the regular engines, so we need the extra space for it. The ships are equipped with multiple redundant back-ups. Let's put it this way—if the ship totally goes off-line, it means we're pretty well fucked regardless, because some major shit's happened to it. It's not like in the old vids where the computers can maliciously take over, or one little short-circuit blows the bird up."

She still felt nervous about going out in space, but these men had spent decades there and survived it just fine. "Is it going to be dangerous?"

The men watched her, but Aaron answered. "Frankly, probably less dangerous than settling down in a house in Old Phoenix and trying to drive to work every day and risking your life in traffic. For some of the explorations we'll pick up military escorts, but even then that's mostly just training for them, not actual protection for us. We'll have a full range of weaponry. Where we're slated to go are places already charted from a distance, but they haven't been closely mapped or explored yet. Mostly unpopulated regions. They're looking for new colony and outpost prospects."

"So there's always a risk?"

He leaned back, his voice softening. "There's always a risk. Any day you wake up in the morning and get out of bed you take a risk. There's acceptable risk, and unacceptable risk. I will never knowingly put my crew in jeopardy. I damn well have a strong sense of self-preservation. Can accidents happen? Sure. Piracy is a possibility, but they won't have near the weaponry we'll have, and where we're going, it's never been reported. I'm not a daredevil, despite the reps we captains sometimes get. I just happen to love my job."

She nodded. "Okay then." His soothing, calm confidence reassured her.

Dinner was excellent. The twins were great cooks. Hopefully they could teach her a thing or two.

After clean-up, Ford rubbed his hands together. "Want the full tour now?"

"I guess I should have asked for that first, but yeah."

Aaron glanced at his watch. "I've got a captain's meeting in fifteen I can't miss." He stood, leaned over and kissed her, then each of the twins. "See you in a few hours."

She watched him leave and blushed when the twins noticed her expression.

"That doesn't bother you, does it, sweetheart?" Ford asked.

Emi started breathing again. It had been a very sweet kiss, like a husband kissing his wife good-bye before going to work...and his husband...and his other husband. Matter-of-fact and brief, but tender.

She shook her head, smiling. "No, didn't bother me, just sort of surprised me. Good surprise. I'll get used to it." Truth be told, she was wondering if she could coax the twins to bed.

The twins' collective sigh of relief made her laugh. "I was worried for a second there, honey," Caph admitted. "Afraid you'd freak out on us. Well, let's get started. We've got a lot of ground to cover."

They showed her the rest of the immediate crew area, including the rec area with exercise equipment and an advanced sim room.

"We've got thousands of programs for it," Ford explained, showing her the console. "Tons of on-Earth places, off-Earth, lots of different things. Make sure you look through the library before we leave. If there's anything you want, requisition it. We have full access, so it's not like it costs us anything."

"Same with the books," Caph added. "We've got a huge book, vid, and music library, but check it out and if there's anything you want, we'll get it. You can get put on subscription services too. When something comes out for keywords you specify, it'll be waiting for us to upload it at whatever our next scheduled DSMC port is."

She shook her head, amazed. "Wow. I mean, it's like a library at your fingertips." She was used to good borrowing access because of the university, but not being able to basically own them and have full and unfettered access. "What about educational material?"

Ford led the way past sick bay. "You'll have the full and most up-to-date medical journals and diagnostic manuals when we leave, with automatic uploads at each DSMC base. Not just human, but known species, especially the treaty races."

"I'll be doing a lot of studying."

They took her up to the bridge next, which was near crew

quarters. "I'm going to be assigned watches, huh?" She stared at the nearly dizzying array of consoles, screens, controls, computers—maybe she was in over her head.

Ford slipped his arm around her waist. "Don't worry. It's not nearly as complicated as it look."

"I hope not."

Caph pointed to one work station, surrounded by a curved console, with a large, comfortable-looking chair. "Captain's chair. Or whoever's on watch. Command console." He waved her over and showed her one main console screen with several readouts highlighted in green. "This is the mini-brain, as we call it. It will tell you everything you need to worry about. There are pre-set alarms, so if something goes out of whack it'll immediately set off the klaxon and we'll all be here in thirty seconds or less, believe me."

"I can't break anything?"

He laughed. "No. Navigation is automatic unless overridden. If you're doing a watch, it'll be set on auto-pilot. Sensors will notify you if there's any reason to change course. If so, it'll either handle it, if it's a minor adjustment like for a single object, or it'll notify us if it's an evasive action, like for an asteroid field. You basically sit up here and stay awake. Good time to catch up on your reading. Sometimes we'll alternate, someone takes the first half of night watch, someone gets up early for the second half. Unless someone had too much coffee and can't sleep." He glared at Ford.

Ford shrugged. "I like my java. What can I say." He winked at Emi. "We won't leave you alone at first. We'll partner up with you. After a month or so, you'll be an old hat at it."

They showed her the observation dome, a small armored bubble at the top of the ship, easily accessed from a ladder in the bridge. "This is usually shielded when we're making jumps or under way, but you can see the whole top of the ship from there, great to check for any damage," Caph explained, making room for her on the small platform. There was enough room for all three of them to stand there and stare out the windows.

She looked out over the dry dock facility. The Kendall Kant and Braynow Gaston were clearly visible nearby. With the observation dome located near the ship's bow, the Kendall Kant's bridge was maybe ten yards away.

Ten minutes later, they threaded their way to cargo. It was huge, almost two hundred yards long and a hundred yards wide, nearly empty. "Where is everything?" Her voice echoed.

"They'll start loading us once the retrofits are complete. Not too much down here now," Ford explained.

The enormity of the situation loomed over her as large as the cavernous cargo hold. "How am I ever going to learn this?"

"Honey, I had no college training when I joined the double-M, neither did Caph. It was all OJT, as they say. On the job training. It's a lot easier to teach someone this—" he waved his arm, indicating the ship, "—stuff than it is what you can do. I promise, in six months you'll be completely comfortable. They don't expect you to be as up to speed on the ship as Aaron or us. Your primary job is to keep us morons alive." He smiled, and she relaxed.

"Thanks."

"It's the truth. That's why they're so far behind launching new missions. There's a few med officers contracted to join once they finish college, but it's hard to find a good crew pairing. This was like fate, meeting you. Seriously."

The tour continued, some of the areas not yet complete where labs would be located. Then another large, unfinished room. "This is going to be the hydro lab," Caph said.

"Hydro?"

"Hydroponics. So we can have at least a few fresh fruits and veggies," Ford volunteered.

"A garden?"

"Sort of," they parroted, then laughed.

She loved it when they did that.

"My parents used to have a garden when we still had a house."
She didn't like to talk about them much, thinking about their death
still hurt, even this many years later. "I used to love that."

The twins grinned. "You want to take charge of it?" Ford asked.
"I was going to try it, but last time I tried plants, I killed them. Maybe
you'd have better luck than me."

Caph rolled his eyes. "He ain't exaggerating. Less than a week,
everything was dead."

She nodded. "I'd like that."

* * * *

They returned to the crew area nearly an hour later, with only part
of the tour complete. She felt tired and wanted to lie down. The day
blurred in her mind. She meant to close her eyes only for a moment,
but when she awoke, Aaron was leaning over, kissing her.

"Hey," he whispered.

She looked around. The twins were asleep, the vid screen on and
tuned to a local TV station, the volume down low.

"Hey." One thing she would ask for was a wall clock, or maybe a
window sim screen. She wasn't used to not being able to sense the
time. "What time is it?"

"After ten. I've been back for a while but didn't want to wake you
guys. I had to take care of some paperwork." He quietly undressed
and slipped into bed next to her, curling around her.

She snuggled against him, amazed how comfortable it felt being
with these men. Ford and Caph both wore sleeping shorts, Ford's arm
slung over Caph's broad chest. They looked so perfect like that, like
they belonged there.

"They're so cute," she whispered.

He kissed the back of her neck. "They are. Told you we're not
always sex maniacs."

She stifled her laughter and closed her eyes, wondering if she'd sleep as well that night as she had the night before.

Chapter Seven

Emi awoke to two pairs of eyes watching her, one blue, one green. The second night in a row she slept like a rock, and it seemed she'd just cuddled against Aaron—

He wasn't there. She reached behind her. The bed was empty, the mattress cool.

"Captain's meeting," the twins echoed.

"What time is it?"

"Seven," they parroted.

"What's next?"

Ford glanced at Caph, then spoke. "You're supposed to be at training at ten. We'll meet you for lunch, and then you've got more training until five. Then we're on our own for the night. They go easy on all of us the first two weeks after a crew pairing, give us time to settle into a routine before they start prepping us and the serious training."

Caph picked up where Ford left off. "And it gives you a chance to get used to where everything is and get comfortable, learn the DSMC basics, all that crap."

"Breakfast?"

"After a shower?" they echoed.

She smiled. "Sure."

The only problem was, she rolled onto her side to kiss them good morning, and ten minutes later she was happily moaning as Ford buried his tongue between her legs while Caph kissed her.

This was a gooood life.

Unlike Daniel's half-hearted efforts to bring her release to not appear like the selfish asshole he was, Caph and Ford were eager and more than willing to take care of her first. Ford took his time laving his tongue over her swollen nub, seeming to know exactly when to back off to keep her on the edge, repeatedly bringing her close until she begged him to let her climax.

When she did she cried out, grabbing Caph's hand and squeezing as her body arched against him. Emi closed her eyes, panting, catching her breath. They were always that good, the other night hadn't been a one-time thing.

Thank the gods!

Ford lifted his head. "Was that okay, sweetie?"

"Huh? Okay?" she gasped, still trying to process his words. "Screw okay, that was amazing!"

Caph chuckled. "He's always like that. Just tell him he's the best, stroke his ego." Caph's hand gently trailed down her body, his fingers teasing her ready entrance. "Ready to feel him inside you, baby?"

Emi nodded, kissing him again.

Ford positioned himself and they both moaned as he slowly buried his full length inside her. Then he lowered his body on top of hers, kissing her, not thrusting. "You...are...soooo...good..." he whispered.

Caph kissed him. Emi watched, fascinated, as the men took their time, their lips exploring each other.

"Wow!" she gasped, wide-eyed.

Caph looked down at her. "You okay?"

"Uh huh!"

"Not freaked out?"

She vigorously shook her head. Ford smiled, nuzzling the base of Caph's throat with his lips. "Maybe we should show her something else while we're at it. She'll see it eventually." He took several slow, teasing thrusts inside Emi, making her moan.

Caph's eyes narrowed in amusement. "You saying what I think you're saying?"

Ford kissed him again. "I wouldn't mind a little bottom action this morning."

Caph's sensual growl startled her, taking her breath away. "Damn," he moaned. "You talk like that, I'll come right here."

Ford met her eyes. "You're gonna have to get used to it sooner or later, right?"

Caph watched Ford, hunger in his eyes. "Don't take all day then, buddy."

He closed his eyes. Emi met his thrusts, almost wanting him to hurry up so she could see this. This was…

Wow.

Emi never thought she'd find two guys being together this sexy, but the obvious love these two men had for each other engulfed her, pulling her in. She felt honored they welcomed her into their lives and were already willing to open their hearts to her.

This was one of the things she loved about being an empath.

Ford dropped his head to her shoulder as she rolled her hips against him and held him tightly.

"Come for me," she whispered, her hands gripping his ass. "Because I can't wait to see the two of you together—"

"Oh man!" She felt his climax in his last, hard thrust, holding still deep inside her. "Damn, baby," he gasped. "That was—"

"Fucking sexy." Aaron's husky voice from the doorway startled them.

Caph grinned. "Busted."

Emi worried for a moment until she looked over Ford's shoulder and saw Aaron's sultry smile. He peeled off his shirt and started toward the bed, soon ditching the rest of his clothes.

"What'd I miss?" he asked.

Ford sat up, taking his weight off Emi. "I think we were just about to move to the shower and give the little lady a show."

Aaron's eyes were dark, nearly smoky with passion, his hard cock standing at attention. "Any other needs we should take care of first, sweetie?" he asked her.

Speech deserted her. What *could* she say? Yes, please?

The men watched her, Aaron's amused smirk capturing her. "I think you guys fried her brain."

"All I did was go down on her," Ford said, his eyes gleaming with wicked humor. "Then I fucked her silly."

"No, you fucked her speechless."

Emi laughed. "You guys are too much."

"Ah," Caph said. "She speaks." He kissed her. "You all right?"

She crooked her finger at Aaron. He leaned over her, kissing her. Ford rolled off her. She sat up, pushing Aaron down to the bed. "I think there's something I'd like to do first." She knelt over him, his eyes burning into hers. "I think it's time I do a little reciprocating." She'd been dying to wrap her lips around their cocks and felt a little guilty that all she'd had to do so far was lay back and enjoy things.

Aaron closed his eyes and moaned as she teased his stiff shaft with her mouth, swirling her tongue around the head before slowly taking him in.

Emi was vaguely aware of Caph getting up and returning a moment later. Ford changed positions, laying on his stomach, his head near Aaron's hip. He reached out with one hand and gently pulled her hair out of the way.

"That's beautiful," he whispered in an awed tone.

She glanced at him, something stirring inside her as she realized why Caph had left—he now held a bottle of lube. He slicked himself and then nudged Ford's ass in the air, gently working lube into him.

It was hard for her to focus on what she was doing, too tempted to stop and watch them. Ford's eyes closed for a moment as both men let out satisfied grunts. Then Ford's blue eyes were on hers again.

"You okay?" he whispered to her, a playful smile curling his lips.

Aaron's hand gently tangled in her hair, his fingers lacing through Ford's. He was also watching the twins. "Dammit that's sexy," he said, his voice hoarse.

He was absolutely right—it was.

Caph gripped Ford's hips, slowly stroking. Emi was so caught up in their hot tableaux that she almost forgot what she was doing.

It didn't seem to matter that she wasn't doing much more than holding Aaron's shaft in her mouth—he was stiff and throbbed against her tongue. She reached out and stroked Ford's hair, resting her hand on his shoulder.

Caph's green eyes looked glazed beneath his heavy lids. "Make him moan, sweetheart," he whispered in a husky voice. "Wrap those sweet lips around him and let me see you make him come."

That was enough to bring her back. She worked her tongue and lips around Aaron's cock. Aaron groaned, his fingers tightening a little on her head as she brought him over. All three men froze as she stayed with him, closing her eyes and wishing she had a cock between her legs because her sex was almost painfully throbbing again. She swallowed every hot drop he pumped out, and when she gently released him a moment later, she looked at the three of them. They sat, frozen, staring, jaws gaped. For a moment she thought maybe she'd done something wrong.

"What?"

"Holy fuck!" the twins echoed in awed tones.

Aaron grinned. "That was fucking hot!"

Now she was confused. "What?"

"You swallowed!" the twins said.

"So?"

Aaron pulled her to him and kissed her. "Not all women enjoy that."

"You know what I'd enjoy?"

"What?"

"Watching those two—" she pointed at the twins, "—then one of you can have me again because I'm so friggin horny I can't stand it."

"I can take care of that." Aaron lowered her to the bed, her head next to Ford's. Caph had resumed his slow strokes. Ford kissed her as

Aaron dropped his lips to her clit.

She suspected Caph reached around and started stroking Ford's cock with his hand, because Ford gasped, then started fucking her mouth with his tongue. Emi let go, enjoying the feel of Aaron's mouth between her legs. She closed her eyes and moaned.

"That's it, baby," Ford grunted, his release close. "See if you can come with me." His hand found hers, gripping it.

Part of her thought this had to be a dream. It felt like she hovered on the edge for hours. When Aaron slipped two fingers into her she exploded, her climax setting off a chain reaction. Ford cried out, squeezing her hand, burying his head against her neck. Then Caph cried out, his last hard strokes shaking all of them.

They collapsed into a heap on the bed, gasping, sweaty. Aaron found his voice first. "I used to hate morning captain meetings, but if I'm going to come back to this every morning, I don't mind so much."

* * * *

They dragged themselves into the shower and then ate breakfast. Surely the novelty of their arrangement would wear off, but until it did, the memory of what they'd done distracted Emi all through her morning training sessions.

The men waited for her outside the classroom. She kissed each of them in greeting before walking with them to the cafeteria. More classes later, and while she thought the time away from the men might drag, it seemed to fly. After dinner, Aaron spent time with her on the bridge, explaining the primary control systems to her. When they all fell into bed after ten o'clock, they immediately fell asleep.

Another solid, dreamless night. If for nothing else, that alone was worth this job. The men, of course, were absolutely fantastic. Having her sleep back was an unexpected bonus.

This pattern repeated for several days. Sometimes they made love in the morning or night, sometimes they didn't. The days seemed to almost merge together, they sped by so quickly. The men patiently helped her study the ship's systems, focusing on one area at a time as she was introduced to the basic workings of each. Life support, shields, engines, sensors, with weaponry saved until later because it was both the easiest and most intense. Every day they spent a little time on emergency procedures, wanting her to memorize those thoroughly.

Two weeks into her new job, during training it was mentioned she had to give the crew their complete physicals despite the fact that they'd already been medically cleared and examined. Because as medical officer, she had to personally know their baselines.

Emi grinned. She already had an intimate grasp of their baselines but understood the need for an official examination.

This could be fun.

Emi called Caph to the sick bay

"What's up?"

Biting back a sexual retort that would no doubt land them both in bed, she smiled. "Physical exam."

He grabbed her hips and pulled her to him. "Mmm. Really?"

"Seriously." Placing a finger on his chest, she stood on her toes and brushed her lips against his. "Get naked, Officer Bates." She winked.

Caph stepped back and pulled off his shirt, immediately triggering flutters in Emi's nether regions. He smiled, dropped his pants.

He was already stiffening.

"Like this?" His playful smirk nearly finished her reserve.

"Yeah, now sit on the exam table."

It was sheer force of will keeping her eyes—and lips—out of his lap. Emi went through the normal routine, his amused gaze following her every move.

"You're gonna play this to the hilt, huh?" he asked.

"I'm the medical officer. I have to have a baseline."

He laughed. "Oh, is that the euphemistic medical term for

molesting your crew?"

She patted his thigh as she noted all the readings in his chart. "Okay, stand up and bend over, please."

He was almost a little too eager. He rested his forearms on the table and spread his legs, casting a glance over his shoulder. She patted his butt and slipped on an exam glove, squirting more lube than she needed into her gloved hand.

"Just relax, Officer Bates," she purred.

He laughed, dropping his head. "Uh, yeah. You are sooo getting fucked hard tonight, girl, I can't even begin to tell you."

Well, that did it. She was officially drenched. "This will only take a moment."

"Take all the time you need, *Doc*."

She put the bottle of lube on the tray and stepped beside him, rubbing a little of the excess lube on her ungloved hand. He spread his legs further as she slipped a gloved finger inside him. What surprised him was her pressing her body against his side and then wrapping her fingers of her other hand around his cock. She did check his prostate, but she was in no hurry to stop there, and neither was he.

His hungry moan as his cock throbbed in her palm sent another wave of moisture to her sex.

"You all right, Officer Bates?" she whispered.

"Mmm hmm." He bucked his hips against her hands as they settled into a slow rhythm. After just a few minutes she knew he was getting close, his breath coming in short, shallow gasps as his hips rocked harder against her hands.

"You close, baby?" she asked.

He nodded, his eyes closed. A moment later he gripped the edge of the table as he groaned, climaxing, coating her hand with his juices.

She kissed his shoulder and withdrew, disposing of the glove and washing her hands. He was still leaning over the table, breathing heavily.

"You okay?"

He nodded, then laughed. "Damn. That was, by far, *the* best physical I've ever had."

She handed him a towel. He wiped himself off, then crooked his finger at her. He wrapped his arms around her and kissed her, holding her tightly against him. "That was fucking sexy, babe. You can examine me anytime you want."

"Don't spill the beans to the others, okay?"

He grinned. "Man, I just thought you were gonna tease me a little."

Emi pretended to frown. "I thought I told you guys at the beginning that I've never been a tease."

Caph laid his palm against her cheek and looked into her eyes. His sudden wave of emotion washed through her. "I love you, Emi," he whispered, placing one last gentle kiss on her lips. "I mean it, sweetie. I love you."

"I love you, too." They shared one last bear hug, and she knew as certainly as she knew that the sun would come up the next morning that she loved these three men. It was crazy and strange and certainly not normal, but she loved them.

He dressed, then turned to her. "Want me to play doctor for a little bit?"

"You'll get your turn later, mister. I'll be in need of your services after I finish with the other two. Go find Ford and send him in, please."

He winked. "I'll hold you to that date, sweetie." He left sick bay and she went to the head to freshen up. Maybe she should have let him have a little solo fun with her.

Ford walked in ten minutes later. She read him without turning to face him, knew that Caph had kept the secret.

"What's up, sweetie?" he asked.

Oh, they sometimes made the comments too easy.

"Get undressed. I need to do your physical." She turned to him and he was already out of his shirt and his pants were halfway down.

Laughing, she shook her head. "Don't have to ask you twice, do I?"

"Come on, Emi. Do you really think I'm going to tell you 'no' when you tell me to strip?"

She went through the same procedure with Ford, only with more of their familiar banter and chit chat. Caph was more quiet when they were together. Ford didn't feel the need to fill silence, their conversations just naturally happened. Talking about any and everything. She suspected her arrival had filled an intellectual need for him that was long unmet. Not that the other two men weren't smart, because they were. However, Emi understood from living with them that Ford frequently suppressed his need for ambling non sequitur conversations around the other two men so he didn't try their patience.

He was a chatterbox.

It wasn't unusual during her talks with Ford for them to start on one topic—a book, for example—then suddenly switch tracks to a completely unrelated topic, bouncing around with light speed until they couldn't remember the original conversation. Caph and Aaron tolerated this in him, but he strongly curtailed his desire to talk around them for their sake, not wanting to drive them crazy.

When she got to the point where she asked him to bend over the table, he looked at her, then smiled. "Sure."

Grabbing another glove, she repeated the same procedure she had with Caph. Ford closed his eyes, sighing.

"Thought you said you weren't a tease." His voice had taken on an arousal-tinged depth.

"I'm not." She stroked him, enjoying the way his body responded.

"Damn," he whispered. He kissed her, his eyes still closed. "Please don't stop."

"I won't." She pressed her body against his, her sex throbbing again. "Show me how good you feel."

"That feels sooo good."

"Caph said I'm getting a good hard fucking tonight after what I did to him."

"Times two…" He grunted, closer to release. "What do you want us to do to you, baby?"

"I figured you'd be trying to get a little revenge, hold me down and tease me, make me beg for it."

"That what you want? Want me to make you beg?"

She was damn close to begging him now. "You know what you do to me." That finished him, his entire body trembled with the force of his release. Emi gave him a moment to recover, cleaned up, and handed him a towel.

Ford pulled her to him, crushing her against him, kissing her. "Dammit you're so sexy, babe. I love you so much. I don't even mind sharing you with those two guys."

"I love you, too. And I don't mind sharing you with them, either."

He grinned. "I still can't believe you're okay with all this. You just fit right in."

"Why wouldn't I be okay with it? Maybe if those other stupid women could have felt what I felt with you guys, they would have kept an open mind."

His eyes grew sad for a moment, and she felt his mood shift. "The three of us, we've been together a lot of years. And I'm not saying I would have changed anything, because I love them, and I know they love me even though I drive them crazy. But it's like…it's like we're complete now, you know? Like we were waiting for you and now that you're here, I can't imagine you not being here. It feels right."

Emi nodded. "I know. And you're stuck with me for at least five years."

He kissed her again. "Hopefully a lot longer than that, babe."

She sent him on with the same admonishment she gave Caph. Before he left he turned, his face clouded.

"Do me a favor, babe. Keep in mind Cap never bottoms, okay?"

She nodded, curious. This wasn't the same thing. Was it? "Okay." He left, and she finished his chart. Aaron walked in a few minutes later, his eyes playful.

"What did you do to the twins?"

Emi went for wide-eyed innocence, knowing her act wasn't fooling Aaron in the slightest. "What?"

"I know those two. They both look like they got laid. Thought this was supposed to be a medical exam?"

"I did examine them, just like I'm about to examine you."

He laughed, shaking his head. "Guess I just have to wait and see for myself, huh?"

"You can undress now, Captain."

He did, sitting on the table and letting her go through the procedure.

When she got to the point where she was going to have him bend over she felt it—his anxiety, stress levels suddenly through the roof. His entire body as well as his mind and soul had tensed, and it was one of the times she wished she was a full clairvoyant.

"What's wrong?"

He shook his head, his playful smile gone and replaced by a grim look. "Nothing. Let's get this over with." He sensed what was up.

She waited, watching him. "Aaron, tell me. Please."

His ragged breath told her she needed to change her plans or there might be serious emotional repercussions for him. "Long story." He looked at her, but his smirk was anything but playful or amused. It reminded her of his hostile response her first night with them, before they started over. "Crew story."

She stepped back, almost physically rocked by his words. "I thought I was crew."

"I—" He stopped, probably mentally swearing. "I didn't mean it like that, Em." His voice softened. "Look, before we leave, after you've signed on the line and all, we'll go out and we'll tell you. The basics, at the very least. I promise."

This was part of his deep grief. She sensed there were two parts to this story, separate, but so entwined they wove the tapestry of his pain.

"You don't trust me yet, do you?"

He stood up. "I do. But it's taken me a lot of years to get to the point where I can even think about it, much less talk about it."

That was the best she would get from him for now, and Ford's words before he left sick bay came back to her. "Okay." She grabbed a glove and carefully and quickly did the exam, professionally, taking mere seconds, without the happy finish she'd given the other two.

Maybe this was tied into why he didn't "bottom."

His sigh of relief when it was over wasn't merely physical, it was mental. She sensed it wasn't that he hated it. It was like he wanted to enjoy it the way the other two did, perhaps even once had, but something stopped him. He enjoyed going down on the twins, she'd watched him do it, and he certainly enjoyed fucking them and letting them go down on him. But this was something different, something preventing him from enjoying it.

His emotional pain.

She had an idea.

"Up on the table and lay down on your back, please."

Puzzled, he did.

She looked at him. "I need to check for any irregularities." She winked, hoping it would relax him.

As if a fog cleared in his soul he laughed, crossing his arms behind his head. "I think I'm going to like this."

She started with a traditional testicular exam—for all of five seconds. Then she went down on him, his moan setting her insides on fire as she laved her tongue around his now-erect cock. The men each had subtle preferences, and they'd had fun teaching her. Always a quick study, she knew just what combination of techniques would quickly bring him over, and that's what she did.

He closed his eyes, one hand going to the back of her head, gently cupping it as she stayed with him until he was completely spent. She looked up to his cautious smile and smoldering gaze.

"You didn't do that to the twins, did you?"

"Not exactly."

He crooked his finger at her, and she kissed him. He sat up and pulled her to him, hugging her. "It's not you, Em," he whispered. "Seriously."

"It's okay. You guys warned me that you don't bottom." She tried to keep her tone light, but despite his smile, she still felt the hints of his grief.

He gently stroked her cheek. "Let's get through training and get the hell off this rock. Then you'll have a lot of time to work on my brain and try to get it straightened out." His eyes searched her face. "I have a feeling if anyone can help me, you can," he murmured.

Then, before she could ask him any more, he was off the table and quickly dressed, planting a quick kiss on her lips, back to playful Aaron. "Don't work too *hard*, Em."

She grinned, catching the barb. He was the only one who called her Em, something special between them. Then he was out the sick bay door, back to work.

It was the best she could ask for, for now.

Chapter Eight

Emi rarely noticed the age difference between her and the men. It didn't appear to bother them, and as the weeks turned to months, it wasn't an issue for her. During training exercises, their age made their skill and experience obvious, comforting her, reassuring her that they knew their jobs and knew them well.

"Her boys," as she'd come to think of them collectively—"boys" being a term of endearment and not the slur the Braynow Gaston crew had intended—were three unique personalities. Aaron was her serious, sometimes brooding, deeply passionate warrior. Ford was the intelligent, sensitive caretaker. Caph was the playful, rowdy protector. Not just with her, but with each other, even though the dynamic was slightly different between the men than it was with her.

However, in training, whether working with her on the ship or in classes, that's when their other sides appeared.

Professional, the men were never unfriendly or cold, but the flip side of the coin, the skills and experience that kept them alive all these years and made them successful in their field. And never condescending, as she suspected both the geeks and the grunts would have been toward her. They were always patient, always careful to make sure she understood something before continuing.

Ford best summed it up when she voiced her frustration at herself one afternoon, mad that she felt like she was holding them back.

He pulled the hand-held console out of her hand and sat on the floor next to her by the emergency override panel in cargo. He grabbed her hands. "Look at me."

She did, fixed by his blue eyes.

"Emi, you're the only one putting pressure on you. Graymard's already told you there isn't a solid departure date. We can't take five years here, obviously, but if it takes a few extra months, we'll do it. Aaron's not going to force you to say you're ready if you aren't."

The fear ran through her again, what had, despite her now totally uninterrupted sleep every night, haunted her dreams, pecked at her brain. "What if I'm not good enough and Aaron replaces me?"

"Oh, sweetie," he whispered, pulling her into his arms as she finally let go and cried. She never let go like this in front of Aaron, and only rarely in front of Caph. Ford was her emotional safety net. He held her, stroking her back, comforting her.

Ford, she knew, understood how she felt. "Don't think that. He loves you as much as we do, trust me."

She trusted Ford to think like that, but not that he was right about it. "He's never said it." The twins said it to her every day—multiple times, usually. And she knew they meant it.

She felt Aaron's emotion, but he'd yet to voice it. She didn't understand the contradiction and didn't know if she wanted to.

"Babe, this is all tied in—"

"I know, crew story." She sat up and bitterly wiped her eyes. Maybe she wasn't ready to do this. The thought of losing her boys ripped her apart, nearly as strong a pain as losing her parents. She belonged on this ship, with these three men. That was one thing she felt through the depths of her soul.

He looked at his watch. "I think it's time for lunch. You need a break." He stood and helped her to her feet, leading her through the ship to the crew area. He seemed perfectly comfortable in the corridors, but she usually got lost at least once a day.

Caph was fixing himself a sandwich in the galley. "Hey, done so soon?"

Emi didn't miss Ford's imperceptible shake of his head. She sighed. "I'm okay, Ford."

Caph grabbed her shoulders in his big hands and gently guided her to a chair. "Sit. We'll make your lunch." She knew Aaron was in the engine room with the refit crew, going through specs on the jump engine. She still wasn't sure how that worked, but knew it would shave months, possibly years off the different legs of their trip.

Caph placed a sandwich in front of her, then sat with his own. "What's wrong?"

She couldn't resist him and knew he'd get the story from Ford anyway. "I'm just being stupid, that's all. I'm okay. I'm just moody."

He reached across the table and caught her chin, made her look at him. "Aaron loves you, sweetie. He just isn't mushy like us two goobers."

That made her smile. "Goober" wasn't the last word she'd use to describe the twins, but it was so far toward the bottom of the list it didn't matter.

"There's my smile." She couldn't say she loved him like a big brother, because that kind of brotherly love was pretty much universally illegal. At least, on Earth it was. But the non-romantic part of their relationship felt a lot like that. Caph was the one who acted closest to her in years in many ways, and he didn't look his age. All of the men were handsome and in shape, but Caph seemed more like thirty than forty. She'd seen him as serious as Aaron while they participated in a weaponry simulation, startled to see his green eyes dark and focused on keeping them "alive" during the battle. When it ended, he'd immediately reverted back to playful Caph.

Ford studied her. She felt his eyes and mind on her.

"Why do you always feel you have to push yourself harder?" he asked.

Caph released her chin and sat back, taking a bite of his sandwich but also interested in hearing her answer.

She shrugged, not wanting to be the center of attention. "I just needed to work hard, that's all. I knew I needed good grades. I didn't have a safety net. I didn't have any family, and I didn't want to spend my life working in a boring civil job just so I'd have a roof over my head and something to eat every month."

"You do now, you know," he said, his voice quiet. "A safety net." When she didn't respond he reached over and gently grabbed her wrist, waiting until she looked at him. "You have all three of us, babe. We won't let you fail, don't worry. Your job is to take care of us and not drive yourself so hard you fall apart. Let us take care of the rest. You think we're letting you get away from us, you're crazy."

Emi mustered a weak smile for his benefit. "Thanks, Ford."

Pain flared in her heart, and she struggled to push it back. She didn't want to think about her parents, about their death and her emotional downward spiral those first months. She didn't tell the men the whole truth. Part of her need to succeed was driven by her fear of failure.

Part of it was to escape her pain.

It was her drug, the thing that kept her going during the bleakest times after the two NSI officials showed up to break the news to her about her parents' death. Work meant not thinking about anything *but* work, no time to grieve, why she drove herself to get an Alpha-ranking, psych minor, and empath training in the same amount of time most Beta-rankings took to get trained.

So she didn't have to think. Not about her parents, at least.

Not about the loneliness.

Not about her grief or pain or if they died thinking about her.

Not about not being able to say good-bye and tell them she loved them.

Emi realized the men were watching her, and she forced another smile. "I'm okay, really."

"You never talk about your family," Ford observed.

Damn him. For someone who wasn't the slightest bit empathic, he was eerily clued into her thoughts. Maybe the chips gave him the extra insight.

"It's not something I want to talk about." She smirked. "Family story. When Aaron wants to tell, we can swap tales of woe."

Apparently sensing she was at the end of her endurance for the conversation, Ford and Caph focused on their lunch and diverted the topic elsewhere.

* * * *

Emi still slept like a rock, and at the four-month mark her training schedule, as well as the crew sessions, were escalated. Emi focused and relaxed when Aaron praised her progress. He made no thought or mention of refusing her assignment or reconsidering their decision to add her to their crew.

All three men constantly encouraged her, telling her how great she was doing, and it didn't fully hit her until one day when she walked from sick bay to the cargo hold to see if a scanner machine she'd ordered had arrived. The entire ten minute walk, she'd had her head bent over her hand-held, looking through messages, checking reports. When she found herself in the cargo hold she looked up, startled.

Usually she got lost going to cargo. Not every day, but twice a week on average. Her navigation skills within the ship were better, but not perfect. She'd learned to focus on the men and use them as a type of homing beacon, knowing where they were helped her orient herself.

Ford walked in a moment later and noted her proud smile. "What'd you do?"

"I didn't get lost! And I was reading my console at the same time!"

He laughed and picked her up, swinging her around. "See, we told you it just takes time. You deserve to be proud of yourself."

Maybe she did.

Would her parents be proud of her taking this assignment? It wasn't particularly scandalous in the grand scheme of things. Intra-crew relationship agreements had been standard for over a hundred years in the various space corps, and polyamorous marriages had been legal for over four hundred years on Earth, even if they were an extremely small minority.

She'd like to think they would, that she went on despite the odds and not only did well in school, but excelled. And that she was part of a group, not just a crew, but a make-shift family. She was, overall, happy.

Now if she could get that one niggling fear to crawl out of her brain and quit distracting her, life would be perfect. No matter how many times Ford and Caph assured her that Aaron loved her, it was increasingly obvious that every time they said it to her, Aaron didn't.

The few times she'd said it to him, he'd smiled that sad smile of his and said, "I know," or something similar, usually kissing her to distract her. It had reached the point where she conspicuously noticed that unless she said it to Caph and Ford around Aaron, the twins only said, "I love you," when Aaron wasn't around. As if trying to keep his lack of saying it from being noticed.

As training intensified, she barely had time to focus on it. While their lovemaking was intense, mind-blowing passion she loved to think about during her few spare moments, there were plenty of nights they were so exhausted at the end of the day that they all fell into bed together and immediately went to sleep, snuggled into one of many familiar configurations.

She was in one of the emergency pods with Caph one afternoon, learning the systems, when he broadsided her with an unexpected comment.

"You know you can talk to me, or Ford, about your parents, if you want. If you ever need an ear."

She froze, her hands nearly crushing the hand-held console she'd been consulting. Forcing a harsh laugh, she shook her head. "Talk about a left-field statement."

"I'm not an empath, but you're getting tense. It's building in you. I feel it, so does Ford. If it's about your parents, you can talk to us."

Relieved at his misinterpretation of her stress, she smiled. "That's not it, but thank you."

"Then what is it?"

Fear. Five years was a long time, but then what? What happened after?

She looked at him. "You guys have been together a long time."

He nodded. "We're like family."

"I'm going to miss this when it's over. I try not to think about that, but I know I will."

Alarm and desperate fear washed through him. "Who says anything about you leaving? You can't leave!"

"Caph, you don't know if Aaron's going to request the DSMC renew my assignment—"

"Damn straight he will! Goddamn, girl, where's your head?" This was the first time she'd ever felt genuine anger from him. "Do you really think he's gonna let you go? That any of us would?" He grabbed her arms, gently shaking her. "You try to leave us, that's pretty hard to do with me hanging onto one leg and Ford on the other, and Aaron blocking the exit."

She swallowed. "But what if he's holding the door open for me to go?" she whispered. "Or what if he decides to refuse my assignment altogether? I'm not 'official,' you know."

He pulled her to him across the seat, holding her. "Sweetie," he pleaded, desperate, "you're one of us. No, there's no way he'd do that. We're used to him, trust me, he doesn't tell us either, but we know he loves us. He doesn't have to tell us. Just let him be Aaron and love him the way he is."

"Is it so hard for him to say it?"

Then she felt a hint of the same sadness she felt in Aaron, and a touch of grief shadowed Caph's playful eyes.

"Yeah. It is," he said, his voice soft as he sat back and released her. "It is hard for him to say."

* * * *

It's not a big deal. It was her silent mantra, and it was a lie. It was a bigger deal every day. Emi was well aware of the irony, that if she'd picked the geeks or the grunts, she wouldn't expect a declaration of love from them because she wouldn't have fallen *in* love with them.

The first time she awoke in the middle of the night since moving in, she realized Aaron wasn't there. She looked at the clock and saw he should have returned hours earlier from a captain's meeting.

Ford and Caph had gravitated toward each other in sleep, making it easier for her to slip out of bed without waking them. Her foot brushed against a shirt. She pulled it on, not caring whose it was. Caph's T-shirt fell nearly to her knees.

In the corridor she closed her eyes and focused. Aaron was back, on the bridge. Barefoot and silent, she made her way upstairs in the dim light and silently watched him from the open doorway.

He sat in his chair. At first she thought he was staring at a console. Then she realized he was staring out the large front view ports. In flight they'd be safely closed behind armored plates, large superimposed vid screens providing them a simulated view.

She watched him for several minutes, his gaze never diverting from the mostly dark dry dock view. There were a few retrofit crews still working, but most of the ships' crews were either sleeping or the ships were vacant.

He was a strong man, but she wished he'd let her in and help him heal. It couldn't be rushed, of course, any more than her own healing could. Yet in this point where their pain intersected, she wished, for once, she could make some headway.

Selfish? Yes. She admitted it.

After a while he stretched his left arm out to his side, palm up, waiting. He'd never turned his head in her direction, could not have seen her standing there.

He'd sensed her presence.

Without a word, she padded across the bridge to him and took his hand. He pulled her into his lap. She curled up, her head against his firm chest. She wanted to talk to him, but sensing his mood—deep, contemplative, melancholy—she changed her mind.

He sighed as he wrapped his arms around her, burying his face in her hair. A sense of calm relaxation gradually replaced his previous tense emotions. He'd always given her a sense of warm strength. Maybe he gained the same from her?

Emi didn't realize she'd fallen asleep again until she felt him lay her in their bed. A moment later he slid under the sheet next to her, holding her.

Despite her confusion over his actions and her desperation to know, she didn't want to ask the question. Part of her feared his answer—that he maybe didn't love her the way she loved him, the way the twins loved her—and part of her didn't want to break his newly-calmed mood.

He held her, his heartbeat soft and strong against her cheek as she closed her eyes again. It confused her that yes, his actions spoke love, but why couldn't he say it?

Chapter Nine

It didn't seem important the next morning. Emi had a day off from training classes, and Aaron still laid wrapped around her. The twins weren't in bed.

"Good morning," he whispered. "Are you feeling better?"

Her eyes must have betrayed her shock. He smiled. "The way you tracked me down last night. And the way you've been acting. Plus the chip. That, and the twins told me."

She closed her eyes and groaned. "They have big mouths."

He leaned over and kissed her, sweet and slow, his tongue lightly tracing the seam of her lips, distracting her the way his kisses always did.

"I *cannot* imagine life without you here," he said, staring into her eyes. "And that's the truth." He started to say something else when the com alert tone sounded.

"Sorry, Aar," Ford apologized, "but Graymard just buzzed. Needs you in his office asap for a consult briefing about a new applicant."

Aaron swore under his breath. "Thanks, Ford," he said, loud enough for the com to pick up his reply. "Tell him I'll be right there." He'd immediately switched from lover to captain mode. He kissed her again and was out of the bed before she could say anything.

"I'm sorry, Em," he apologized over his shoulder, jogging for the head. "One of those times it sucks to be captain."

She flopped back in bed, staring at the ceiling. "Yeah," she mumbled. "Sometimes it sucks to be the crew, too."

He gave her a quick kiss five minutes later as he rushed out the door.

The twins worked on the bridge while she ate breakfast. Emi considered seeking them out but knew they were busy and didn't want to distract them. She tried calling Donna at work. They talked for a few minutes, but Donna couldn't take a long lunch break.

Emi walked over to the cafeteria with her hand-held console, wanting time out of the ship, at least. She spent an hour eating a leisurely lunch, reading a book on her console, occasionally chatting with some of the other crews. They didn't do a lot of socializing, not because it was discouraged but because they were all so busy.

When she'd finished eating she moved outside to the cool, shaded gardens to read some more. The middle of winter, but New Phoenix was balmy if you stayed out of the sun. Not so much during the summer, unfortunately, when it was scorching hot outside even in the shade.

On her way back she thought she heard angry voices. In the distance she saw Aaron stalking to the ship, away from the Kendall Kant's Captain Elloy, who looked smug and arrogant. By the time she reached the gangway, he'd also disappeared.

She found Aaron storming around the galley, alone, the twins giving him wide berth.

"What's wrong?" she asked.

He set his jaw as he slapped a sandwich together. "Nothing. Just assholes running their mouths, that's all." He looked at her and his face softened. He leaned over and kissed her. "Nothing you need to worry about." He took his sandwich with him. She suspected he was off to the engine room to work on something, or at the very least to calm down. That was his place to relax, where hers was the hydroponic lab.

* * * *

Emi decided to make good use of her time and went to the retrofit construction office to put in plans for some final modifications she wanted for sick bay and the hydro lab. She stood at the counter, talking with the foreman in charge of their ship, when she heard amused male voices floating from an open office door.

"I cannot believe those...*faggots* got that ship. They have no business getting a full heavy. What have they done to deserve it?"

Emi froze. She knew that voice. Captain Elloy from the Kendall Kant.

The horrified foreman tried to distract her but she held up a staying hand as she listened.

Elloy continued his rant. "Not only they get a ship that's too good for them, they get an Alpha-ranked med officer? A *female* Alpha-ranked med officer? Screw that. I could understand her picking the Braynow Gaston over us, that wouldn't bother me. But the TB? Fuck, that should stand for 'The Buttfuckers.'"

Hoarse, braying laughter, and Elloy continued. "She's probably a friggin dyke, picked them so she never had to get laid..."

The voice trailed off. The foreman had walked over and quietly pulled the door shut, his face red. "I'm sorry," he whispered. "He's an asshole. Aaron and the guys are good at what they do. The K-2 guys are just jealous, that's all. Aaron and the guys got the better ship and they got the beautiful girl." He smiled, trying to diffuse the situation.

Emi held onto her rage and somehow made it through the rest of their talk. When the office door opened minutes later, Elloy and another foreman stepped out. The captain only paused a second when he saw her.

She glared at him. He had the nerve to smile before talking to the foreman. "Get the hover lift, I'll show you what I mean. Up on the top of the ship, I want to..." The door closing behind them cut him off.

Sudden pain in her palms made her look at her hands. She'd dug her fingernails into her skin with her clenched fists, almost drawing blood.

Emi quickly finished and returned to the Tamora Bight, in full run as she hit the gangway to the main hatch. She'd glanced at the next berth. Sure enough, Elloy and the foreman were up top with one of the other grunts looking at something.

She glanced at her ship and grinned, her idea now fully formed.

Racing down the main corridor, she tried to find the guys and located Ford in the secondary corridor. She grabbed his arm, pulling him behind her. "Come on!"

"What?"

"I don't have time to tell you. Follow me."

He easily jogged behind her up to the bridge. Caph was in the common area, but she didn't have time to get him. She wanted to do this while she still had an audience. Racing up the ladder to the observation dome, she waved Ford up behind her. "Hurry!"

"What is going—"

She grabbed his hand as he reached the platform, pulling him to her and kissing him.

He only resisted for a second, then got into it. She turned them around so she could peek and waited until the men on the top of the K-2 were finally looking their way.

She jumped up and wrapped her legs around his waist. "Just play along, Ford," she said, careful to keep her face turned from the window. They were about thirty feet away from the other men, but she didn't want to risk them being able to read lips.

When he tried to speak she laid a palm along his cheek as if to turn his face and kiss him. She mumbled, "I'll tell you later. We have to give the K-2 crew a really dirty show." They were visible from the waist up from the other ship's vantage point.

"Okay," he murmured against her hand. "You'd better tell me later. I gotta hear this."

He set her down. She worked his shirt off, dropping it off the platform to the bridge below, kissing his chest. "Don't be obvious, but are the K-2 guys watching?"

He must have glanced. "Holy shit, yeah, their jaws are dropped," he muttered out of the side of his mouth.

"Good. Make it look real." She dropped to her knees, pushing him back against the side of the dome. "Pretend I'm giving you the best blowjob you've ever had."

He threw his head back like she'd just deep-throated him. "Why fake it, sugar?"

"I'll tell you later. They still watching?"

"Oh, yeah. Now there's two more guys up there. We should charge admission."

She stood up, kissed him, then worked her way back down his body. His cock was rock-hard, and it was tempting to do it for real. Instead she gently squeezed him through his pants. His responding growl wasn't faked.

"You said you're not a tease, babe."

"I promise I'll put out when we're done, sweetie. Just play along for now."

He pulled her to her feet and kissed her. "If we're going to give them a show, we'll give them a damn good show. I ain't gonna fake it." He lifted her shirt off, knowing she wore a sports bra underneath. He dropped her shirt off the platform.

Caph's voice startled them from below. "Hey, why the fuck is it raining clothes? What's going on?"

Ford glanced down at him. "I don't know. Emi wants to give the K-2 assholes a peep show."

"Oh. Well, in that case." She heard Caph's feet on the ladder, and he appeared a moment later.

Ford knelt down and undid her pants while Caph kissed her. "Mmm, I didn't know you were wild. You said you weren't."

"I'm not," she gasped as Ford's tongue found her clit. "Don't be obvious, are they still watching?"

Caph glanced sideways. "Five of them. Looks like some refit crew with the grunts."

"Good."

She glanced down, finding the com panel and positioning her finger over the external PA button. Ford worked in earnest, meaning it when he said he wasn't faking it. Caph kissed her and Emi felt her climb to release, suddenly not caring there were several men a few yards away watching.

At the last moment she hit the com panel, ensuring her passionate cries—she didn't fake it, but she'd admit to enhancing them a little—were broadcast to the entire dry dock.

"Yes!" she screamed. "I want that sweet cock in—" Gasping, she hit the switch again.

Ford and Caph froze.

"Um, honey? What did you just do?" Ford asked, looking up.

She smiled, crooking her finger at him. "Come here, we're not done yet." She wrapped her arms around him, sandwiched between the men. Caph was shocked into silence, but she felt his erection pressing against her through his pants. "Pretend like you're fucking me."

Ford ground his hips against her, then nipped her earlobe. "Sure you don't want me to do it for real?" he growled.

"In a few minutes, in bed. They still watching?"

"Yep."

A moment later she heard pounding footsteps running into the bridge below them. "What the fuck is going on up here?" Aaron yelled.

"Uh oh. Busted," Caph said.

Emi laughed. She noticed Aaron's surprise when he looked up and saw her lean over the ladder.

She was about to respond and explain when their ship com signaled. Aaron frowned and answered. "Yes?"

"Captain Lucio, this is Dr. Graymard. I'd like a word with you and Dr. Hypatia in my office, please. Now."

Aaron glared at her, and her heart thumped in an unpleasant way.

"On our way," Aaron said, his eyes on her.

Shit. Maybe this wasn't such a good idea. She hadn't thought about the consequences. She'd been too pissed.

She pulled her pants up, and they all descended from the observation platform, then she put herself back together.

"What the hell where you guys doing up there? And do you realize the whole dry dock knows?"

She smirked. She wasn't apologizing. "Good. I hope they know. I hope they *all* heard it." She pushed past him, but he caught her arm and spun her around.

"You *will* give me an explanation."

She shrugged him off. "I'm sure Graymard will want to hear it too. Might as well only tell it once."

The twins stared in stunned silence as she stormed off the bridge, Aaron angrily stalking behind her.

* * * *

Aaron tried to talk to her on the way. As she passed the Kendall Kant, she saw there were still four men standing on the roof. She smiled, waved, then flipped them off.

Aaron grabbed her arm. "What the fuck are you doing, Em? What the *hell* has gotten into you?" he whispered angrily.

"Something I should have done a while ago, *Captain*," she said.

He didn't speak, confused by her tone.

Dr. Graymard's face looked an unhealthy shade of peach. The vid screen on his office wall was frozen on a frame obviously taken from a security camera mounted in the dry dock rafters.

She winced. She hadn't considered it being captured for posterity.

Dr. Graymard didn't speak at first, studying her, then apparently evaluating Aaron's angry stare as he glared at her. Graymard addressed her. "Well, Dr. Hypatia?"

With a glance at Aaron, she told the story. By the time she finished, Aaron had a hand over his eyes, shaking his head. He was upset, but also trying not to laugh.

She hoped.

Graymard leaned back in his chair. "I see." He turned from her to Aaron. "You didn't know, Captain?"

He looked up. "I heard the PA like everyone else. I was down in the engine room. I had no idea what was going on, but that's no excuse, because I'm responsible for what happens on my ship." He glared at Emi again.

Emi turned to Graymard. "Look, if you're going to punish anyone, punish me. Don't give them demerits because of me. I wasn't going to let that bastard get away with that. I'm sick of him and his crew of merry assholes talking down to my boys."

"You know, I thought you would be a good assignment to their crew, Dr. Hypatia. They haven't earned a single demerit since you joined them, and that in itself is a miracle. I thought you'd be a good influence on them. Now it looks like just the opposite." He studied her for a long moment, then finally laughed. "No, no demerits this time. Just don't do it again. I have to admit, you're very devoted to your captain and crew, aren't you?"

"Fucking A."

"Dismissed."

She followed Aaron out and thought he'd talk to her, but when she tried to speak he held up a staying hand, not meeting her eyes.

Now she couldn't read him clearly, his swirl of emotions scaring her. Oh gods, she didn't fuck this up, did she? He wouldn't get rid of her over this, would he?

Aaron didn't speak on the way back to the ship, his angry wall thick and impenetrable. Once there, he returned to the engine room to whatever it was he'd been doing.

Scared, she found Ford and Caph waiting for her in the rec room. Then she burst into tears. The men pulled her down to the couch, finally calmed her, and got the story of what led up to the incident out of her.

Ford laughed. "That was pretty quick thinking, sugar. Inventive."

Caph agreed. "The dry dock will be talking about this for years."

She shuddered, her breath coming in hitching gasps. "But what's Aaron going to do? He's really pissed. He wouldn't talk to me all the way back, then he went downstairs." She closed her eyes. "I wish I hadn't done it. Now he'll get rid of me."

"No!" they echoed, hugging her.

"He won't do that!" Ford insisted.

Caph tried to reassure her. "Honey, what you did is nothing compared to some of the shit we've pulled over the years. If he hasn't gotten rid of us, trust me, he won't get rid of you. He just needs to cool off, that's all."

She shook her head, tears falling. "I'm almost sure he will. You didn't feel how pissed he was." She pushed up out of their laps and headed to their cabin. They started to follow. She shook her head, unable to face them. "No, please. I need to be alone for a little bit."

Ford caught her hand, waiting until she looked at him. With his thumb he gently brushed her tears away. "Hey," he said. "Someone told me they'd take care of me after we got done with our little impromptu performance." He said it gently, teasingly, trying to break her funk.

She let him pull her in for a hug. "I'm sorry, Ford. I will. Just not right now." The men let her leave.

She curled up on their bed. Aaron had been so…angry. That's the only way she could describe how tense, nearly vibrating he'd been. She would have to confront him sooner or later about it, get it over with. Maybe he'd let her spend one more night on the ship with the twins before she had to leave.

* * * *

Emi waited until she felt Caph and Ford return to the bridge. Then she sought out Aaron in the engine room. He sat, cross-legged, his back to her, on the floor by an access panel. After consulting the hand-held console on the floor next to him, he reached in and did something.

From the change in the set of his shoulders and the feel of his energy, she knew he sensed her presence.

Once he finished his task he sat back. She spoke. "I'm sorry, Aaron."

He flinched. He didn't turn, and somehow, that made it worse.

After another moment of silence, she spoke again, almost desperate. "Please, let me stay one more night, at least."

"What?"

He turned. While angry, he was also confused. "What are you talking about?"

She looked at the floor, unable to take the weight of his gaze. "Let me have one more night so I can say good-bye to the twins. Please."

"You're leaving?"

She blinked, not anticipating his shocked and questioning tone of voice. "What?"

He closed his eyes and took a deep, steadying breath before looking at her again. "All right, Em," he said in a calm voice that didn't match the energy flowing from him. "What are you talking about? Let's start over."

"You're not kicking me off?"

His energy shifted again. While still angry, now he was…amused? He leaned back against the wall. "Why would I do that?"

"After what I did."

He studied her, throwing his head back and closing his eyes. "I'm not getting rid of you. Not over this. Pissed? Yes. I'm very pissed. But I'm not getting rid of you."

"You're not?" He wasn't just yanking her chain, was he?

After a few long minutes, he met her gaze. "I'm not getting rid of you. I am pissed because I expect more from you than I do from the twins. The twins could walk alone into an empty room and manage to earn demerits for something. They attract trouble like the moon pulls the tide. You're responsible. Besides needing a med officer and the fact that your personality fits with ours, I hoped having you with us would help me keep them out of trouble, a second set of eyes on them giving me more time for my duties. I never in my life imagined *you'd* be the instigator!" His voice climbed in volume and strength toward the end of his monologue.

"Em, you're responsible. You're an Alpha-ranked healer, for chrissake. They don't just hand those out in fortune cookies. I expect the twins to get into trouble because they're the twins. I expected you to keep them out of trouble, not lead them into it. Am I pissed? Yes. I don't need you fighting our reputation battles for us. We've dealt with shit worse than that for years. There probably isn't a single fucking slur we haven't had hurled at our faces or invoked behind our backs, but our record speaks for itself. And that's why the DSMC gave us the Tamora Bight, and Elloy and his grunts are stuck in a mid-heavy."

"You're mad because I got back at them?"

"I'm mad because now the dry dock is going to be talking about it for years. Em, while I appreciate your heart being in the right place, you don't have to fight our battles for us. We're happy with our arrangement, it works for us, and we don't feel a need to justify it to anyone else. We never have." He sighed. "You're not off the ship. If I didn't bounce the twins for putting a truck in the middle of the cafeteria, I'm not bouncing you for this."

"But you're mad at me."

"Yeah. I'm mad. And I'm disappointed."

That was worse. She'd rather he just be mad. She didn't want to disappoint him. She didn't speak, didn't know what to say.

"Talk to the twins. They understand. They'll probably be better at explaining it to you. I'm the captain. I'm *always* the captain, I have to be—it's my job. Until the day we're no longer on a vessel and we're all civvies, I'm captain first. I can't have crew running around doing shit like that. That isn't the twins getting into a bar fight or something.

Yes, your heart was in the right place, absolutely. But don't do anything like that again."

She nodded.

He tipped his head to the doorway. "I'll be up in a few hours. I want to go through these schematics for a while longer. Give me more time to calm down."

Relieved, she returned to the crew area. *He's not getting rid of me.*

That set off another round of tears.

Before the twins could see her mental state she made her way down to the hydro lab. She'd found a good combination of nutrients that slightly accelerated plant growth, and she'd experimented with which plants thrived under the grow lights.

She currently had several tanks of tomatoes, several kinds of greens and lettuce, squash, carrots, bell peppers, beans, a variety of herbs, and two types of melons. Because of the controlled environment, seasons were irrelevant. She used seed stock that would keep well, and the men had been very pleased with her efforts. She also had test flats of other vegetables started, trying to find as many varieties as she could so she could alternate them during the trip. And she grew several small fruit trees in individual tanks—papayas, bananas, two types of oranges, grapefruit, and lemons. It wasn't possible to enhance their growing season as much as it was with the smaller plants, but it would be welcomed supplements to their mostly pre-packaged diet once in space.

Working in the hydro lab had become her favorite way to relax, even though it was technically work. Sometimes she could think of her parents without wanting to cry, her childhood in Montana, the house in Bozeman before her parents took the job requiring them to spend over half their year on the moon at the research facility.

Caph whistled as he walked in. "Hey, they're looking great!"

"Yeah, just keep Ford away from them."

He grinned. "You ain't kidding." He pulled her to him. "You okay?"

"Yeah. I'm not booted."

"I knew you wouldn't be. We tried to tell you that." He rubbed her back. "I think you could behead the K-2 crew and as long as you weren't in jail, Aaron would keep you on board. You're good for us."

Emi couldn't hold the bitter comment back. "Yeah, the crew slut."

His reaction startled her. He grabbed her shoulders and held her so he could look into her eyes, his face severe. "No," he said, sharply. "Stop that. That's *not* what this is about. We love you. If you never slept with us, or if you said that's it, no more, he'd still have you on board. You're a damn good doctor, your personality is perfect for ours, and you don't give a shit about our personal lives. Seriously, you say, 'Sorry boys, no more nookie,' and that's fine."

He wasn't lying, but he spotted the doubt in her eyes. "Seriously, Emi. You say the word, we'll get the refit crew in here today and have them build out a private cabin and head for you. I'll go get them right now, it'll be ready by tomorrow. You can't leave us—we need you." He gently shook her, punctuating his last words.

There was more behind his comments, she felt it, but he carefully hid it. Not the same way Aaron buried his, but his playful side masked it well.

"What happened to you guys?" she asked.

He pulled his hands away and dropped his gaze. "I can't talk about it."

"Crew story?" Her acidic tone returned.

Caph nodded. "That, and I *can't* talk about it. I don't like to even think about it." He turned and walked out of the hydro lab, leaving her speechless.

Chapter Ten

Emi spent over an hour in hydro and decided to do a little digging into their past. The thought had crossed her mind before, but usually she didn't have time or the boys were working with her and she didn't have privacy.

She went to sick bay, and, using her secure med officer terminal, she pulled up their full personnel and medical records. Nothing jumped out at her at first, until she realized there was a time gap in all three service records, starting approximately two years after they started with the Merchant Marines, lasting about eighteen months.

She dug further and found an interesting message.

Records locked by joint order of Merchant Marine and ISNC Tribunal.

The medical records showed the same gap. The only thing listed was that Aaron had received a Silver Service Star, and the twins both received Bronze Service Stars.

All three had graduated training at the same time. Before the gap, Aaron had been appointed as second officer on a ship named the Wayfarer Margo. At the end of the service gap, Aaron was promoted to the rank of captain, with the odd standing order that he and the twins were "bonded crew," by declaration of the joint tribunal.

She looked it up and found the term listed in the confidential officer manual, accessible only by ranking fleet medical officers such as herself, captains, and higher ups.

Bonded crew members are those that, for whatever reason deemed, may not be separated despite wishes to the contrary of ranking superior officers. This designation is applied by the Joint

Tribunal and is irrevocable except by request of the crewmen involved. Bonded crew might or might not be married to each other or others, and be any number from two members or more, and can be any combination of genders. If a crewman ever wishes to unbond from the others, they may do so without it affecting the status of the other bound crew unless it's only two members bound. This designation is used when valuable crew members with specialized training or experience wish to stay in the service but might suffer irreparable psychological damage by being separated...

Hmm. What happened to her poor boys?

She researched further and found fewer than one hundred current designations of bonded crew, most involving in-laws or blood relatives, and no others involving unrelated men in the way Aaron and the twins were together.

More digging, and she discovered the captain of the Wayfarer Margo when Aaron and the twins had been assigned to it was executed about four months after the time gap started, the details, again, locked.

Executed?

She searched out information on the crew manifest for the Wayfarer Margo and tracked down the other five crew members, except one. Kelsey D'ambroise.

She was listed as deceased, killed in the line of duty at the time the service gap started, and she had been posthumously awarded a Silver Service Star. Details of her death were locked.

Was this Kelsey D'ambroise the source of the "crew story" and their shared grief? She couldn't confront them about it, because she shouldn't have been snooping. They had promised to tell her.

Now with more questions than answers, Emi closed out the files and went to cook dinner for the boys.

Aaron joined them for dinner. He was quiet, frequently glancing at Emi. The twins nervously made small talk, and when dinner was over they jumped to volunteer for clean-up. Emi excused herself and returned to the cabin. Aaron wasn't as upset as he had been, but he was still not back to his normal self, and neither was she. She meant to stay awake, but when she felt the twins crawl in next to her later, she closed her eyes and went back to sleep.

* * * *

She awoke before the twins. Aaron was already out of bed, most likely at an early meeting. She cooked them breakfast, and in a few minutes the smell of coffee and bacon drew them out. They hugged and kissed her.

"How you feel, sweetie?" Ford asked, concerned.

"I'm okay. I'm sorry I left you hanging yesterday."

He brushed the hair out of her face and smiled. "That's okay. You can make it up to me."

Caph stood behind her and wrapped his arms around her waist, nuzzling her neck. "What can we do to make *you* feel better?"

She patted his hands. "I'll be okay. I just need to get through it. That's all."

"I love you," they parroted, glaring at each other.

That made her laugh, which in turn made the twins smile. "I love you too, guys," she assured them.

They ate breakfast, and Emi left for her morning training class. She ate lunch there instead of returning to the ship, and her short afternoon class was over before she knew it. She'd felt better being away from the ship. As she returned to the Tamora Bight, Emi's funk returned.

The twins must have ratted her out to Aaron. He found her staring out at the dry dock facility through a port in the observation bay.

He laid a gentle hand on her shoulder. "What's wrong?"

She stood up and quickly wiped her eyes, hoping he didn't notice. "Nothing. I'm fine."

His worry shadowed him even more than his pain. "You're not

still upset, are you?"

"Not at you guys."

He hesitated, and she spoke again. "No, I'm not reconsidering my decision." She forced a smile. "You're stuck with me for five years."

Aaron pulled her to him. "Then what's wrong, Em? I thought we'd settled this."

She closed her eyes and relaxed against him. He was her rock, grounding her, his strength flowing through her. "What happens after?" she whispered.

"What do you mean?"

"What am I going to do with my life after this is over?"

His body tensed. She suspected he didn't even realize he'd done it. "After?"

She looked up at him. "I don't want to leave you guys after five years."

He relaxed, every ounce of tension draining from him. His broad smile lightened his face. "Em, you don't have to leave."

"You guys said you'll be doing short hops and stuff."

"So?"

Realization dawned. "I can still go with you?"

"Damn straight, sweetie. You're my crew. I don't split up my crew."

The bitter word was out of her mouth before she could stop it. "Crew."

"Em, babe, I didn't mean it like that—"

She pulled free and ran down the corridor away from him, blindly turning and twisting, trying to lose herself in the bowels of the ship.

He couldn't say it. The other two could, freely and without reservation. Yes, Aaron cared for her, she sensed that. Maybe he did love her. But the three little words—how clichéd—she desperately wanted and needed from him, no matter what his actions, were the ones he couldn't bring himself to say.

She shouldn't take it personally.

An hour later, Ford found her in the corner of the hydroponic lab, curled in a ball and staring at her tomato plants. He sat next to her and pulled her into his lap, not speaking, letting her sob against his shoulder and cry it out.

"Why can't he say it?" she whispered in a tortured voice.

He nuzzled the top of her head. "He's a hard nut, honey. He's the Cap. He has to be. It's how he survived, how we've all survived."

"If he's so tough, why can't he say it?"

"That's not my story to tell. We might be friends and lovers and soul mates, all of us, but never forget he's our captain first and foremost, especially when we're on this crate. It's kept all of us alive together a lot of years when other crews with 'skills' beyond ours are space debris. He takes care of his crew."

"He's not taking care of me."

Ford gently shifted her in his lap so he could meet her puffy eyes. "Sweetie," he said gently, "what's more important? That he shows you how he loves you without telling you, or that he tells you how he feels without showing you? Personally, I prefer showing to telling. Are three little words really that important?"

She couldn't answer that.

"I just wish he'd say it."

"Don't ever doubt how much he loves you. He'd die for you in a second, for any of us. Crew first, before himself. I've been with him a lot of years."

"Why didn't you ever become a captain?"

"I didn't want the responsibility. Caph and I switch off first officer duties between runs. It's just a title. He's like me, he'd rather have Aar taking care of the big picture. We trust him. He's saved our asses more times than we care to count." Something shifted in Ford's face, a deep sadness she didn't want to explore right then. "Times lesser captains would have backed down and been willing to sacrifice something, or someone. Aaron will die before he loses crew."

Ford's gentle presence always calmed her. He was a multi-faceted man. Brainy, quick-witted, and steady. Fiercely loyal. A different kind of settling strength than Aaron. Just as Caph's huge presence pushed away her stress.

After another half-hour, he patted her shoulder. "Chow time. Why don't you come with me? Help me in the galley."

She nodded, rubbing her still-sniffling nose on her arm.

He stood and gently pulled her to her feet, not releasing her hand, knowing she drew comfort from him. He took the long way back to the galley, most likely avoiding Aaron's brooding presence on the bridge. They were far enough away he wouldn't come seeking them out.

Caph joined them a few minutes later. By his forced, almost manic attempts at playfulness, she knew he'd heard what happened and was trying to help cheer her up.

It didn't work.

She slipped out of the galley while they were distracted and returned to their quarters. Not that she could escape them on the ship, and as much as it would almost physically hurt to be away from the men for a night the way she felt about them, she grabbed a couple of things and her pillow and quilt and went to sick bay, closing the door behind her. Hopefully they would take the hint.

Physician, heal thyself, she thought miserably. This was stupid. She'd better get over this childish need, and fast. Ford was right that Aaron was a damn good captain, and obviously what he'd done for years worked for him and the twins. After a few months in space, she would most likely feel the same way as Ford and be able to let go.

For now, it hurt.

An hour later, the door chime sounded. She was curled on the bunk, the quilt wrapped around her, staring at an aquarium vid screen while trying to zone out. She sensed it was Caph.

"Come."

The door slid open. He walked over to her, the plate practically dwarfed in his hands. "We didn't want you to go hungry, sweetie."

She nodded, sitting up and letting him set the food on the tray, sliding it into place in front of her. He'd also brought her a mug of hot tea, made perfectly.

The goddamn grunts would never have done this for her.

Then again, she never would have fallen in love with the grunts either. Hearts as hard as their bodies, no doubt.

"Thanks, Caph." She picked at the food more for his sake than hers. She wasn't hungry but knew if she didn't eat he'd sic Ford on her, who would most likely worry and call Aaron into the mix.

And Aaron was the reason she was here.

He watched her eat without speaking for several minutes. "You gonna sleep in here tonight?" he softly asked.

She nodded, trying not to cry, afraid it would set him off. She couldn't pit the twins against Aaron, it wasn't fair to him. This was her problem and she knew it. She just had to figure out how to deal with it.

He tenderly tucked a stray hair behind her ear. "It's gonna be lonely without you cuddled up next to me."

She took a long, hitching breath. "I just need to get my head on straight, that's all. No reason to torture you guys with it." Emi forced a smile she didn't feel, hoping it would fool him.

It didn't.

"Ford and I are gonna hit the town tonight. Why don't you come with us?" She started to shake her head, and he added, "Aar's already said he's staying home, so someone needs to come keep us out of trouble."

The last thing she wanted to do was go out. She wanted to curl up under her quilt and mope and get it out of her system so she could start fresh tomorrow and face Aaron. But tonight…

Tonight the lesser of two evils was going out with the twins and not spending it dodging her captain. Besides, he did say he wanted her to keep them out of trouble.

"When do we leave?" she asked.

His smile lit his face, lifting her mood a little. "In an hour." He hesitated. "Aaron's in the engine room. Why don't you finish eating and then go get ready?"

"How fancy?"

"Aw, crew outing, babe. We'll all match." His green eyes twinkled.

Chapter Eleven

Aaron didn't put in an appearance while they got ready. Emi donned her casual uniform, matching the twins. All the cars were checked out from the motor pool, so Ford requisitioned one of the pick-up trucks. With all three of them riding in the front seat, Ford drove them five miles into New Phoenix.

She'd spent plenty of time at school in Tempe and Old Phoenix, but had never really explored New Phoenix. They pulled up to a bar with a nearly full parking lot. An old-fashioned blinking neon sign in the window identified the bar as the Dry Port.

"Dry Port?" she asked, an unsettled, nervous feeling overtaking her.

Caph grinned. "Yeah, it's a little irony. This place has been here for years. It's a regular watering hole for crews." Sure enough, when she looked closer she realized several of the vehicles in the lot bore DSMC, MM, and ISNC motor pool license plates on the back.

Ford grabbed her arm. "C'mon, sugar. Another crew experience for you."

She balked, holding out her palm. He laughed and dropped the keys into her waiting hand. "You drive one of those things before?"

"Enough to get a license and know I won't kill us on the way back to base." She pocketed the keys and let the men lead her inside.

Inside was crowded and noisy. Over half of the patrons were dressed in crew uniforms. With Ford in the lead, they snaked their way through the throng to a table near the back where three of the six chairs were already occupied by crew from another ship. They wore casual uniforms similar to theirs, only in different colors, with a different ship's crest on the shirt.

The largest of the three men looked up, his momentary surprise immediately concealed behind a calculating mask.

"Hey, Ford, Caph. Where's Aaron?" His question really was, "Who's the chick?" but he didn't voice it.

Ford held Emi's chair for her, and the twins sat, flanking her. "He wasn't up for a night out. This is Dr. Emilia Hypatia, our med officer. Captain Rick Garcia of the Angor Bay, his first, John McReiny, and mate William Baxter."

The men nodded in turn and shook hands, still eying her.

"You get a med officer yet, Rick?" Caph asked.

He shook his head. They're setting us up as an eight-pack this time, detailed explores. Cleaning up y'all's messes." He grinned, then took a swig of his beer. "Said it'll probably be another six to eight months at least before we ship out."

A waitress took their order, Ford and Caph both getting beer and Emi sticking to soda water. She felt Rick's eyes on her, and not in a comfortable way.

"When you guys shipping out?" Rick asked.

Ford shrugged. "Still going through final retrofits, training, all that. Emi's got another weaponry simulation on Friday. She could blow your balls off from here to Flagstaff," he proudly boasted.

She blushed, wishing the boys wouldn't engage in a pissing contest. Not with these three men, at least.

"I bet she can," McReiny said, his eyes never wavering from her.

She blushed again. He meant that in a way totally different than the twins took it. Sometimes it sucked being a trained empath.

Emi sat back and tried not to pay attention to the conversation, preferring to keep her mind on the twins and how drunk they were getting. They quickly finished their first beers and, knowing Emi would safely drive them home, ordered another round.

The more they drank, the more the twins loosened up, and the more she tensed. The Angor Bay crew rarely took their eyes off her.

She hoped they weren't drunk enough to try something stupid.

After an hour she had to use the bathroom. When she stood, she uncomfortably realized she was the only female patron in the bar. How had that fact escaped her earlier?

Keeping her gaze down, she carefully worked her way to the hallway leading to the restrooms, doing her best not to brush against anyone. She needed to get the boys out of here asap. She could claim she was sick. Even drunk, that would motivate them to leave. She hated to ruin their evening, but the rock hard feeling in her gut was quickly swelling to the size of a boulder, and she knew until they were safely back at the ship the feeling wouldn't dissipate.

When she left the bathroom, McReiny was making his way down the hall toward her. The hall was barely wide enough for two people, and when she turned to let him pass, he stepped into her, pressing her against the wall.

From his eyes and breath, she knew the whiskey he'd been drinking was overriding his common sense.

"Well, hello, Doc," he slurred.

The hallway wasn't visible from their table. Emi tried to read McReiny, to find anything she could use against him short of physical force.

Considering he was nearly a head taller than her and outweighed her by at least fifty pounds, she didn't know how practical that option was.

Mustering her cool, professional voice, she threw up a wall around her nerves. "Hello, Officer McReiny." Now she had to meet his eyes, stare him down.

He hesitated, perhaps rethinking his evaluation of her weaker personality.

"Why don't you come crew with us?" He flicked a lock of hair off her shoulder. "I bet you'd have more fun with us."

She slid her hand down to her pocket and found her cell phone, then wrapped her fingers around it. It wasn't a weapon, but she knew enough to know she could smash it in his face to buy a second or two if she needed it. "I'm perfectly happy on the Tamora Bight, McReiny."

He stared her down for a moment. When she thought he was going to back up, he pressed harder against her. His erection dug into her hip. Emi realized if she didn't do something fast, she was going to have a serious problem.

He wasn't chipped.

"We transferred over from the Merchants a few weeks ago," he said, smiling. "I'm not a healer, but I had plenty of training in negotiation science."

Fuck. He was an empath too. Apparently stronger than her, because he'd hid it well despite being drunk.

He bent his face to her ear and whispered, "We know how to take care of a lady better than those guys do, I guarantee you."

From somewhere, she summoned her strength and pushed him back. He staggered, allowing her to bolt, right into another man.

Baxter.

He grinned, grabbing her wrist. "What are you doing, Mac? Starting without me?"

She twisted, trying to pull away, and knew she had a very limited window to make a decision. Try to fight and risk getting raped, or scream her head off and trigger a bar fight when the twins waded in?

The twins were drunk, drunker than these two assholes. Praying for a miracle, Emi fell against McReiny, surprising him. She kicked out, nailing Baxter squarely in the nuts.

He fell to his knees with an agonized groan, and McReiny loosened his grip on her long enough for her to stomp his foot and break free. She dodged Baxter's hand and ran down the hall and into the barroom. For a second she panicked when she didn't see the twins at the table, then spotted them at the bar talking to another crew.

She raced to them and grabbed their hands. "Come on. We're leaving. Now." She'd call Graymard from the truck and file charges against the other two, but she had to get the twins out of the bar.

Ford's eyes gleamed. He was wasted. "What's wrong—"

"Officer Caliban, that's an order," she barked, hoping to shock him through his alcohol haze.

She pulled them toward the door, but the men balked. "Emi, what's going on?" Caph asked.

"Officer Bates, we are leaving. *Now.*"

It was her bad luck that he wasn't quite as drunk as Ford. He was larger, meaning it took more to put him in the tank. And it was also her bad luck that he turned at that moment and spotted McReiny and Baxter at the hallway entrance, both obviously in pain and sending murderous looks her way.

Caph pulled free from her desperate grasp. "Oh, *fuck* no!" he growled. "What the hell did they try, babe? Did they hurt you?"

Bad luck seemed to flow as freely as beer tonight. Ford immediately picked up the source of Caph's outrage and realized how upset Emi was. "Fucking bastards!"

"Guys, I'm okay," she pleaded, frantic. "They're not chipped. Let's get the hell out of here, we can handle this—"

The twins moved as one away from her, pushing through the crowd toward where the Angor Bay crewmen stood. She didn't see Garcia and suspected he wasn't in on his crew's plan. No captain was that dense, to risk death and a ten million dollar return bonus over an unwilling piece of ass.

Was he?

Caph was taller and outweighed the other two men. Baxter was approximately Ford's size. As the patrons realized a fight was brewing, they cheered and formed a circle around the men.

"No! Caph, Ford, no!" Emi screamed, trying to push after them. It was useless because, sensing blood in the water, the other customers were eager to see a fight.

From the sounds of the cheers and impromptu betting she heard, apparently her boys had quite a reputation in bar fights.

The four men faced off, circling. She finally spotted Garcia sitting at a nearby table, his arms crossed, an amused expression on his face. She ran over to him. "Captain, go get your men!"

He shook his head. "I'm not fucking stupid. They'll blow it off in a few minutes and be laughing and joking and friends again."

Barely controlled rage shook her body. "Your men nearly raped me!"

He looked at her and rolled his eyes. "If you're gonna play with the men, girl, you need to learn to take care of yourself. This isn't the kiddy pool. You're not even off-Earth yet. This is a church compared to some of the spaceport bars."

"Captain Garcia, go get your *fucking* crew, and that's an order!" Emi didn't know where the depth and force of her voice came from, but even Garcia reappraised her.

"You aren't in a position to order me around—"

"I am a ranking DSMC fleet medical officer, and I can have your license pulled for dereliction of duty and medical soundness. How would you like to spend the rest of your life driving a taxi in New Phoenix? Get your men—now—or tomorrow morning you will find yourself in front of a duty fitness board. When I'm finished with you, your next view of space will be through a telescope. And get your goddamn crew chipped first thing in the morning, or I'll get them neutered by lunch!"

He glared, but reluctantly stood and headed for the crowd. "Fine!" he spat.

She trembled, following him, afraid once she did make it back to the truck that she wouldn't be able to drive. It was adrenaline and shock combined, she knew, but she had to hang on, had to get her boys out of there.

Caph pounded on McReiny, and Ford looked like he was holding his own against Baxter. Every time one of Garcia's men landed a punch on her boys, Emi felt it as if they'd hit her. She followed Garcia, trying to get in there. If she could get the twins out—

A loud shout, and Caph went down. Emi screamed, trying to force her way through the gathered mass of drunks. The crowd flowed closed behind Garcia as he pushed through, leaving her to find her own way to her men. Finally, she managed to shove her way through to them. Garcia was trying to pull McReiny off Caph, who had his hands wrapped around the other man's throat.

She started toward Ford and Baxter, with every intention of forcing herself between them despite the risk of personal injury, when a firm hand clamped onto her shoulder and dragged her back. Spinning around, prepared to fight, she stared into Aaron's iron glare.

"Go grab Caph as soon as Rick gets Mac off him," he ordered, his voice soft, firm, calm, all business. "He'll still be able to walk. I'll meet you with Ford at the truck."

She didn't have time to express her shock, disbelief—and relief. She nodded. Garcia pinned McReiny's arms behind him and slung him off Caph. Emi immediately jumped on Caph, grabbing his face in her hands and locking onto his green eyes.

"We're going. *Now*," she ordered, pouring as much mental force into her words as she could.

He hesitated, then nodded. She stood and grabbed his wrist with a death grip. Instead of trying to get through the crowd, she pulled him down the hallway to the back door. He followed, nearly docile. She prayed this entrance led to the parking lot.

Thank the gods, it did. She had the keys in her hand and nearly dropped them as the shakes threatened. She didn't know how Aaron got to the bar, and she didn't care, but it was easier to shove Caph into the truck bed. She opened the tailgate and pushed him toward it.

"Get in. Now." He did after stumbling and staggering around the back of the truck. Emi turned to see Aaron carrying a nearly-unconscious Ford, slung across Aaron's shoulders in a fireman's carry. Apparently Baxter got in a few last punches. Aaron unceremoniously dumped a groaning Ford into the bed next to Caph and closed the tailgate.

Then Aaron turned to her. "You okay, Em?" he asked, his eyes burning, searching for any injury, his hands on her shoulders. "Are you hurt?"

"I'm okay," she said. She started to walk toward the driver door when her knees unhinged. Aaron caught her, scooping her into his arms as she sobbed against his shoulder.

"Shh, it's okay, babe," he soothed. "I've got you, honey. You're safe." Holding her tightly against his chest, he carried her to the passenger side and gently placed her in the seat.

Medical diagnoses floated through her mind. Shock was the main one, and Aaron seemed to sense it. He buckled the seat belt around her and jogged to the driver side, turning up the heat for her as he peeled out of the parking lot.

Her teeth chattered. He grabbed her hand, holding it, his flesh hot against hers. "You're not hurt?" he asked again.

She shook her head, unable to talk. She slumped against him as much as the seat belt would allow, sobbing, and he put his arm around her and gently rubbed her shoulder. They quickly made it back to the dry dock where he backed the truck into the loading bay slot near their cargo hatch.

He left it running and put it in park. "Stay here," he ordered, turning up the heat full blast for her. "Don't move." She watched as he walked around to the tailgate and dropped it. Both Caph and Ford stirred, but neither made any obvious moves to get out.

Aaron uncoiled the fire hose and opened the valve, then stood by the cab and blasted Caph and Ford with the full force of the water.

The men yelled, floundered, and fell out of the back of the truck. From the look on Aaron's face, she knew he was beyond pissed. She didn't bother trying to intercede on the twins' behalf. It would only make matters worse at that point.

He hosed them down until they were standing, yelling, trying to hold their hands in front of their faces to block the spray. Convinced they were conscious enough to walk, Aaron hosed out the truck bed

Apparently one or both of them had puked.

He shut the hose nozzle off, his barely restrained rage clearly evident in his deceptively calm voice. "Get your asses in the ship. I'll deal with you later, goddammit. Don't show your fucking faces until you're sober tomorrow morning." The twins stumbled toward the cargo hatch.

Aaron turned his back on them and shut the water off, coiled the hose, and returned to the truck.

He looked at her again, his firm mask slipping to concern. "Are you sure you're okay, sweetie?"

She nodded. How could she have ever doubted how much he loved her?

Ford was right. She didn't need to hear it. What good was hearing it if he didn't show her? Tonight he'd shown her. It'd washed off him in nearly panicked waves when he grabbed her shoulder in the bar.

He drove around the dry dock facility to the motor pool office and left her waiting in the truck while he turned the keys in. Then he opened her door for her and helped her out. She tried to walk, but her legs gave way again. She didn't object when he scooped her into his arms and carried her back to the main hatch and all the way to their quarters.

He gently laid her on their bed, and that's when she felt his sad but determined thought.

"No!" she gasped. "You can't cancel my assignment!"

He closed his eyes and knelt beside her, holding her hands. "I can't risk you getting hurt."

"Please, no!" she begged. "Aaron, I'm okay. It was stupid, I should have made them leave sooner."

He shook his head, his eyes sad and heart heavy. "Em, I couldn't live with myself if you got hurt."

"I didn't get hurt." She sobbed, clinging to him, resisting his attempts to peel her off him. "Please don't make me go. I love you, I love all of you, you're all I've got...you're my family!"

After a minute he relaxed and finally enveloped her, his face buried in her hair. "We've got to sit down and talk about this. I can't focus on my job if I'm worried every second you're out of my sight that something's going to happen to you."

Relief flooded her, nearly as strong as her adrenaline shock. He wouldn't send her away. He'd already changed his mind back. He didn't want to lose her any more than she wanted to lose them.

Because he loved her.

"How did you get there?" she asked.

"I changed my mind and went down to the motor pool to check out a car. Thought maybe I could apologize to you. Ford told him they were taking you to the Dry Port for the first time, and that over half the crews including Rick's were there. I also remembered overhearing Rick saying that they weren't chipped yet, so I grabbed a cab."

She clung to him, relaxing as he soothed her.

"What happened, Em?"

She shivered, and he pulled a blanket around them both as she told the story.

His voice hardened. "I'll call Graymard myself, have him haul Rick and his gorillas in for disciplinary action." Then his voice lifted, amused. "You really threatened to yank his license?"

"And get them neutered."

He laughed and her last bit of worry drained from her. She closed her eyes. "Where's the twins?" She was too tired to try to find them.

"They'll sleep it off in cargo. Even as drunk as they were, they won't dare come up here until morning." He hesitated. "I'm sorry about earlier."

"Me too."

"I didn't mean for you to think—"

She kissed him, surprised that after the evening's events she could feel even remotely romantic. They weren't together alone very often, and any solo time she got to spend with one of the men was time she treasured. Through the scorching touch of his lips, she felt his easing desperation and fear, residual effects of his worry. He took his time, slowly, gently caressing her skin as he cupped her breasts and went from one to the other, circling her taut nipples with his tongue and making her moan.

"I almost left them there," he whispered against her neck. "I saw the fight, and I panicked when I didn't see you. Then I realized you were about to get between Ford and Baxter, and I was afraid I wouldn't reach you in time."

"You would have left them?"

"Wouldn't be the first time the MPs brought them back drunk and disorderly," he laughed. "Would have scared the crap out of them when they sobered up enough to realize you were missing."

"I don't think I could have done that. I don't think I could have left them there."

"I know." He nuzzled her ear, sending another dizzying wave of sensation through her body. "That's why I didn't. I didn't think you would let me."

"You're the captain," she teased. "Don't you get to make that call?"

Aaron raised up on one arm to meet her eyes, now serious. "Yes. But smart captains also know when to weigh what's in the best interest of their crew before making a decision. I knew if I did that, you'd be fighting me and screaming to get back in there to protect them, then you'd be pissed at me. I pick my battles carefully."

His hand drifted between her legs, his fingers knowing exactly what to do to bring her close to release. He stopped short before she came, entering her and taking long, sweet strokes that kept her breathless and wanting more.

Then he sat up, still deep inside her. His thumb found her clit, tracing little circles around it. "The only screaming I want to hear from you right now is when I make you come for me. I've got you all to myself, and I want you to scream for me."

His deep, growling voice triggered a waterfall inside her. She closed her eyes, her muscles squeezing him as she climaxed, crying out his name.

"That's it," he said, slowly fucking her. "Let me hear what I do to you."

The last spasm left her gasping for breath and he thrust hard, his release not far behind. When he recovered, he rolled to his side and pulled her tight against him, spooned together.

He kissed her shoulder. "Extra training for you," he mumbled. "You're going to be a kick-ass fighter before we leave here."

"Okay," she sighed. She would do it for him. "Did you mean it earlier, that we could all stay together after this mission is over?"

He hugged her tighter. "Of course I did. I want to spend the rest of my life with you, baby girl. I can't lose you any more than I can lose those two assholes sleeping it off downstairs."

More than relief—satisfaction—washed over her. Wanting to spend his life with her was as good as telling her he loved her, right? Maybe better. You could love someone and not want to spend your whole life with them.

"Good. Because I want to spend the rest of my life with you, too."

* * * *

Ford and Caph weren't in the crew area the next morning. Aaron wasn't in bed, and she found him in the shower. He pulled her in with him and held her.

"I already talked to Graymard. We meet in his office in an hour."

Fear coursed through her. He smiled, touching her cheek. "Disciplinary action, Em. I won't cancel your assignment, quit worrying. You're here to stay. You have to tell them what happened, though." He smirked. "Personally, I'd like to push for letting you get to neuter those two assholes."

"What'll happen to them?"

He shrugged. "Hard to say. They'll have to go through extra

psychological checks at the very least. That alone will cost them time and assignments, not to mention bonuses. And they probably won't get assigned female crew."

She snickered. "So what does that mean?"

He laughed. "Either they bend over and take it like men, or they get well-acquainted with their hands."

Emi toasted them bagels while Aaron dictated a preliminary report for Graymard. Caph and Ford still hadn't appeared.

Emi worried. "Don't we need to get them up here? I should check them over."

He shook his head. "They cleaned up downstairs, I'm sure. They were howling last night when I hosed them off. They couldn't have been too fucking hurt. I'm sure they dug into the spare lockers down there for uniforms." He reached across her and hit the intercom button, flicking the volume up full blast. His voice loudly echoed through the ship, and she winced.

"Gangway, ten minutes, in uniform." He turned it off and smiled, taking her hands. "Look, Em, I know you're worried about them. Chances are they'll have some pretty good war wounds from what little I saw when I got there. But don't you dare baby them before we get back, okay?"

"Why?"

His face had transformed to captain firm again. "They put you at risk. I know it wasn't intentional, and I know it wasn't their fault what happened. I'm not blaming them. But they are experienced officers. They should have damn well remembered that one of them needed to stay sober to keep an eye on you. They should have been protecting you. I want you to be very angry and quiet with them this morning, promise?"

Reluctantly, she nodded. "It'll hurt them." That's the last thing she wanted to do to the twins.

"Yeah, but it'll hammer home the lesson, and they won't forget it anytime soon." He touched her chin and turned her lips to his, brushing them with a gentle kiss. "Trust me. This is far kinder for them in the long run. Better they feel horrible for a couple of hours than to feel horrible forever because they fucked up and cost you your life. You need to be the ballsy bitch who stood up to Rick last night."

That made her laugh. "I didn't feel very ballsy."

Emi couldn't read his glare. "Trust me, it was. Seriously, please do this for me. Practically ignore them. Don't break down and hug them. Be very cool and professional toward them. Let them think you're really pissed."

"Is this a captain thing?"

He hugged her. "They have to learn it now, Em. They can't ever forget again. Next time we might not be so lucky."

* * * *

After emerging from the hatch, Aaron spoke before the twins could say anything. "Keep your goddamn mouths shut. We'll deal with this as a crew when we get back. Not a word out of either of you assholes. She's fine, no thanks to you two."

It was hard to keep her promise. Ford and Caph looked miserable, and not just because of their injuries and hangovers. Both had black eyes, Ford's upper lip was split, and Caph had several bruises on his face. They looked hopeful when they saw her. Then she felt both of them sink into despair when they thought she was angry. She wanted to reassure them that she still loved them and didn't blame them, but she'd promised Aaron.

She had to listen to her captain.

Emi pulled it off, glaring at them, letting Aaron take her hand and silently lead them across the facility to Graymard's office.

Garcia and his men were already there. She noticed with smug satisfaction that both Baxter and McReiny looked worse than the twins. Her boys had done good.

Aaron pointed to two chairs along the wall, and Ford and Caph sat, their eyes on the floor. Aaron held a chair at the table for Emi and sat next to her, across from the Angor Bay's crew.

Furious, Graymard directed his ire at Garcia. "Well, Captain, tell me why I shouldn't yank your commission?"

Garcia paled, and the other two fidgeted. "Look, I didn't know they were going to do that. Believe me, if I'd known, I would have stopped them."

"They shouldn't need chips to not rape a woman," Aaron growled, finding Emi's hand under the table, his thumb stroking her. "They'd be dead right now if it wasn't for her getting away from them." Rape by commissioned officers was an immediate executable capital offense if the victim demanded that punishment. "What kind of men are they if they think it's okay to go after a woman like that? They're a couple of fucking animals."

Both men reddened, looking at their hands. Garcia glared at them. "Well? You tell them."

"We're sorry," the men mumbled.

Under the table, Aaron squeezed Emi's hand. She briefly met his glance.

Knowing what he wanted, she looked across the table. "Why should I forgive you? Why shouldn't I demand they pull your rank and toss you on your ass?" She pointed at Garcia. "And you weren't going to do anything about it until I threatened you, asshole." If Aaron could swear in here, so could she. "You're responsible for your fucking crew, Captain."

Graymard nodded. "She's right. Captain Garcia, I took a risk allowing you and your boys into the program based on your psych evals, and frankly, I'm disappointed but not too surprised." He looked at Emi. "It's your call, Dr. Hypatia. What do we do with them?"

She took her time, knowing they grew more worried with every passing minute. Now knowing McReiny was an empath, she held a strong block against him so he couldn't read her.

"For starters, they get chipped immediately. And I want it set so at least for the next six months, every time they get the urge at all, even to masturbate, they get zapped." She glared at them. "All three of them, including the captain. Depending on their behavior, maybe if they're good I'll consider rescinding that."

Aaron's hand tightened around hers slightly. She knew he was trying to contain his laughter, not shut her up.

Graymard leaned back, considering it. "It's unusual. But I like it. That, and twenty-five demerits."

The Angor Bay men looked horrified. "But—"

"Take it or leave it, gentlemen," Graymard said. "I think she's being very generous. By statute she has the right to demand permanent chemical castration. It was attempted rape by commissioned officers. Consider yourselves lucky."

"Maybe next time they'll think twice about trying to rape someone," Emi spat.

"I'm sorry," Baxter pleaded. "We were drunk! It won't happen again."

"Oh, thanks for reminding me." She looked at Graymard. "Also an alcohol restriction. The chips can handle that too, right?"

He smiled. "Dr. Hypatia, I'm glad you're not mad at me." He looked at Garcia. "Well?"

The three men deflated. "All right."

Graymard called in a technician, gave him the orders, and the men were escorted out of the room. Then he turned to Emi. "Are you still sure you want to stay assigned to this crew?"

She looked at Aaron. "I like working with Captain Lucio." She specifically didn't mention the twins and felt their remorseful pang from behind her. It took every ounce of will she had to keep her promise. "He's going to get me extra personal combat training before we leave."

"Very well. Then we're done. No demerits for your crew, of course."

Aaron led her by the hand. Caph and Ford silently fell in behind them. She wanted to throw her arms around them and cry, kiss their wounds, love them. They'd stood up for her, belatedly, but they'd been willing to fight the men who tried to hurt her. She hated doing this to them but understood why. Aaron was right.

She had to trust her captain.

* * * *

Aaron forced her to keep up the silent treatment all the way to the ship. Once in the crew area, he ordered the twins to sick bay. "Get your asses in there and wait for her to come check you out."

When they were out of sight, Aaron pulled Emi to him, tightly hugging her. "You did great, Em," he whispered. "Now when you go in there, don't fall all over them. Make them work their asses off to get back in your good graces. It's the only way they'll remember."

"Okay. Where are you going?"

"To the bridge to work on my logs. They'll come sucking up to me after you're done with them, and I'll make them pay big time. Remember, make them work for it." He kissed her one more time and left for the bridge.

She forced herself to wait another five minutes, brewing a cup of coffee before going to sick bay. Ford and Caph looked even more miserable, but Aaron's words echoed in her brain.

She examined them, silent except to ask about their symptoms and injuries, checking for concussion even though she didn't suspect it, refusing to meet their eyes. After twenty minutes of cold professional treatment, Caph grabbed her hand.

"Emi, please, baby. We're sorry," he said, his green eyes near tears.

She wanted to hold him, rock him, comfort him. Instead, she pulled her hand free. "That's very comforting, Bates."

He recoiled as if slapped. It hurt her as much to say it as it did him to hear it.

Ford tried next. "Please, honey. How can we make it up to you?"

This was so hard, his aching voice shattering her heart. "Caliban, to be honest, I'm not sure."

They silently watched her. She gave them both medicine for their hangovers and pain from their beatings. When she dismissed them, instead of leaving they sat and watched while she filled out her log reports and their medical charts.

Aaron made this cold and calculating attitude look easy, but then again, he'd had nearly twenty years with these men.

Maybe this was why he never "bottomed." He needed the extra emotional advantage over them to hold onto his professional veneer. They had to listen to him, not question him, to keep them all alive.

"Was there something else, gentlemen? You're dismissed."

They looked practically broken. Both men stared at the floor and shook their heads. How long and hard did she make them work for this?

After another couple of minutes, they filed out, looking dejected. Once the door slid shut behind them, Emi paged Aaron on the private bridge com and told him what happened.

"Good," he said. "They'll come here next. That was perfect."

Emi hated herself for adding to the twin's pain. "It didn't feel perfect, Aaron."

"I know, honey. I'll lay into them, and then they'll come back to you and you can give in. Just play along a little bit longer."

She fought her tears, wanting to race after them and hold them. "I don't know how you do this."

He hesitated. "I don't enjoy it. It sucks. I fucking hate times like this because you know how I feel about those two assholes, they're my life. I hate having to be like this. But it's better they get this lesson now than in the middle of the mission in a spaceport where I don't have the DSMC honchos to help me deal with crap. You might not like hearing this, but we have to protect you. All of us. They forgot that last night. They can't ever forget again. Remember to play along when they come back."

"Okay." He hung up, and she waited.

And waited.

Nearly an hour later, she was going over her inventory when the sick bay door slid open. She knew it was the twins, but didn't turn.

"Yes, gentlemen?"

They walked in together. She let them stand there in silence for a few minutes before she faced them. They looked even worse than before, even though they'd changed clothes. Whatever ass-chewing Aaron gave them had the desired effect. They approached her, stopping a few feet away.

Ford spoke first, his voice ragged, choked. "Emi, please, don't leave us."

She hoped she masked her surprise and didn't say anything, unsure what response was appropriate. What had Aaron told them?

Caph nodded, reaching for her hand. "We love you, sweetie. Please, whatever we've got to do, please don't leave us. We need you."

Settling for what she hoped was a cold, appraising mask, she studied them. "I don't *want* to leave you." She hoped it came out the way she meant to say it, so they'd think that was what she was going to do anyway, even though it was the truth.

She *didn't* want to leave them.

Ever.

The men looked horrified. Ford took her other hand, desperate. "Emi, babe, please. Tell us. Whatever you want, we swear, we'll do it. We were assholes—we never should have taken you out there. It would serve us right if you left us..." His voice broke. "Honey, we're so sorry. We never thought you could get hurt, not there."

Caph looked near tears. "Please, Emi." He kissed her hand, holding it to his cheek. "We're begging you, please don't leave us."

What was the right thing to do—to give in immediately, or to gradually relent?

The door slid open. Aaron strode in, looking upset and miserable. He pushed in between her and the twins, and she had to fight to stifle her nervous giggle when he winked at her.

"Look, Em, please, listen to me," he said, pulling her hand from Ford's grasp. "I know you said you'd pretty much made up your mind, but can I talk you into staying? Can I talk to you one more time?"

Wow. He'd *really* pulled a mind fuck on the twins. He wasn't kidding when he said he would make them pay for this.

She glanced over his shoulder at the twins, who looked like they didn't dare hope.

Emi made a show of sighing. "I don't know what to say, Aaron." That *was* the truth. She searched his eyes, trying to feel for his guidance.

He winked again. The twins couldn't see from where they stood behind him. "I think they understand, Em. And I don't think they'll ever repeat last night's incident."

The twins frantically nodded behind him. She fought the urge to giggle. They were so cute, bless their hearts.

Emi rolled her eyes to the ceiling as if trying to make up her mind. In reality, she was trying not to laugh.

After a long minute she sighed, as if resigned. "All right. I'll stay."

The twins swooped, hugging her desperately, relieved, almost overwhelming her with the force of their gratitude. Aaron stepped out of the way and winked at her again, nodding slightly.

"*Good job,*" he silently mouthed, turning to leave her alone with them.

She nodded, closing her eyes and wrapping her arms around the twins.

After a few minutes, she patted them on the backs. "Let's go to the cabin and you can show me how sorry you are."

She thought Caph would toss her over his shoulder, he was in such a hurry to go. Desperate to make her happy, the men held her between them in their bed, covering her body with kisses, apologizing, murmuring to her, wanting to make amends. She felt guilty she'd deceived them, but she would trust Aaron's judgment and sensed the twins would not only guard her with their lives from that moment on, but they would most likely never willingly expose her to anything more dangerous than a sunburn.

Emi lay cradled in Caph's arms as Ford kissed his way down her body. He slowly laved his tongue over her clit while Caph kissed her and played with her nipples. It was heaven letting these men have her, and while she wished Aaron were here, too, she understood why he stayed away for now.

It didn't take long for Ford to make her climax, reading her body and drawing the sensation out as long as he could for her. When she lay, spent, in Caph's lap, the men smiled at her.

"How was that, sweetie?" Caph asked.

Emi smiled. "As wonderful as always." She crooked her finger at Ford and he leaned in, kissing her, then Caph. She loved watching them play together almost as much as she enjoyed what they did to her.

Which gave her an idea. She sat up and grinned.

"Uh oh," Caph said. "She's planning something. I know that look."

Waggling her eyebrows at him, she pushed him down to the bed. He was hard and ready and felt good as she lowered herself onto him.

Pulling Ford close, she whispered in his ear and he grinned. "Anything you want, babe."

Caph's large hands rested on her hips. "What?"

Ford leaned over and kissed Caph again. "She wants a little show."

Comprehending, Caph grinned. "Well, get over here then."

Ford knelt beside him. Caph wrapped his lips around Ford's cock. Both men let out content groans.

Emi had to remember what she was doing, because the sight was so hot. She resumed her sultry bump and grind on Caph. "That's it," she whispered. "Show me what you can do to him." She stroked Caph's chest, playing with his nipples, then leaned over and kissed Ford.

Ford's eyes squeezed shut as he lost himself in the feeling. "He's so fucking good," he moaned.

Emi's hand drifted down Ford's back, between his legs, stroking his sac. "Well, show me how good he is. You know I love hearing you come, baby."

Caph's hips bucked under her. He was loving every second of this, his fingers tightening on her.

Emi smiled, gently brushing her nails against Ford's balls, making him moan again. "He's going to swallow every drop, isn't he? I bet you're about ready to explode for me right now."

His forehead was damp, his body tense and trembling. He was damn close.

"Suck him deep, Caph," she purred. "I want to hear you make him come for me—"

Ford cried out, his body tensing as his hips bucked against Caph's face. She slipped her arm around his waist as he came. Then he carefully collapsed next to them.

"Damn!" he whispered.

Caph kissed him. "Good?"

"Yeah. Your turn." They kissed, and again Emi almost forgot what she was doing. Caph grabbed her hips and thrust into her, hard, lifting her body with his larger frame.

"Yes," she said, leaning forward to suck his nipples. "It's your turn now, baby. I want to feel what we do to you."

He was caught in his passion, quickly rolling toward release, and his loud moan was muffled by Ford's mouth. But she felt him as he pulled her hips tight against his pelvis, his entire body tensing as he climaxed.

When he finished, he pulled her down on top of him, his arms around her, kissing her. Then he wrapped an arm around Ford and held him against his side as they all napped.

She wasn't sure how long they laid there when she felt Aaron's presence. The twins were asleep, and Aaron's playful smirk lit her heart. He leaned in the open doorway, arms crossed, taking in the scene.

Emi lifted her head and crooked her finger at him. He silently crossed the room and knelt on the floor close to her, leaning over and kissing her.

She raised an eyebrow at him, an invitation to play. Sensing her meaning he smiled again and shook his head, then pressed his lips against her ear and breathed, "Later. Take care of them for now. They need you."

He kissed her again before leaving, shaking his head in amusement.

When the twins awoke, she led them to the shower and enjoyed the royal treatment of the two men soaping her up. Once they'd been reassured she wasn't leaving them their tension had dissipated, although she still sensed their guilt. She suspected they would deal with that for weeks, if not months.

The twins spent the day catering to her, doting on her, including cooking her favorite foods for dinner. When Aaron joined them in the galley, the twins looked at his stern face and apologized again.

He nodded. "Don't ever forget again, guys." He leaned over and kissed Emi's cheek, whispering, "Well done, baby girl," in her ear.

She barely concealed her smile. Emi had a feeling she'd share many moments like this with Aaron over their hopefully many years together. While still crew, he saw her in a different light than the twins, would count on her to be his eyes and ears and a good influence on them in his absence.

Aaron sat at the table. "So what's for dinner, guys?" The rest of the meal passed in a lighter mood, and by the time they went to bed later, Aaron curling up with Emi while Caph and Ford snuggled close, they were back to whatever passed for normal between them.

Chapter Twelve

With the confidence that Aaron not only loved her, but wasn't going to refuse her assignment at the end of training, Emi threw herself into her work. Aaron personally went with her to the hand-to-hand combat classes, not holding back as her sparring partner. The twins were good for practice, but both she and Aaron noticed they were too careful, afraid of hurting her. She understood Aaron's need for her to be effective in this way, and he always felt bad about the bruises she incurred. But after several weeks she was giving back as good as she took.

Most of the retrofits were complete. They'd started major testing of the ship's systems, including the power generators and life support. While she wouldn't say she was confident with her ability to perform her non-medical duties, she was more comfortable with them than she had been at the start.

The men were right that some things became second nature. As her tension eased, she felt her libido rise. There were a few nights the men were worn out from their duties and had fun taking care of her, never failing to leave her satisfied.

A tentative departure date was set, giving them six weeks to finalize preparations. It wouldn't be confirmed until several days before they left. They would spend two weeks at the orbital docking complex, allowing for last-minute load checks on the systems, real-life simulations with life support and defenses, then an escorted six-week shakedown cruise to the Mars station to ensure there weren't any problems. There they would pick up their final supplies and equipment before heading out of the solar system to their first destination.

The crew shifted into a nightly watch pattern. In space they would still emulate the twenty-four hour daily cycle, so at night they alternated shifts. The men took turns on watch with Emi, wanting her completely comfortable with the systems before turning her loose on her own. The computer simulated various conditions, benign and dangerous, to give her experience with what to look for and how to respond.

She enjoyed this alone time with each man. While she knew she could easily spend time with any them if she asked, it was a guilt-free excuse to have their undivided attention without worrying if someone's feelings were hurt. She admittedly enjoyed her watches with Ford the best, his body slim enough they could sit side-by-side, tucked snugly into the command seat, cuddled together and talking.

Staying awake with Ford was never an issue. Between their talks and his frequent, playful groping, nights with him flew by. Aaron was always casual with her but took time to go over the different systems, answering any questions she had, making sure she understood the settings. Caph was too willing to let her drift to sleep and do her job for her. She frequently had to remind him to keep her awake, not protect her from what they were doing.

* * * *

With four weeks left, Dr. Graymard called her into his office one morning. "So how are you getting along, Emi?"

Her confidence wasn't faked anymore. "I'm nervous, obviously, but the guys have been great. I know if I have any questions they'll help me."

"No second thoughts about backing out?"

"Not on your life."

She sensed there was something else he wanted to discuss. "Are you aware of the term bonded crew?"

She stiffened. She didn't want to hear the story from him, not really. She wanted her boys to tell her, even though she was desperate to know. "I ran across it."

He nodded, eyeing her. "The men of the Tamora Bight are bonded crew. It's a very specific designation, meaning they cannot be separated unless they desire it. Since they are bonded crew, they can add to their number if they wish. Now, I have not spoken to Aaron about this yet, because he is the one who has to make the request, speaking for his men. Should he make the request, however, I would prefer to know your answer in advance, if at all possible. I won't tell him your answer because that's between you and the men. But there are paperwork issues to take care of, and the more advanced knowledge I have, the easier it makes my job."

She nodded. "I'd like that."

"It doesn't make you married to them or anything. It means you cannot arbitrarily be transferred out of his command by outside officers unless you request a transfer." He made a notation in his computer. "That's all, Emi. I just needed to talk to you about that."

A few hours later, Graymard paged the ship and requested Aaron come to his office, alone. He didn't seem nervous, but she was. Would they be talking about her?

It was her night to cook. She was preparing dinner when the boys walked into the galley, smiling.

That had to be a good sign, right?

Aaron took her hands in his. "Em, we wanted to talk to you about something."

She nodded, hopeful, expectant.

Aaron glanced at the twins, who were remarkably silent. They nodded their encouragement.

"We'll be shipping out soon, and we're going to have one last crew day together in the city, followed by dinner. Someplace nice where they don't ask if you want fries with that. It's our tradition. But we'd like to know if you'd start a new tradition with us."

"What?"

"We'd each like a day and night away from the ship with you, alone. We'll be together for a long time, and we agree it'd be nice to get a chance to have you to ourselves."

Not exactly what she'd expected, but nearly as good. "I'd love that."

They set the dates, and each man made his plans. Aaron decided Ford could have the first night, Caph the second, and he'd take the night before their crew day together.

"Where are we going?" she asked Ford the night before her day with him began.

He grinned. "Secret. Not telling. I've already packed for you. We all have."

She eyed their nearly identical smiles. "Okay. I'll let you have your fun."

* * * *

The next morning, Ford requisitioned a car. The men would trade off each day, and he loaded two bags into it. They had packed for her, not wanting her to have any clues as to their plans. She stood in the galley and hugged Caph, kissing him good-bye.

"I'll see you tomorrow," she said, feeling a little sad but knowing this was a good thing.

"You'd better believe it." The playful gleam in his eye indicated he'd planned something fun.

Then Aaron. He hugged her tightly. "Keep them out of trouble, Em," he whispered. "I'll miss you."

She felt his wistful pang and knew it would be even worse for him than it was for her. He would have to go two days before seeing her, and she'd at least have the other guys distracting her and keeping her busy. "I'll miss you, too." She hesitated. "I love you."

He smiled and met her eyes, nodded, then touched his forehead to hers for a moment. "Me too."

The wave of emotion she felt from him screamed his love. Ford was right—she didn't need to hear him say it.

She hugged him tightly. Ford returned. "All set. Ready?"

She nodded.

"Have fun," Aaron and Caph parroted. Aaron groaned while the others laughed.

"Great," he playfully groused. "Now I'm doing it."

* * * *

None of the men revealed their plans to her. Ford had laid out a casual outfit for her to wear that morning, a blouse and linen slacks, comfortable sandals to go with them. He looked sharp in khaki slacks and a freshly pressed button-up chambray shirt.

He held the car door open for her. Then, once he was inside behind the wheel, he grabbed her hand and kissed it. "I've got you all to myself for a whole day and night." He grinned. "I can't believe it."

He was so playful, his sweet personality infectious. "I can't believe you guys aren't jealous of each other."

He snorted. "Why? I mean, if you suddenly picked one of us over the others for good, maybe. But we love each other, we know you love us, and we love you. We've been together too many fucking years to be like that."

She watched the scenery as he drove them to town. Then a horrible thought struck her. "You wouldn't add any other crew, would you?" She knew it was selfish, but she didn't want to share her boys with any other women. And frankly, she didn't want any other men in the mix, either.

Ford looked at her, then realized what she meant and laughed. "No, sweetheart, you're our limit, trust me. I mean, never like that. We might have to add crew in terms of working on the ship, but never like that. While we don't mind sharing you between us, we're not about to share you with anyone else. I know that's a weird double-standard, but there you have it."

At a traffic signal he stopped and looked at her. "You're all ours, babe. As long as you'll put up with us."

They checked into the hotel first, an expensive hillside retreat with a stunning panoramic view of the valley below.

And a very large bed.

"What's next?"

He glanced at his watch. "Our first stop on today's adventure is one I've been wanting to make for a long time, and I hope you enjoy it as much as I think I will."

It was a short drive to the New Phoenix Museum of Art and Science, a large, sprawling facility associated with one of the local universities. They had a wide variety of exhibits from fine arts to historic relics from the twentieth century and earlier.

She loved it.

She walked hand-in-hand with Ford, losing herself in his enthusiasm, enjoying this uninterrupted time with him. He was still the same man, but this side of his personality could fully emerge. She loved it. After a long lunch, their next stop was the nearby Botanical Gardens.

"I thought you'd appreciate the irony," he said as he bought their tickets.

She grinned. "The plant killer taking me to see plants?"

His blue eyes twinkled. "Exactly."

The sun was dropping behind the western mountains when they finished. She rested her head against his shoulder, his arm around her waist as they returned to the car. "This day is going too fast," she said.

He kissed the top of her head. "Tell me about it. You feel like dinner?"

"Yeah."

When they returned to the room later, he stopped her at the door. "What?" she asked.

He scooped her into his arms and carried her inside. "Not the same thing, I know. But my first night all alone with you."

She wrapped her arms around him, kissing him. "You don't have to rush."

"I don't have to share." His smile belied his words. "I know you like watching, but every once in a while it's fun to be a little selfish."

He gently laid her on the bed, stretching out beside her. "I mean, once we're in space, every so often the three of us will put our heads together, if you don't mind, and we'll do like a double night watch or something so we can take turns alone with you. If you want that."

"That would be okay every once in a while. I don't want to do that every night. I'm selfish. I like having my boys with me in bed."

He laughed, kissing her. "You just like it because you know you've got us wrapped around your fingers. You've got a male harem at your disposal." He held her hand, kissing her fingers. "Are you really happy with us?"

Emi nodded. "I can't wait to make it official."

"There is no chance of Aaron refusing your assignment, you know."

"I know. I just want it in writing."

He took his time unbuttoning her blouse. "We'll tattoo it on our backs, how's that?"

She ran her fingers through his hair. "That's a little excessive, but appreciated."

Ford was her slow, sensual lover. With an entire night in front of them, he took his time, gently coaxing two orgasms out of her before rolling her over onto her knees and carefully entering her from behind, his arms wrapped around her waist.

She loved the way his body perfectly molded to hers. All three men were fantastic lovers. But in this way it was as if he was completely attuned to every nuance of her body. She noticed this when he made love to the other men as well.

He laid his cheek against her shoulder. "Can I get one more from you, baby?" he whispered.

"I can't promise it."

"Good enough for me." He stilled his strokes, his cock buried deep inside her. Keeping his weight off her, he reached around her waist and his skillful fingers gently stroked her clit. She gasped.

"Damn, I love the way you squeeze my cock like that. I take it that's a strong maybe," he joked.

"You keep that up, it is."

His lips traced the contour of her spine as he slowly teased her toward another orgasm. She loved the feel of having one of them inside her when she came. When her release started, he gently encouraged her, murmuring to her.

"That's it, sweetie, give it to me. Let me have it."

Emi ground her hips against him. He took that as his cue to resume his thrusts, taking his time, drawing sensual moans from her as he let his climax gradually build. Then he exploded, gasping her name as he held still inside her, taking a long, deep breath before wrapping his arms around her and rolling to his side, taking her with him.

"Good?" she asked with a teasing smile.

He laughed. "You have no idea, baby. So good." He turned her to face him, kissing her. "So good," he mumbled, brushing his lips along the base of her throat, tracing her jaw. "Perfect."

The men had never once asked her to do the one sexual activity she was increasingly curious about. Or asked her to do anything, actually. They were always careful to let her set the pace of their lovemaking sessions. With her trust securely placed in them, she asked Ford.

"Tell me how it feels…back there."

His lips froze in place, and then he laughed. "You want to broaden your horizons a little, honey?"

She tipped her head so she could see his eyes. "I think so, yes."

He blinked. "You're serious? Really?"

"Yeah."

A slow, surprised smile crept across his face. "That would be fun, getting to do that with you."

"I've never done it before."

His eyes widened. "Oh, wait...wow." He laughed. "We get to pop your cherry!"

"I suppose. You didn't answer my question."

"I mean, it's fun."

"Aaron doesn't think so, apparently."

Ford froze, tension filling him. She wished she hadn't mentioned it. After a long, hesitant pause, he said, "It's not that. Again, it's not my story to tell, sweetie."

"When do I get the crew story?"

His smile returned, but it was sad. "After the crew dinner we'll all come back here for one last night away from the ship, and we'll let Aaron decide how he wants to tell it." He kissed the tip of her nose. "We *will* tell you, though. There's parts of it that are his alone to tell...or not."

"But it's tied in, isn't it? That whole thing?"

His sad eyes glistened. "Yeah," he whispered. "It's all tied in."

She wished she could take the words back as soon as she said them. "It has to do with Kelsey, right?" They'd told her plenty of stories about their exploits, but she'd never heard her name mentioned before, or anything about their time on the Wayfarer Margo.

When Emi spoke her name, Ford's body tightened. "How did you know about her?"

His reaction told her all she needed. "All I know is she died. I looked up the crew records. I don't know anything beyond that. The records were sealed."

Ford's eyes looked past her, nearly twenty years distant. "Yeah. She died." He rolled over on his back and stared at the ceiling.

She wanted to pull him from his pain, wishing she'd never said anything. "Tell me how you three guys met, at least." She rested her palm over his heart, trying to will him to calm down. "That's not classified, is it?" she snarked.

It worked. He rested his hand over hers and smiled. "No, smarty. That's not. We were in training and just sort of...fell in with each other. We worked well together, and we requested assignment to the same vessel after we were certified. Me and Caph, we were fine following Aaron around. He didn't have aspirations to make admiral or anything, he just had a good head on his shoulders and we wanted to follow him." Ford laughed. "He saved our asses so many times. I'm surprised he didn't get sick of us. We knew he'd keep us alive, and he knew we'd back him up. It just sort of worked out for the three of us."

She rolled over on top of him, enjoying the feel of his hands sliding down her back and resting on her ass. "Back to what we were talking about." She wiggled her hips against him. "Taking care of broadening my horizons."

He immediately pulled out of his funk. "There's part of me that wants to tell you to bend over right now. However..." He kissed her. "Something that special, as much as the selfish part of me wants to have you all to myself, I'd like that to be a group event, if you don't mind."

He was so sweet. "I don't mind." She kissed him. "Do you think it would bother the others if I asked you to be the first?"

Emi would kill for the broad, happy smile he bestowed on her. "I doubt it would, but can I ask how I managed to be the lucky one?"

She'd watched the men together many nights, how gentle Ford always was. Not that the others weren't, but so many times she noticed Ford put everyone else before himself. This was something she wanted him to have first, something special between them that he could always remember. "Because I do. Maybe that's something else we can do after our crew dinner."

Her hips were in just the right position to feel him rubbing between her legs, against her slick cleft. He grew stiff again. "Wow. A cherry for dessert. What a sweet treat."

She raised herself up just enough to slide him inside her. He rolled her onto her back. "You want one more, sweetheart?"

Emi wrapped her arms around him. "I think you've worn me out. Why don't you come for me, baby."

He dropped his head to her shoulder, taking his time, varying his strokes. "I promise you'll love it," he whispered against her neck. "We'll make you come so hard you'll think your head's going to explode."

"Someone's head'll explode, at least."

He chuckled. "Your first time. Damn, that's a sexy thought. I can't wait to do that for you." His breath came in shorter gasps. She knew he was close.

"Maybe…" She felt safe voicing this fantasy with him. "Maybe two of you can have me at the same time—"

"Fuck!" He came, hard, crying out, his eyes squeezed shut. She held him as he collapsed on her, wrapping her legs around his so he couldn't get away.

After he caught his breath he laughed and lifted his head to look into her eyes. "You mean it?"

"No promises. We'll see how it goes."

He shook his head, smiling in wonder. "You're amazing. It's no surprise why we love you so much."

* * * *

Emi awoke with dawn peeking through the window, one of the few things she missed about life outside the ship. The window sims they'd installed did an okay job, but just weren't the same, didn't give the same brilliance, cast warm light on the floor or catch dust motes dancing in sunbeams the way sunlight did.

Ford's mouth was latched onto one of her breasts, gently teasing her awake. "There you are," he murmured. "I thought you were going to sleep all morning."

"When will Caph be here?"

"Three hours." He kissed her. "Just enough time for us to take a long bubble bath and have breakfast."

The deep tub was perfect for romance. It was another of the things she would miss while living on the ship. With water a precious resource, water showers were a luxury they would rarely partake in, and they had no bathtub.

Ford made slow, sweet love to her again, leaving her breathless. After she made him come, they cuddled in the warm water for several long minutes.

He sighed. "Ah, my dream is about to end."

"Not exactly. Remember what you get to look forward to."

"Oh!" He grinned. "Damn, you're right! Can't get here soon enough." He nuzzled her neck. "Do me a favor, please, babe," he said, his voice soft and serious. "Don't mention anything to Caph or Aaron about Kels, okay?" He hesitated, and she sensed he was trying to find the words. "We all loved her, and it tore us all up to lose her. But you know how different people handle that differently. You'll hear the story soon enough, okay?"

"I understand. I won't."

He kissed her. "Thanks. You're the best." He drained the water from the tub. "Well, let's go eat."

"Any hints what Caph has in store?"

"I'm sworn to secrecy."

* * * *

Ford laid her out an outfit—jeans, a T-shirt, and sneakers. She felt underdressed next to Ford in the hotel restaurant, but he assured her it was fine. "Nope, this is what you wear today."

Caph arrived soon after they finished eating. He kissed her, then Ford. "You didn't wear her out, did you?" he teased. He was also dressed in jeans and a T-shirt and sneakers. Whatever they were doing, they matched.

She gently nudged him in the ribs. "No, smartass."

"I'm leaving her with you in perfect condition. See she stays that way."

Caph rolled his eyes and winked at her. He was playful in a different way than Ford. Caph tossed a set of keys to Ford. "It's parked next to the other car. Pick-up."

Ford handed him the car keys. "Let me go get my bag from the room."

They waited for Ford in the lobby. Caph hugged her.

"All mine," he playfully growled, goosing her ass.

"For a day. When do I get to hear the plans?"

"When we get there."

Ford returned with his bag, handed the room key to Caph, and they walked to the parking lot together. Caph retrieved his bag from the truck and gave Ford another hug and kiss. Then Ford took one last private moment with Emi, whispering in her ear, "I can't wait to do that, sweetie. I'll be looking forward to it."

"Me too."

He stepped back. "Have fun. Love you." He looked at Caph. "Love you, too."

"I love you, too," Caph and Emi parroted, then laughed.

Ford grinned. "It's contagious!" They watched him drive away. Caph dropped his bag in the trunk.

"You don't want to take that to the room?" she asked.

"Nope, I want to get on with our fun."

* * * *

He wouldn't even give her a hint about his plans. They drove nearly a half-hour north into the mountains. She had an idea what was up when he pulled into a stable.

"Let me guess," she said.

"Ever ride before?"

"Yeah. When I was a kid. I don't think Aaron will like it if I'm too sore to do anything tomorrow, though."

"Hey, I'll kiss your saddle sores for you, how's that?"

"Like I could really keep your head out from between my legs even if I wanted to."

He grinned, kissing her. "Ooh, hadn't even thought of it like that."

They followed their guide on a horseback ride along a beautiful trail through the mountains. After two hours they arrived at a private clearing where a picnic tent and folding table had been set up.

"Early lunch?" Emi asked.

Caph shook his head, smiling. "Not yet." He grabbed a backpack from the small folding table under the tent and took her hand, leading her alone down a trail. After twenty minutes of walking, they arrived at a tree-shaded area along the bank of a small stream.

"Wow! I didn't know there were places like this. I thought it was all dry and arid around here."

"There's little oases here and there, if you know where to look." He took a blanket out of the pack and spread it out in the shade. He sat and patted the ground in front of him. "Come here."

She sat in front of him and he rubbed her shoulders. "How's that?"

Emi groaned. He had magic fingers, always able to soothe her. "Wonderful." She was surprised she wasn't the least bit sore from their ride and hoped she wouldn't be sore tomorrow, either.

He had her lay down and massaged her back, then slipped his hands under her shirt. "We're all alone, sweetie. I promise." He pulled her shirt off. She closed her eyes, enjoying the feel of his hands on her. "I've been coming to this place for years, since I was a kid. I grew up about ten miles north of here."

Caph was always a bit of a surprise for her. She knew one thing for certain about him, and that was that he could catch her off-guard. She would have expected a movie, or a sporting event, or maybe an amusement park. Not a private ride to a personal haven.

After a half-hour of heavenly sensations, he stretched out next to her.

"This is nice, Caph, really. Very relaxing."

He brushed the hair from her eyes. She made no move to don her shirt, knowing if she needed it he'd have it on her in a heartbeat.

"We'll be on a ship for a few years. We'll get shore leave here and there, but it'll be a while before we get back here."

Emi held his hand and kissed it, pressing his large palm against her cheek. "Promise to bring me here again when we get back?"

He smiled. "It's a date." His green eyes traveled her face, as if taking in every detail. "I love you so much, Emi. The other guys do too. Life's a lot better with you around, and I don't mean just sex. I'm talking everything."

"Sex, too, though."

He grinned. "Well, yeah, okay, that's good too. But you know what I mean."

She did. His earnest intent was as clearly there as the smile on his face.

A brief blip of sadness from him again. "You're good for Aaron, too. Man, me and Ford, we were so worried about him…" He looked down, picked at his fingernails. "I shouldn't talk about that now. I don't want to ruin the mood." He met her gaze and winked. "Ever made love in the great outdoors?"

He rolled on top of her, kissing her.

She laughed. "No. But are we really alone enough to do that?"

"Oh yeah. The guide is ours for the day, and he'll stay back there with the horses until we're ready for lunch."

He nuzzled the side of her neck. As the warm breeze caressed them, she ran her hands up under his shirt, lifting it over his head. The feel of his smooth, firm flesh beneath her hands ignited a fire deep in her belly that she knew from experience only his touch could put out.

"Then why don't we have a little fun?" she asked.

He worked his way down her body, his deceptively large hands intimately aware of how to stroke and caress and tease her flesh. Every brush of his thumbs against her nipples left her gasping for more. By the time he reached the waistband of her jeans, she was more than ready to finish getting naked.

He helped her off with her shoes and socks, then ran his tongue down the inside of her leg as he removed her jeans and underwear. When she was naked before him, he stood and kicked off his shoes and dropped his pants.

This view of him always took her breath away. As large as his body was, knowing how gentle and loving and all hers he was made her lower belly quiver with anticipation.

After gently nudging her legs apart, he knelt between them, then pulled her into a sitting position and lifted her into his lap. He was hard, and she was ready. With a happy sigh she lowered her body onto him, enjoying the feel of his thick cock gliding inside her, parting her lips and sliding home as if he was perfectly formed to her body's shape. She wrapped her legs around his waist and kissed him, her hands tangling in his hair as his hands skimmed down her back to her hips.

They fit so well together like this. So far no luck in the unassisted orgasm for her, but not for lack of trying on his part.

And Caph was always willing to try.

It was a lot of damn fun trying, too.

Almost as if he read her mind, he whispered, "I'd like to give you that." He nipped her ear, knowing that sent shivers down her spine despite the warm, mesquite-tinged air.

Rocking his hips, he slowly fucked her, gently adjusting positions and taking his time as she clung to his body and enjoyed the sensations. At one point he shifted just right, and she felt his body brush against her clit.

She gasped, spreading her thighs a little wider, trying to duplicate the sensation.

"Like that, baby?" he asked.

"Mmm hmm." He had to be going crazy—they'd been at it for a while with her writhing, impaled on his sweet muscle.

He found a rhythm that worked for her. While it wasn't perfect, and not nearly as intense as when one of them used their mouth or hands on her, she found herself climbing toward release.

He held her against him, working his hips in sharp thrusts that sent pleasant jolts through her core every time his pubic bone hit her just right. Caph let her set the pace. Before long she was thrusting, her eyes closed, desperate to make it over this time, wanting it not just for her, but for him, too.

"Come for me, Emi," he whispered, trying not to break her rhythm. "I want to feel it, baby."

Their skin slick with sweat, he held her, letting her use his body as she needed. She closed her eyes and rested her head on his shoulder, still rocking, moving, grinding.

When the fireworks went off behind her eyes it shocked her, startling her. He groaned with her.

"That's it, baby. Come on, give it to me."

She cried out, sobbing as her orgasm hit, going limp against him as he lowered her to the blanket without breaking his hold on her. In three quick thrusts he came, moaning her name.

Emi clung to him, crying, gasping for air.

Never before. Ever. Not like that.

"You okay, honey?" he asked, almost worried.

She laughed despite her tears. "Happy tears, honest, Caph."

"Oh, okay," he said, relieved.

When she let him go he pushed up and looked at her. "You were worrying me there for a minute."

"I just…it's just…I never—" He kissed her, silencing her.

"I know," he whispered, nuzzling her nose with his. "I thought maybe out here in the great outdoors, all alone, no one to bother us, maybe it would relax you."

"Wow."

He grinned. "You liked that?"

She nodded, eager. "Maybe we can set up the sim room for that."

"Sex in the desert, huh?"

They cleaned up in the stream, laying on the blanket until they were dry, Emi cuddled against him. She closed her eyes and sighed. "That was so good, Caph."

He laid his palm on her belly. "You're not getting off that easy…no pun intended."

Spying his playful grin, she laughed. "I didn't break anything, did I?"

He reached down and shook his limp cock. "Nope. I think he just needs a rest. He'll be ready to play by the time we get back."

Caph was her goofball. That was a good way to describe him. When he didn't have to be serious or working, he was her big, sweet goofball, always trying to make everyone smile, his sense of humor never harsh or hurtful.

Laying her palm against his cheek, she kissed him, long and sweet. "Thank you," she said.

"Well, I figure Aaron got to have you first, Ford'll probably get something else first, so I got to do that for you. It all works out."

Her mouth gaped in shock.

"What?" he asked.

"Did you guys, like, compare notes or something?"

He laughed and rolled to his side. "Well, I know Ford. We've been together a lot of years. I'm also guessing he didn't do *that* with you last night, because knowing him, he would have said he wanted to wait until it's the four of us together."

Still speechless, she stared at him.

"Oh, come on, Emi. It's not spooky. Am I right?"

She nodded. "It *is* spooky. I thought *I* was the ship empath."

When his gaze left hers for a moment, she suspected his mind's eye was briefly focused on a piercingly sad point in the men's collective past. "It's only right." He looked down. "History repeating itself in a way. Only with a happy ever after ending for us this time." He closed his eyes and rolled onto his back. "It should be Ford who gets to have you first. He's got a special touch. He won't hurt you."

"You and Aaron wouldn't hurt me!"

"I don't mean like that." Caph searched for the words. "Not hurt. But that first time…it should be perfect. Like I said, he's got a special touch. It's better he's first, because I know you'll enjoy it." He finally looked at her again and winked. "I know I did." The twins both enjoyed the top and bottom roles and never had trouble changing it up. He looked at his watch. "Let's get dressed and head back. Lunch is waiting."

They shook out their clothes and shoes to check for any bugs before dressing. She helped him shake out and fold the blanket. Then, before they started their return hike, he hugged and kissed her again. "Really, tell me the truth. Was that good?"

"It was great, Caph. Seriously."

He looked proud of himself. "We'll have to see if we can do that again."

* * * *

They hiked back and ate, then followed the guide to the stables. They held hands on the return drive to the hotel and took a long, sultry shower to rinse off the sweat and horse smell. He tossed her a bathing suit. "Part two. Let's stay close to home."

It was the middle of the week, so the hotel wasn't full. With the exception of two people sunning on the pool deck, they had it to themselves. Emi dove into the deep end. When she came up for air Caph grabbed her, kissing her.

"Looks like I caught me a mermaid," he teased. She let her leg brush against the front of his swim trunks, making him harden immediately. "A mermaid who doesn't fight fair." He laughed, easily tossing her into the air. She landed with a splash a few feet away.

He was strong, diving under and cutting through the water with swift, hard strokes, surfacing behind her. Before she could turn, he reached out and goosed her ass, then quickly dove out of reach.

They horsed around in the pool for an hour before climbing out, laughing and out of breath. They took two lounges at the far end of the deck in the sun. They lay there, eyes closed, holding hands and quietly talking.

"Admit it, you probably thought I'd take you someplace else," he said.

"Yeah, I'll admit it. You surprised me." She looked at him. "In a good way. This has been a great day, Caph."

The sun hung low in the sky, but they still had a few hours before dark. "For me too, Emi." He squeezed her hand and took a deep breath. "Promise you won't leave us. Please."

"I'll never leave you guys. I promise."

He looked at her, then nodded, satisfied. "Good. I can't stand to lose twice in one life, babe. I might as well cut out my heart."

* * * *

Emi didn't ask for clarification on his comment. They changed clothes, ate dinner in the hotel restaurant, then returned to their room. At the door he stopped her and grinned.

"Let me guess," she said. "You want to carry me in."

He shrugged. "You don't mind, do you?"

She threw her arms around his neck. "Of course not."

He carried her to the bed and that was the extent of the similarity to her night with Ford. Well, that, and the fantastic lovemaking.

All alone and without any distractions, Caph wanted to experiment with positions and strokes and techniques. After an hour he discovered a slow, grinding slide that perfectly stroked her clit on each downward thrust.

Once she moaned he wouldn't stop, taking his time, watching her face, softly encouraging her. It took her a while, but when she came he waited long enough he knew he wouldn't be cutting her release short to slam home, his own orgasm right behind hers.

Feeling like an idiot, she burst into tears again. His gentle laugh reassured her and he kissed her.

"Happy tears again?"

"Yeah. Sorry."

"Don't apologize!" He held her, cuddling with her, lying next to her with her head tucked into his arm and their fingers laced together. "I just feel good I can do that for you. Something special for us."

"Would you feel bad if one of the other guys figured out how to do it too?"

He laughed. "Fuck, no. Sweetie, being able to make you feel good, it's what we live for." He brought her hand to his lips and kissed each finger. "You know, if we stick to our plan to switch to moon runs or short hops after this, we can be home here on Earth most of the time. You can go with us, obviously, but we'd live here. Or maybe, with all of our money pooled together, we'll just retire and spend every day fucking your brains out. Build a house with a pool and a huge tall fence, and we can spend all day playing mermaid."

She giggled. "Be a kept woman, huh?"

"It'd be your money too, kiddo. And we could switch it off. You know, we'll play kept men for a week, you play kept woman for a week, back and forth. Equality and all that."

He sucked her fingers, one at a time, into his mouth.

"You could spend all day naked, couldn't you?" she asked.

"Is that a problem?"

"No, not for me it's not. I like looking at you guys running around naked."

"Maybe we should have a clothing optional rule on board." His teasing smile made her laugh.

"Nightly strip poker."

They made love again, and this time he knelt between her legs and slowly traced the contour of her sex with his tongue. He took his time and wrapped his arms around her thighs, driving his tongue deep into her wet entrance, keeping her spread wide open.

He wouldn't let her come at first, spending nearly an hour bringing her close to the edge repeatedly before backing off, blowing on her mound, chuckling as she writhed against him.

"You're all mine, babe," he whispered as he let her cool off yet again. "I live to hear you come."

Emi reached down and found his hands, their fingers twining. "How long you gonna torture me, baby?" she gasped.

He swirled his tongue around her throbbing nub. "As long as I can, honey."

Caph's hands kept hers trapped and she let herself go, relinquishing control of her body to him. When he finally let her come, she turned her face into the pillow to muffle her scream. That was a good thing about the ship, not having to worry if anyone heard them or not. They could make wild and passionate monkey sex sounds as loudly as they so desired.

Caph sat up, still holding her hands, and raised her arms above her head. He lowered his body over hers, kissing her. Nudging her legs wider apart, he rubbed his stiff shaft along her wet cleft. "Ready for me, baby?"

She nodded, still recovering from her last mind-blowing orgasm.

Letting go of her hands, he sat up and grabbed her thighs, pulling her hips to him. "Gonna fuck you real good, sweetie," he whispered, his eyes locked on hers.

His strength, his unbridled power always melted her. When he thrust home they both moaned. He paused for a moment, enjoying the feel of her body sheathing him.

Knowing she had reached the limit of her endurance, he played with her, leaned forward to kiss her as he stroked, his tongue's movements matching his hips.

Their skin damp, slipping against each other, he whispered, "Are you ready?"

Emi nodded. Caph let go, his release taking him.

She pulled him down to her, and they fell asleep cuddled together.

* * * *

Caph ordered room service the next morning, and they ate, naked, in bed.

"We ought to do this at the ship," Emi joked.

"Hmm. I'd make you breakfast in bed every morning if you'll look just like this." He leaned over and kissed her tummy.

They made love again, gentle and slow. Emi was surprised she wasn't the slightest bit sore after their ride or…Caph's riding her. She must be in better shape than she thought.

When they finished their shower, Caph laid out another outfit for her, a blouse, linen slacks, and sandals.

"No hint?" she asked, batting her eyes at him.

He snickered, playfully swatting her ass. "Like that really worked before. No way in hell would I tell you Aar's plans. Don't want him going all captain on my ass again, babe."

She was dressed when Aaron knocked on the door and Caph let him in. Aaron gave him a hug and kiss and looked at her.

"You didn't wear her out, right?"

"She's not even saddle sore."

Aaron grinned. "Good."

She went to him and hugged him, kissing him. "Missed you."

His eyes crinkled. "Missed you too, Em." He swapped keys with Caph, who pulled her to him for one final hug and kiss.

"We'll see you tomorrow, babe. Have fun. Love you."

She'd miss him, her buddy, her big goofball. "Love you too."

When they were alone, Aaron wrapped his arms around her, staring into her eyes. "I love Ford, but I forgot what a day alone with him is like."

"Did he talk your ear off?"

"Yeah, poor guy. I don't know which one of us was more miserable. So are you having fun?"

"A lot of fun. What do you have in store for me today?"

"A couple of things." He set his bag in the closet, then turned. "First, we go shopping."

They drove to a gigantic indoor shopping complex and walked inside, hand in hand. He stopped at one of the guide maps, found what he was looking for, and continued on their journey. A few minutes later, they stood in front of a jewelry store.

"Aaron—"

"Shh." He held both her hands. "It's okay. The guys loved it when I told them." He took her inside. An hour later, he'd nudged her toward a diamond and sapphire ring. Aaron paid for it, and then the sales clerk took it in back to size it. While they were alone Aaron turned to Emi.

"I know you know a little of the basics, Em," he said, his voice low. "There's a trigger every time our personnel files are accessed. It lets me know, regardless of who does it."

She reddened, ashamed. "I'm sorry, Aaron. I—"

"Shh. It's okay." She forced her eyes back to his face and found him smiling. It really was okay, he wasn't upset. "It makes it a little easier. You know what bonded crew is, right?"

She nodded.

"We want you to join us, Em. If you want to. I don't just mean join our crew. I mean become bonded crew with us."

"Really?"

"Yes, really. Do you honestly think we're letting you out of our sight now that we all love you?"

She froze. He hadn't said it exactly, but more than close enough for her. She burst into tears and threw her arms around his neck. "Yes!" she gasped, trying not to look like an idiot.

His soft chuckle reassured her. He held her, gently rubbing her back. He kept his voice low, murmuring in her ear. "It also means we won't share you, sweetie. Even if we ever have to have a larger crew, because of our status, we get to set our own rules like that. DSMC honors bonded status rules. You don't have to share us, and we don't have to share you with anyone else."

"I don't want to share you, and I don't want anyone else but you guys."

He hugged her tighter, kissing her neck. "I was hoping you'd say that. I'll tell Graymard." He kissed her, touching his forehead to hers. "There's a lot of the story I still can't talk about yet. Not all at once. I told you I think that if anyone can help me, it's you. We'll tell you the story tomorrow, but I'm going to have Ford tell as much of it as he can. He was the strong one for a while there. I think that helped him process it differently than we did. Maybe Caph and I will let you guys go out for a while or something. Is that okay?"

"Yes." She felt his keening pain returning and didn't want his day with her ruined.

He nodded. "Thank you, babe." The clerk returned, smiling, with the sized ring. Aaron took it and slipped it on Emi's left hand.

Automatically making the wrong assumption, the clerk said, "Congratulations! I hope you'll be very happy."

Emi met Aaron's deep brown eyes and nodded. "I know we will."

* * * *

They had an early lunch, and then he surprised her by taking her to a performance of the ancient play, *Macbeth*. It surprised her, something she'd never thought he would be interested in.

"I love old classics," he explained.

"So what's in store later?"

"Secret, sweetie. Let me have my fun."

She stared at the ring all day. It was beautiful, and she wondered if this was what newly-engaged brides felt like. That's basically what it was—she was, for all intents and purposes, marrying these men, just not in name or legal designation.

When they returned to the hotel from the play, he went to the closet and pulled out a garment bag. Apparently one of the men had snuck it in when she wasn't looking. He handed it to her.

"For the next part, please? Go take it into the bathroom and get ready. I'll get dressed out here."

Inside, she found a long, formal black evening dress, shoes, make-up—everything she'd need to dress to the nines. When she emerged nearly a half-hour later, she gasped.

Aaron was dressed in a tux and looked devastatingly handsome. "You like?" he asked.

She nodded, stunned. He was always a good-looking man, but now...with the total incongruity from his normal manner of dress, it was amazing.

He took her hand and nodded approvingly. "You are gorgeous, sweetie."

"I'm guessing we're not going hiking, horseback riding, or to the botanical gardens or museum?"

"Not quite."

Their destination was the opera house, where they watched a performance of an Italian opera whose translated title meant, *"Heart of Gold."* Fortunately, they had subtitles on a screen over the stage so she didn't get totally lost.

Emi tried to subtly study Aaron's face during the show. They held hands the whole time, his thumb gently stroking her knuckles.

When it was over, she stopped him outside. "You're a mystery man."

His amused smile twisted her heart around his. They might think she could lead them around, but the truth was they had the same effect on her.

"Did you have fun?" he asked.

"A lot of fun. I've never been to anything like this before."

"Then let's go get dinner." Dinner was at an upscale Japanese steakhouse. They had a grill and cook to themselves, and she wondered if Aaron had arranged that in advance. When they returned, she wondered if he'd carry her over the threshold too. He did, but he surprised her, throwing her over his shoulder, laughing, playfully dumping her on the bed.

He landed next to her with a bounce. "So what now?"

Emi laughed and rolled over on top of him. "Do you really need to ask?" She kissed him and felt him stiffen beneath her. "That was really sweet of you to let the twins go first."

He shrugged. "They've kept me alive all these years. It's the least I can do."

"They say the same thing about you."

"I think it's more I've kept them out of the brig and from facing a court martial."

"They're devoted to you."

"I'm devoted to them." His sadness broke through again. "They saved my life. They refused to give up on me and let me die. If it wasn't for them…" He didn't finish.

"Truck in the cafeteria, huh?"

Aaron laughed. "You're distracting me."

"It's a fair question."

He stood up and undressed, told her the story of how the twins were pissed at another crew for being jerks, so they stole the pick-up the other crew had requisitioned for a week and put it in the cafeteria of the Merchant Marine building when they were in dry dock a few years prior.

"How'd they get it in there?"

He hung up his jacket. "Beats the hell out of me. They never did say, and for some reason, the security cameras malfunctioned that night."

She shimmied out of her clothes, and he hung her dress for her.

"Maybe I can get it out of them."

"You have ways of making them talk?" His playful smirk warmed her.

"I'm sure I do."

Their talk, however, ended as he made love to her for several hours before they fell into an exhausted sleep. The next morning, she studied him while he slept, his face and soul completely relaxed, perhaps more than she'd ever seen him.

No, not relaxed.

Content.

He felt different today than he had even yesterday. Maybe he was finally starting to heal?

She hoped so. She wanted to be the one to bring him peace.

"So tell me about your parents," he said, startling her.

"I didn't know you were awake."

He opened his eyes and smiled. "You didn't ask." He watched her face. "You don't have to if you don't want to."

She cuddled in his arms, and, feeling secure, she told him.

"They loved what they did. They were good at it. I missed having a house with a huge yard and garden, but they promised in another two years, when their contract was up, they'd move back Earth-side and buy us another one." Emi closed her eyes, conjuring their faces. "They came back once a month to visit. I never went up there. I was afraid to."

"And now you're getting on a spaceship for five years?"

"Yeah. Tell me about it. The official story, as far as I could learn from the government report, is that they were outside the main compound, in a research pod. Do you know anything about how they have it set up there?"

"I'm only familiar with the commercial and residential settlements."

"The research compounds have defense fields and sensor systems. Fail-safes, you know? Even if something gets past the sensor, the defense field takes care of it, repels it."

She tried not to think of the pictures she'd foolishly demanded, filing Freedom of Information Act lawsuits to get all the answers. "They'd taken the sensors off-line for maintenance. Not a big deal, right? Because of the defense field. But the problem was, no one bothered to tell the research pod that the sensors were off-line."

Her voice softened. "The engineer at the research pod needed to replace a power generator and had to take the defense field off-line to divert the energy to life support. Normally not a problem, but they had no warning."

Emi fought the tears. "A small meteorite slammed into the research pod. Normally not a huge problem, because the skins they use on the pod buildings are double-hulled, another safety feature. Well, this one hit right at one of the hatches, and the inner airlock door was open because someone was getting ready to come out.

"It was one of those freak accidents on top of a freak accident. Any part of the equation, if it was different, they would have been okay. If they'd been at the far side of the pod, behind one of the back-up air-tight bulkhead doors, they would have been okay. Or if the sensors or defense fields had been on."

He let her lay there silently for several long minutes. "Twenty-two people died, including my parents. They offered all the families cash settlements, as well as fully paid tuition to any university for minors and dependents. They issued me emancipated minor status, because I had no family. I was in boarding school, so I stayed there. I could have stayed in college for the rest of my life, and they would have paid for it."

"I'm glad you didn't." He pulled her tighter against him.

"Me too." She sighed. "Or I can always go back one day for another degree."

He nuzzled her ear. "Maybe after we get back from this mission." Her heart chilled until he clarified. "If you didn't want to go with us every day, we could do moon runs, be home here every night. It would give you something to do during the day while we were gone. Or you can go with us."

"You mean it, right?"

"Of course we mean it. We aren't letting you go. Get that through your thick head. In fact, if you were to cancel on us at the last minute, we'd probably resign and stalk you wherever you go and beg you to stay with us."

"No need to do that. You're stuck with me."

"Good."

They also took a long, romantic bath. "Do you mind if the twins join us for breakfast?" he asked.

"You don't want me alone for a little longer?"

"That didn't answer my question."

Emi tipped her head back to look at him. "I don't mind if you don't." Truth be told, not having all three men with her for more than a few hours at a time was downright weird, even though she had enjoyed the alone time with each of them.

The twins arrived an hour later. It felt good to have her men together again. The twins hugged and kissed her.

"Good morning," they parroted. Emi laughed.

Aaron rolled his eyes. "Twenty years. I'm telling you, Em, you'll stop thinking it's cute at some point."

"It's freaky, but it's still cute."

"Why don't you go get us a table downstairs? We'll be right down," Aaron said.

She met his eyes and knew he wanted to talk to the twins alone. "Okay." She kissed all of them and staked out a quiet corner booth away from other patrons.

The men followed a few minutes later. They all looked happy, but a slight haze of melancholy hovered over them, especially Ford. She already knew he'd agreed to Aaron's request and wondered when they'd have their talk.

"Ooh!" Caph said, grabbing her hand. "Let me see!" He studied the ring, then leaned over and kissed Aaron. "You did good, Cap."

Aaron blushed, the only time she could ever remember seeing him do that. Ford looked at the ring next, and smiled.

"It's perfect." He also gave Aaron a kiss. "This makes it official. Well, not that we needed a ring, but we wanted you to have something from us."

They ate breakfast. When they finished, Aaron glanced at the other men then turned to Emi. "Why don't you and Ford take another run over to the Botanical Gardens, see if there's anything else over there you might want for the hydro lab? I need to talk to Graymard for a little bit. We'll all catch up here for lunch."

They weren't fooling her, but if that's how they wanted to do it, she'd play along. "Okay, that sounds fine."

Ford grinned. "A little more alone time."

Ford and Emi took the car, while Aaron and Caph took the truck. Once they were alone she leveled her gaze at him. "You guys didn't have to go through this much trouble, sweetie."

His blue eyes clouded, sadness threatening. "It'll make it easier on me."

She hadn't thought about it like that. "Okay."

They found a shaded bench deep in the Botanical Gardens, secluded, quiet. They could almost be in the middle of a forest.

He held her hand in both of his and stared out into the distance. Not in space, but in time. Someone passing by might have thought he was looking at the huge eucalyptus tree in front of them. Emi knew he was looking back at their voyage on the Wayfarer Margo so many years ago.

Chapter Thirteen

"We were assigned to the Wayfarer Margo after we'd been in the Merchants for a year," Ford started. "The captain was sort of a jerk, but sometimes they are. No big deal, right? The three of us were close friends, of course. We never minded rooming together, so when space was short we usually ended up in the same cabin, sometimes in the same bunk depending on who had watch and if the ship was short on space. So we get to the Margo, and there's this one girl on board with the other guys. But she wasn't involved with them. The Merchants don't have the same rules about that like the DSMC does. There's no expectation of involvement, even though if it happens, it's fine.

"The captain was, we found out through the grapevine, pissed that Kelsey wouldn't get involved with him. She didn't like him. Can't say as I blame her. When we were assigned, she had a cabin to herself, the other cabins were full. She volunteered to let us bunk with her. It was that or she'd have to bunk in a storage closet.

"I mean, we all had chips, like in the DSMC. It prevented force. So it's not like she was worried. We liked her immediately because she was so funny." Ford paused, thinking, reliving the past. "Smart as a whip, she was a Beta-rank med. Grew up on Mars, so she'd been used to dealing with military brats. She kept us in line, but we sort of felt protective of her.

"We were all together about a month and we're on shore leave one night at a spaceport. Had a little too much to drink—well, a lot, we were tanked—but she was sober. She rounded the three of us up and got us back to the ship. Started to pour us into bed, then she pulls the bunk mattresses onto the floor." He laughed. "We thought we were really drunk, couldn't believe it was happening. She locks the cabin door and sits in the middle of this makeshift bed and rips off her shirt. Says, 'Okay, boys, you've kept me waiting long enough.'"

He paused again, a sad smile caressing his gentle lips. "Well, she didn't have to ask us twice. Even with us drunk, the chips would have kept her safe, but she was willing. She turned us every which way but loose that night." He looked at Emi. "That's also the night she broadened our horizons, so to speak. We'd never done anything like that before. We were close friends. Brothers, even. We'd never...you know."

Emi didn't want to speak, didn't want to interrupt him, so she simply nodded.

He continued. "We woke up the next morning, hung-over and all of us a wee bit...worried. She's sitting there, smiling at us. Kissed all of us and said, 'I hope you boys will give me a show like that every night.'" He laughed. "We weren't sure exactly what happened at first, so she filled us in. Before we could start freaking out, Kels said, 'If you're gonna be my boys, you've got to let me have a say in what happens. It's obvious you all liked it, what's the problem?'

"Why not?" He kissed Emi's hand and looked across the path again. "We never realized we were like that. And to be honest, I don't think we'd be like that with anyone else. We had to admit being bi with each other—and her—felt right. She sure as hell got a kick out of it. We didn't talk about it with others, obviously, but it only took a couple of weeks for us to realize it was right for the four of us. And if she wasn't feeling in the mood, she'd curl up in bed with us while we took care of each other.

"We pulled the mattresses down every night. It was nice being able to all be curled up together like that, you know? Just sort of tangled together. That was her idea. We all fell in love with her, but we didn't feel jealous. She fell in love with us, too. She made us promise we'd all stay together."

He went silent again, his thumbs gently tracing her knuckles. "The captain was pissed. Here he'd been trying to nail her, and then the three of us come on board and she picks us. No one else cared, some of the guys on our ship were married or involved, but that captain, man, he was an asshole after that.

"We were together for a while on that vessel, about a year. On one mission we were sent out with the ISNC to do some explores in a sector where there'd been some problems with raiders. The captain, Aaron, Kels, and two others including the first went planet-side, left me and Caph on board with two more. The ISNC ship had gone to check out a distress call nearby."

He took a deep, shuddering breath. His voice grew hoarse. "It was a decoy. The raiders grabbed the landing crew. They wanted Kels, obviously. They told the captain he had to hand over at least one other crew for ransom or they'd kill them all. Aaron demanded they take him, because he wanted to try to protect Kels. Aar was the second officer at the time.

"Fucking asshole let him go." Ford's voice dropped almost to a whisper. "The first officer tried to get the captain to go instead, or to let him go, thinking they wouldn't hurt Kels if they had a high-value hostage, right? Or to try to trade himself for Kels, to protect her. Captain refused. Fucker told them, 'No, he volunteered, let him go with her. Why risk our lives?' He ordered them to not volunteer, to let Aaron go with Kels."

He closed his eyes. Emi knew he struggled not to cry. "The grunts were trying to get back to us. When we got the landing party on board, the first officer relieved the captain of duty, locked him in a storage room because we didn't have a brig. Fucking bastard. We tried to follow them, not lose them, but they had a small, fast skiff, man. Hit and run group. That's why they only took two, that's all they could take. Ransom gang." He fell silent again for a long moment. When he next spoke, his voice sounded haggard and drawn.

"Took the grunts three days to find them. They were playing hide and seek in an asteroid field. Grunts used a tractor beam on them, caught the ship, but Kels was hurt bad in the firefight." Then his tears fell, and Emi leaned in close, her head on his shoulder. "Aaron was still alive. Barely." He swallowed hard. "The fuckers didn't rape Kels, didn't hurt her. If she'd been in a different place on the ship, she would have survived."

He looked at Emi. "Aaron traded the raiders. Himself for Kels, to not hurt her, not touch her." He looked at Emi, not wanting to voice it, and her heart caught in her throat. "Aar begged them to leave her alone. They fucked him over hard, man, literally. Damn near beat the life out of him. Nearly killed him the way they used him." He shook his head. "He crawled to her during the firefight—she was dying. She told him she loved him, to tell us she loved us, and asked the three of us to stay together because she knew we loved each other. He told her he loved her, and then she went. Died in his arms."

He closed his eyes again. "We nearly lost Aaron. He had a lot of internal bleeding. I'd spent enough time in sick bay helping Kels, I'd learned some stuff, and I had basic med assistant training. They had a medic on the grunt ship, but not a doc. Between the two of us we managed to keep him alive until we got him to a spaceport with a hospital. The first became captain and asked the Merchants to keep us together, to let me and Caph stay with Aaron while he recuperated. He was a decent fucking guy, we really liked him. The captain was the only one on the Margo who didn't like what we had, no one else gave a shit.

"Aar wanted to die. Between losing Kels after all he went through, he thought he failed her, thought he failed us. Took us three months to get his body healed enough to get him into physical rehab. He tried to kill himself a couple of times. At least one of us always had to be with him, they let us stay with him in rehab. Eventually, he got to the point where he started wanting to live again. When he was ready to return to work, the Merchants offered us bonded crew status and gave him a promotion. We took it, and we've been together ever since.

"Don't tell him I told you this, but me and Caph, we were fucking sneaky there for a while. We'd deliberately get into trouble so he'd have to bail us out, right? Bar fights, do something stupid to a superior, anything. Not enough to get us busted on our asses, but just enough to make sure Aaron felt he had to keep us out of trouble."

"And you're still doing it," she said with a smile.

"Well, not intentionally all the time now. Old habits die hard. It worked though. He started feeling responsible for us. We knew we wouldn't have to keep an eye on him every second to keep him alive, he was starting to move on." Ford squeezed her hand. "Aaron swore he would never do what that fucking bastard did to them, he would never leave crew behind, never give up crew unless he was dead already. You already know the captain was executed for dereliction of duty, because Kels died and Aaron nearly did. You don't fucking do that. You don't sacrifice crew. You don't leave people behind."

Ford took a deep, shuddering breath and looked up at the tree canopy. "Caph and I thought maybe after all Aar'd been through that he wouldn't want the sexual part of our relationship anymore, you know? We understood. But he still wanted to sleep together like we had before, all in a bed. It was a comfort for all of us. We'd think about Kels, we needed each other for support, we still loved each other and by that point it was stupid for us to try to deny it. She'd asked us to stay together. It would have been like spitting on her grave to split up. We didn't have sex over a year, any of us, because Caph and I didn't want to put Aar through anything that might trigger flashbacks, right? Aar had fucking horrible nightmares for a long time.

"Then one night he woke up and kissed me and Caph and we figured he wouldn't want...you know, us to fuck him. We never even thought about asking it of him. And he didn't. If he wanted to, he'd have said so. But he was ready to try to live again a little, he wanted what we had back, as much as we could have it. Took us a long time to convince him he wasn't hurting *us*, to get him to relax when he fucked us, even though he knew we liked it and me and Caph did it to each other anyway. He was so afraid at first, we had to beg him. His emotional wounds eventually healed enough he could enjoy it with us again. At least, some of it."

"Captain doesn't bottom," she whispered.

Ford looked at her and sadly shook her head. "Would you, after something like that?"

"No." Thank the gods for her empath training. She shuddered to think how it might have emotionally wounded Aaron if she'd done to him what she'd done to the twins during the physical exam.

"Caph and I wished we could have ripped the dicks off those sick bastards for what they did to him. There were still two left alive after the fight, the grunts shot them out an air lock. Alive. At least Kels didn't suffer the way Aar did. They would have killed her like that. They forced her to watch though. I know that would have been almost as hard on her as him going through it, but at least they didn't physically touch her."

He sadly smiled. "Before that, the four of us used to have fun together, didn't matter who was top or bottom, we mixed it up all the time. I know this is weird to talk about. She used to love it when he'd be inside her and one of us would get behind him and that just really got her all hot. Any of us, but especially Aaron. It was sort of natural, me and Caph and her and Aaron, even though we were all together, like we are now."

Emi nodded, understanding.

He kissed her hand. "So there's our crew story. That's why I say you're good for him. He's happier now than he's been in a long time. We all love you, but you're healing his heart in a way me and Caph can't."

"When was the last time you guys were with a woman beside me?"

He shook his head. "There was Kels, and there was you. No other men, either. We had each other—it was enough. All or nothing, babe. We don't cheat on each other, even if we could, and we weren't interested in one-night stands. We always knew if it ever happened, that if we had a woman assigned to us we'd be open to it, but we all agreed she'd have to be willing to be with all of us, no one left behind. Not even like that."

He kissed her. "You're the perfect woman for us," he said. "That's why we knew Aaron would never refuse your assignment." He laughed. "We never believed the DSMC would ever find us a fourth who would put up with us. We agreed that if we got pulled from the line for no fourth, we'd settle for short hops. Then you walked in and the future changed for the better."

Emi wanted to cry, for them—and for a woman they'd loved that she'd never met, a woman who'd loved her boys as much as she did now. "Do you have a picture of her?"

Ford froze, then reached to his back pocket for his wallet. He removed a picture card and scrolled through the pictures, then handed it to her.

The three men, Aaron in the middle, the twins flanking him, with a woman in front. Aaron had his arms wrapped around her, and the twins each had a hand on her shoulders and Aaron's. All four of them were smiling, the men looked nearly twenty years younger. She was cute, dark blonde hair worn in a bob, hazel eyes.

"She's pretty." She handed the picture card back to him.

He looked at it, his voice sad. "Yeah, she was. Mouth on her like a grunt though. You'd think she had a set of balls on her the way she talked." He shook his head and returned the card to his wallet. "You're a lot like her in some ways, totally different in others." Ford met her eyes. "That's good. I think it would be too weird if you were just like her in every way. No offense."

"None taken." Emi leaned against him as he put his arm around her shoulders.

He pressed his lips to the top of her head. "And that's our crew story, babe. Like I said, I don't know everything that happened while he was on that ship. I don't think I want to. It kills me I wasn't there to help him, me and Caph both. If we'd been on the landing party, we'd been fighting those fucking raiders. They'd have to kill us all down there."

He took another deep breath. "I saw what Aaron looked like when the grunts got him back to us, I had to try to keep him alive. I can connect the dots. I don't need to know unless he ever wants to tell us. Damn near killed Caph losing her, then as bad as Aaron was, he wouldn't leave Aaron's side for weeks. I thought I was gonna have to have him admitted and doped up to get him to sleep. You know what a softie the big guy is."

She nodded.

"I mean, it was bad for me too. At least I could sort of push it away. I had to keep Aaron alive. I had to make sure Caph didn't collapse. I could put my energy into them and not think about things for a while." He patted her hand. "Look, when we get back, don't go all moonie over either of them, okay? I know you feel bad for them, and that's okay. They understand. But they're at a point where they don't want to go back there. In some ways they're not strong enough to go back there, not to talk about it. Not right now. Maybe one day."

"Okay."

He ran his thumb over the ring and smiled. "It looks beautiful on you, babe."

"They can't split us up, can they?"

"No. Not bonded crew, they can't. Aaron will put the papers in and you'll be all ours."

"You're sure? I mean, there's no loopholes or anything? I don't want to be anywhere but with you guys."

"That's good, because you're stuck with us."

* * * *

They returned to the hotel and had lunch in the restaurant, then spent the afternoon at the pool. Ford's mood lifted almost immediately. Aaron and Caph were both playful, tossing her back and forth between them in the water and roughhousing with each other. She spent time napping in the warm sun, watching her boys as they lounged, talking, along the pool's edge.

Dinner was casual, again in the hotel restaurant. They split a bottle of champagne, not enough to get them tipsy. Aaron held up his glass in a toast, and they all joined him.

"To the Tamora Bight, may she bring us all safely home. Crew first."

They clinked glasses, and the others repeated, "Crew first."

Pleasant anticipation tensed Emi's body. Several times during dinner, Ford's eyes met hers, and he playfully winked. She still wanted it. In retrospect was glad Ford insisted on waiting. It was something the four of them should share together. After dinner, they returned to the room, and she started to walk through the door when Ford grabbed the back of her shirt and pulled her to him.

"Where are you going?" he asked.

"Oh come on. All of you have carried me in."

"Not together," Aaron said.

Before she could complain, all three had picked her up and carried her together, dumping her with a round of laughter onto the bed.

Emi sat up. "Happy now, boys?"

They nodded with broad, beaming smiles and started undressing. "Oh, yeah," they all echoed.

Aaron grimaced. "Here we go again."

They ended up in the bathroom, in the large sunken tub. There was plenty of room for all of them. Emi relaxed in their arms as Ford took over and started seducing her, his lips tenderly exploring hers while his fingers gently stroked her between her legs.

He traced her jaw with his tongue, then whispered in her ear, "You still want to?"

She nodded, her eyes closed, her passion stirred by the feel of their hands on her.

He kissed her again and turned her around so she faced Aaron. He took over care of her lips her while Caph snuggled in close and played with her nipples.

Emi didn't open her eyes, enjoying the sensations, giving her body to them, trusting them.

Ford positioned her hips above the water, her knees resting on the steps on either side of Aaron's legs, and she felt something cool and wet against her ass.

Aaron reached down and spread her cheeks as he kissed her, distracting her. Then Ford carefully, gently massaged her virgin rosette, not penetrating, taking his time, his other hand lightly stroking her back.

When he felt her relax he added a little more pressure, still not penetrating. Caph reached between her legs and found her clit, started circling it with his fingers, drawing a low moan from her. She wanted more and rocked her hips against Ford's hand.

"That's my good girl," he whispered, resisting her attempts to rush him. "Just relax and enjoy it, sweetheart."

After what felt like hours of hovering, he added more lube and one finger easily slipped in her tight rim. She gasped and he paused, making sure that was a good gasp and not a pained one.

"Don't stop," she begged before sucking on Aaron's tongue again.

The men chuckled. "I told you he's got the touch, sweetheart," Caph said.

After a few minutes of this, Ford added more lube and a second finger. "You okay?"

"Fuck yes!" she gasped, and the men laughed again.

When he thought she was ready he withdrew his fingers and pressed his stiff and well-lubed cock against her. "Relax. Breathe, baby." She briefly tensed as he pressed in past the first resistance, then he stopped, waiting.

Between Aaron and Caph distracting her, she soon flexed her hips against him, wanting more. When he felt that, Ford slowly sank his full length into her with a low groan.

"Jesus, you're tight, baby. You're so good!"

Caph had two fingers buried in her pussy, his thumb stroking her clit. Her body vibrated against them, every sensation rocking her.

"You okay?" Ford asked, not yet moving.

She broke her kiss with Aaron again. "Yes! Don't stop!"

Emi closed her eyes and enjoyed every second of it, the feel of their hands and Ford carefully thrusting. When her climax hit she screamed and bit down on Aaron's shoulder to muffle the sound.

Ford held her hips. After a few more thrusts, he was also coming. He held still for a moment, then wrapped his arm around her waist, kissing the back of her neck.

Caph and Aaron cradled her in the water, supporting her. "You okay, baby girl?" Aaron asked.

She nodded, beyond speech.

After a few minutes, Ford carefully untangled himself from her. "I didn't hurt you, did I?"

She turned and kissed him, sinking into the water with him and wrapping her legs around his waist. "Did it sound like I was in pain?"

"Not sure. Did you bite a chunk out of Aaron?"

She winced and turned to examine the bruise forming on his shoulder. "I'm sorry, Aar."

Aaron smiled. "It's okay. I'll consider it a war wound."

"Who's next?" she slyly asked, looking at Aaron and Caph.

Ford grabbed her around the waist again and pulled her into his lap, splashing water on the floor. "Nope, not tonight, babe. We don't want to hurt you." He kissed the back of her neck again, making her shiver with pleasure. "We can do that every night if you want, but until you're used to it we're not going to risk hurting you. Besides—" He cupped her breasts, pulling her tight against his chest, running his thumbs over her pebbled nipples, "we can do lots of other things to you tonight."

Aaron flipped the drain lever. "Yeah, and let's get in there and do them," he playfully growled. He leaned over to kiss her again and his stiff cock brushed against her leg.

She grabbed it, slowly stroking him. "Anything you say, Captain," she teased.

* * * *

They spent a long night making slow love to her and each other. When she drifted to sleep in Aaron's arms, Caph and Ford were still at it. The next morning they were all in bed, snuggled tightly together because it was a little smaller than their one at the ship.

Ford winked at her. "You okay?"

She did a quick inventory. "You did good," she whispered. "I'm not a bit sore anywhere."

"Good." He kissed her. "It's not fun if it hurts, and I don't think you're into kink."

She tried to stifle her laugh, but Aaron awoke, his hand cupping her breast. "Someone go turn off the window sim," he groaned. "I want a few more hours."

Ford leaned over her and kissed him good morning. "Wish I could, but that's a real window. Reality calling—we've got a ship waiting."

Caph stirred, stretched. "I have to admit I love the tub, but miss our bed. I feel like I'm going to fall out."

Aaron and Caph headed to the bathroom first, and Ford took the opportunity to hog Emi for a few minutes. "You really okay?"

"I'm fine. Wonderful." She gripped his hand and pressed her lips to his palm, flicking her tongue against his flesh. "I feel great."

"Tomorrow the countdown begins." His blue eyes studied hers. "You nervous?"

"Of course."

He smiled. "Good. I'd be worried if you weren't. We all get nervous, it's pre-flight jitters."

"I'm not scared, though."

"There's nothing to be scared of. You know we'll take care of you."

Ford was always the easiest for her to read. She didn't know why, but he was. And right now she felt his love, his protective urge—and not the slightest hint of jealousy for the other two men. Sometimes she sensed a little envy from one of them if they were busy and couldn't spend time with her when another could, but never jealousy.

"I know."

Chapter Fourteen

As their time on Earth shortened, Emi had dinner with Donna and a few other friends one evening. Then it was back to the ship to immerse herself in last-minute details.

Her job, after ensuring the sick bay and hydro lab were all set, was to help the men as needed. Mostly with last-minute inventory, loading some equipment and supplies, and running through pre-departure checklists. She still wasn't clear on the sequence of events. Ford filled her in one afternoon as she helped him go through an engineering electrical panel, checking circuits one final time.

"They use hover lifts to move us out of the dry dock to the launch pad. From there, the heavy lifts, we call them tug boats, take us up. We can't use a jump engine here, it's too populated. A ship like this isn't designed to land and take off unassisted on a planet like Earth, we'd use up too much energy against the gravity trying to lift ourselves. Once we're up about five kilometers, the orbital docking station takes over with a tractor beam and does the heavy lifting for us. Then we can negotiate our way to the designated berth."

"But how does the grav-plate system work? I still don't understand that, and I watched the stupid vid at least three times."

He paused and thought about it. "It keeps us and everything else on this boat from floating around once we're in zero G. We won't be at full gravity, so it'll feel like you lost about fifteen pounds all of a sudden. It's enough to keep stuff in place. It's designed to run off either the gennies or the solar arrays on the ship's skin. If we're close enough to a star, it'll feed off that. If not, the ship's engines run it. I don't know the exact details of why it works, something to do with creating an artificial gravitational field."

While Aaron spent a lot of time in engineering, one of Ford's primary duties was engineering and defense, while Caph oversaw life support and weaponry systems. The three men overlapped in most areas, vital with a crew as small as theirs. They gave her small reading assignments every day to help her learn the ship's systems, afraid of overwhelming her.

The morning they were scheduled to leave, Dr. Graymard met with them in his office and gave them a final briefing and well-wishes. "I'm sure you'll all do well." He leveled his gaze at Emi. "Relax. You have a lot to learn, but you know your job inside and out, and that's all we can ask of you at this time. Give yourself a break."

She forced a nervous smile. "Thank you."

She stood on the bridge and watched the men work, going through final checklists as the dry dock crew prepared to disconnect their utility umbilicals from the facility. While fully loaded with basics such as food, fuel, water, and other essentials, they still didn't have a complete payload for their expedition. They would pick some of that up from the orbital hub, the rest from the Mars station once the shakedown cruise was a success. The men were focused, professional, business-like.

After a half-hour, Aaron looked up from his station and nodded to Caph. "Looks like we're ready." He signaled the dry dock crew. Emi watched as they slowly moved out of their berth. She'd been standing behind Aaron's chair, her fingers wrapped around the back. They tightened, her knuckles white, as the cavernous facility was slowly left behind.

The tedious process took over four hours just to clear the building. She tried to keep herself busy but kept returning to stand behind Aaron's chair. Once outside on the tarmac, they progressed a little faster until she saw the launch pad ahead, heat waves shimmering off the asphalt in the bright afternoon sun.

Aaron reached back and squeezed her hand. "This is it, baby girl.

You okay?"

She nodded, unable to move or take her eyes from the front ports.

Ford and Caph called readings back and forth to each other and Aaron as they set up the systems for the lift and ran through final status checks. Then, the last order.

"Close front plates," Aaron said.

Ford nodded, and the plates slid into place over the front ports. Almost immediately the built-in vid screens came to life, nearly duplicating the view without the real light shining in.

Emi saw the tugs waiting for them on the launch pad, six of them.

Aaron pointed. "The lift process takes about ten hours, and they'll stay with us as back-up when the tractor beam takes over."

Going into space. It didn't seem real.

Emi didn't feel it when the lifts loaded them onto the tugs.

The com link signaled. "Tamora Bight, this is lead tug, Desert Sun. Captain, are you ready?"

Aaron looked at Ford and Caph, who nodded. Then he turned to Emi, and the smile lighting his face washed all her fears away like water down a drain. The emotion she felt from him, a different kind of almost pure joy, easily overcame any hesitation on her part.

All of the men were happy to be going back to space. This was why, even after the horrors they lived through, they returned to their job.

Because it was their life, and they loved it.

"I'm ready," she whispered.

He pulled her into his lap and flicked the com link. "Desert Sun, this is Tamora Bight. Take us up."

"Roger, Captain. Have a safe journey."

Caph and Ford sat back and watched the front vid screens as the ground slowly disappeared beneath them. Emi thought it might feel like flying in traditional air transports, but it wasn't. It was smooth, as if the Earth fell away, not that they were climbing.

Aaron patted her on the thigh. "Now, we wait. Caph, you want first watch?"

"Yeah, I'll take it. I'm assuming you want to be on deck when we're in docking range."

"Right. Do short watches. You, then Ford, and I'll be here." He squeezed Emi's hand. "Not trying to leave you out, babe, but this isn't like a normal night watch."

"I understand." Her stomach growled. It would be dinner time soon. "I'll go make supper."

He helped her out of his lap. Twenty minutes later, Aaron and Ford joined her in the galley. They helped her finish preparations, and she took Caph's dinner to him, then slid into Ford's seat while he ate.

"Aren't you going to eat, babe?"

"Yeah, in a little bit. I wanted to sit with you for a while."

He pointed at the vid screens, where purple dusk had overtaken the western landscape beneath them. "Amazing, isn't it? I never get sick of this."

"How many of these have you done?"

"Four like this. We've had other ships, smaller ones, that could lift on their own, or that could be tractored from lower. We've also had ships where we took command at a hub or space-side somewhere else. This is the biggest, though, the Tamora Bight."

"Do you miss it? When you're in space, do you miss being on Earth?"

He shrugged. "Not so much. I'm usually too busy. It's easy for me. My family's scattered all over, so it's not like I'm leaving a bunch of people behind."

The men rarely talked about their families. Aaron was almost as alone as she was, with only a cousin who worked on a space station near Saturn. Ford had a brother and sister on a Jupiter outpost, he wasn't close to his father, and his mother was deceased. Caph's parents were colonists in a different solar system—she couldn't even begin to pronounce the name—and his three siblings were split around the known universe.

This truly was a ready-made family they'd become.

"What about after?" she asked.

He shook his head in mock disgust. "We're not having this conversation again, are we?"

"No, I meant if we decide to settle on Earth later, not take another mission, would you be okay not being in space?"

He finished his dinner and handed her the plate, playfully pulling her in for a long, passionate kiss. "Honey, it doesn't matter if I'm on Earth or in space or in some distant rat-hole spaceport as long as it's the four of us there together. My home is with you three, not any place or ship or planet."

She could agree with that—she felt it too.

"Go eat your dinner before it gets cold, sweetie."

Emi took his plate back to the galley and ate her dinner.

She thought she'd be too excited to sleep, but started yawning an hour later.

"Nerves," Ford said with a smile. "Go to bed, watch the vid or something."

She did, thinking she wouldn't sleep. She awoke to find Aaron stretched out next to her, fully dressed, watching the vid screen.

"Little formal for bed, aren't we?" she joked.

He shrugged. "Just a precaution. In case the twins need me on deck."

"Thought they were going to trade off?"

"They are. Caph will be along in a little while."

Cuddled against Aaron's side, she drifted again. When she awoke, Caph was stretched out next to her, dressed, and Aaron was gone. This was one of the very few nights she didn't sleep all the way through since joining her boys.

He pulled her to him, tightly snuggled. "Go back to sleep," he whispered. "It's late for you. You'll need to get used to sleeping without a set sunrise and sunset."

"Doesn't it bother you?"

"I'm used to it." He pressed his lips to her temple in a sweet, chaste kiss. "You'll have plenty of time to settle in on the docking hub."

"I want to see it when we get there, before we dock," she mumbled, already falling asleep again.

"I promise, we'll wake you up."

"Okay…"

Ford gently nudged her awake. "Hey, Sleeping Beauty. We're close to the hub."

She rolled over. The window sim looked like early dawn. "What time is it?"

"Almost six a.m."

She sat up and he kissed her. "I'll have your coffee waiting."

"Thanks."

She grabbed a quick sonic shower and dressed. Ford had her bagel toasting and her coffee ready, perfectly prepared. Emi hugged him from behind. "You're the best, you know that?"

"Keep talking." He grinned, playfully bumping her with his hip.

Emi helped him make breakfast for Caph and Aaron and they carried it to the bridge. Outside, the sky looked black, punctuated by pinpoints of stars, clearer and more breathtaking and in far greater quantities than she ever remembered seeing from on Earth. Ahead of them lay the large orbital hub facility, several dozen ships berthed on each side and a flurry of traffic at one end, where the smaller transport and passenger vessel terminal was located.

Caph chuckled. "It's neat, isn't it?"

Dumbly nodding, she stared.

Space. She was in *space.*

Was this how her parents felt the first time they traveled to the moon? She wondered if they'd ever passed through this same orbital hub. There were fifteen of the large ones and twelve smaller, passenger-only hubs.

She jumped when Aaron touched her shoulder. "We'll be docking in about an hour, just waiting for an available pilot tug to come get us." He looked at her. "It's amazing, isn't it?"

"Big." Pictures and vids had not prepared her for the reality.

"Not the biggest. Third biggest. They had an open berth, otherwise we'd have to wait three more days for one of the other hubs to be in the right position for us to lift."

There wasn't anything she could do but watch. The pilot tug hooked onto them and slowly guided them into their berth. Once they were secured, a docking crew hooked up utility umbilicals and a portable gangway to their front hatch.

The com signaled. "Tamora Bight, welcome to Orbital Hub 0-7-Alpha. Captain, your hook-ups are complete. You and your crew have permission to debark as needed. A dock foreman will get with you on your schedule."

"Thank you." Aaron looked at Emi. "And that's all there is to it." He smiled. "They've got a great restaurant here."

Ford lit up. "Oh yeah! I forgot about Charlie Tacos. I'll make a reservation."

* * * *

Barring any unforeseen issues, they'd be at the orbital hub for two weeks. The first night there the boys took Emi out for dinner and she was amazed at the view of Earth from the hub's huge observation room. Staring down at the planet slammed home the finality of her decision. She'd never give up these men or what she'd chosen, not for that hunk of rock and water beneath them.

Two weeks at the hub seemed to fly by. She learned more about the ship's systems and took her turn at solo night watches. When the pilot tug guided them away from their hub berth, Emi watched the orbiter slip away in the front vid screens.

Two ISNC cruisers accompanied them and three other ships—freighters—to Mars. They had to test their jump engine, something Emi didn't even try to understand. It almost frightened her to contemplate how fast it transported them from one side of the solar system to the other, but in their case they were only using it to jump short distances to check the power loads on the various systems.

The Mars trip took six weeks. Emi settled into a comfortable routine with the men. As they closed in on the red planet her eyes widened, fascinated, at the sight.

Ford laughed as he watched her. "Amazing, huh?"

"Yeah. It doesn't feel real."

"We've seen it plenty of times," Caph said. He turned. "Hey, Aar, do you think that karaoke bar will let us back in yet?"

He grinned. "Not a chance. They were pretty pissed at you guys."

Another story Emi knew she'd need to hear. For now she was content to sit and watch the planet grow in their front vid screens.

Lots of work had been done to introduce ice and water to the Martian surface in hopes of stimulating an atmosphere. Several large residential and research settlements had been built in addition to the station they were en route to. Experts believed Mars might have a self-sustaining, natural ecosystem within three hundred years, but the atmosphere was still extremely thin compared to Earth.

Because Mars didn't have much of one yet, and because of the reduced gravity, it was easier for the Tamora Bight to take off and land from the planet under her own power. More pilot tugs arrived to assist their drop, as they called it, to their station berth. Once safely docked and their cargo and main hatches were connected to the gangway, Aaron ordered the front plates raised.

Caph flicked the switch. The plates retracted, leaving a natural view as the vid screens deactivated.

Emi sucked in a sharp breath. It was daylight, giving her a perfect view of the Martian landscape.

"Wow!" she breathed, walking to the front ports.

The men gathered behind her. "Beautiful, isn't it?" Ford asked.

Unable to form a coherent word, she simply nodded.

"Much of the base is underground," Caph explained. "Protects it, helps regulate the temperature."

Pictures never prepared you for the first-hand sight. She stared for over an hour, amazed.

Eventually she was aware of Aaron slipping his arm around her waist. "You want to stand here all day, sweetie?"

She leaned into his warm body, shaking her head, pulling his other arm around her. "Just trying to take it all in, that's all."

His lips brushed the back of her neck, sweet and tender. "I have something else you could take in, you know." He rubbed his hips against her ass, his cock firmly pressing against her.

She slid one of his hands lower, between her legs. "You do, hmm?"

"Yes, I do."

Emi writhed against him, encouraging. "You don't have something to do now that we're here?"

"Not for a few hours." He slid his other hand up to her breast, running his thumb over her nipple through her shirt. "I could do you, if you're in the mood."

She closed her eyes and threw her head back against his shoulder. "That sounds great."

He scooped her into his arms and carried her to their cabin. "Where's the twins?" she asked as he lifted her shirt.

"I don't know. Frankly, I don't care right now. I've got you all to myself for a little bit." He sucked one nipple into his mouth, flicking his tongue over the hard peak.

Emi squirmed under the firm attention from his eager mouth. "So what are you going to do with our time?"

He sat up and yanked his shirt off, then stood and dropped his pants. His stiff cock sprang free, the action sending a flood of moisture straight to her sex. The sight of one—or all—of their ready members wanting her always did that to her.

"I'm going to fuck you until you beg me to make you come."

It took her only a second to shimmy out of her pants. He knelt in front of her and grabbed her arm, pulling her to him, thrusting his tongue into her mouth.

Sometimes he was like this, forceful, almost aggressive—and she loved it. Emi squirmed against him and he flipped her over, his hands skimming down her body to her hips, positioning her.

"Do it," she begged, wiggling her ass at him.

"Oh, baby, I'm going to do you, all right." He dipped his fingers into her, making sure she was wet and taking a moment to tease her, thrusting them into her. "I'm going to do you real good, baby girl."

He pressed his cockhead against her pussy, not entering, his fingers gripping her hips. "What do you want? Tell me."

"Fuck me good, Aar."

He slammed home with a growl, forcing her to hold still and not grind against him like she wanted. "You want it, baby? I don't think you want it that much."

Gripping her pillow, she tried to thrust backward against him, but he held her too tightly. "I do, I want it."

He chuckled and leaned over her, one arm wrapped around her waist. "No you don't. I don't think you want it at all."

Playful didn't begin to describe his mood. All the men had been happier since leaving the orbital hub, eager to be on their way. "Please fuck me. I want you to fuck me with that sweet cock."

"Mmm." He flipped them onto their side, still inside her, and hooked one leg around hers. "I'm going to fuck you good and slow, sweetie." His hand found her clit. She groaned as he stroked it, slowly fucking her at the same time. "Gonna keep you right on the edge." He ran his lips across her shoulder, gently nipping her, sending shivers through her.

"Oh, nice!" At the sound of Caph's voice, Emi and Aaron looked up. Caph stood in the cabin doorway, his pants tented.

"I guess I don't have you all to myself anymore," Aaron murmured in her ear. "How you feeling, baby?"

"Horny," she gasped.

Caph laughed and shook his head. "Is this an open party, or should I come back later?"

Emi thought Aaron might ask for more alone time, but he lifted his head. "I think she needs a little assistance."

Caph crossed the room in two strides, and was naked by the time he dropped to the bed. Aaron moved his hands to her breasts, rolling her nipples in his fingers and sending spasms straight to her pussy. Caph spread her legs wider, cool air brushing against her throbbing clit.

"Are we keeping her begging for a while or going for a fast explosion?" Caph asked.

"Ah, let's keep her begging for a while," Aaron said.

Emi whimpered, closing her eyes and loving the sensation of them taking control.

"Cool," Caph said, his lips closing around her clit.

Heaven. She'd died and gone to Heaven.

Aaron groaned. "Jesus, you should feel the way her pussy throbs when you do that." He fucked her agonizingly slow, taking his time.

She moaned, squirming, wanting release. "Fuck me, please!"

"I am, baby. What's your rush?" He kissed her jaw, nuzzling her.

Caph lifted his head and met Aaron's eyes. "She's awfully chatty today."

"Yeah, why don't you give her something else to do."

Caph snickered and changed position. Emi sucked his cock into her mouth with a greedy moan.

"Oh, yeah," Caph said with a growl. "That's it, honey. You know what I like." He licked her clit, flicking his tongue over her, making her moan around his shaft.

"Jeez, I'm down in engineering working, and you three are up here fucking around." Ford's good-natured ribbing startled them.

Aaron looked up. "Then get your ass over here."

Ford stripped and stood over them. "This is like one of those friggin' puzzles," he said with a grin.

Aaron reached over and patted Caph's ass. "Right here, buddy."

"Mmm. Good idea." He grabbed the bottle of lube and slid into position behind Caph, nudging his cock against his rim.

Caph lifted his head for just a moment. "Do it, goddammit. Don't tease me."

"Such a romantic," Ford joked, thrusting his hips. Both men moaned as Ford sank his full length into him. "Like that?"

"Yeah."

Emi wanted to explode, but all the men had learned how to keep her hovering, enjoyed prolonging her pleasure. She wiggled her hips against Caph's mouth, trying to get more pressure on her clit to send her over the edge.

He laughed and lifted his mouth. "Baby, you don't get off that easy."

It was hard for her to vent her frustration with her mouth full of man-meat, but she groaned.

"Take your time, Caph," Aaron grunted, keeping his thrusts slow. "I'm having fun."

"You ain't the only one," Ford said.

Every stroke Ford took brought another low moan from Caph, and his cock throbbed in her mouth.

After a few minutes, Ford grabbed Caph's hips. "Someone better do something soon, or I'm gonna go off."

"Gotta love that sweet ass of his," Aaron said.

"Yeah, man, you know I do," Ford agreed.

Emi neared desperation, dying for release. She whined and wiggled her hips, trying to get them to let her come.

Aaron kissed the nape of her neck. "Maybe you should let her come, Caph. I can't hold out much longer." His voice had dropped, husky with passion.

She moaned in agreement.

Caph's gifted tongue and lips worked her clit. The familiar

fireworks started, sending her over. She sucked Caph's dick deep into her throat, triggering his climax.

The chain reaction set off Ford and Aaron, and a few minutes later they were all panting, breathless, trying to recover.

"Welcome to Mars, sweetie," Ford snarked from somewhere behind Caph.

They all laughed.

Chapter Fifteen

Emi stood out of the way, watching while Ford and Caph supervised the loading of cargo and equipment. She loved this part of their personalities, the all-business attitude they had when working. They could be playful and funny and definitely sexy, but their confidence and dedication comforted and reassured her.

Most of the equipment was totally foreign to her. One piece was a landing vehicle that could be launched from a special hangar bay at the front of the cargo hold. It functioned as a small ship and as a land vehicle. Aaron assured her she'd get a chance to practice with one on Mars before they left.

The Martian day was only slightly longer than an Earth day, but they were still running on a twenty-four-hour Earth cycle. Their day cycle started in the middle of the Martian night. Aaron decided to switch them over to the Mars cycle for the duration of their stay, giving Emi time off to sleep away some of her nervous tension. They would be on Mars for at least four weeks, possibly longer, allowing them time to run final systems checks and fully test the solar arrays under low atmosphere conditions. There was no set departure date, taking some pressure off of them.

Emi was both thrilled and terrified by the thought of exploring Mars, a place she'd only seen in books and vids. Five other complexes were connected to the facility they were docked at by a series of transport tubeways, partially buried tram routes that allowed safe and easy movement between the locations. The other Martian settlements were reachable by ground or air transports.

She wanted to sightsee, especially to visit the huge agricultural dome, but Aaron set some ground rules. "I don't want you going alone, hon."

"Why not? Isn't it safe?"

The men exchanged a glance. "It's safe enough, but not everyone around here is chipped. I'd rather not risk it," Aaron said. "There are some private transient freighter crews that pass through, and while the risk is low, it's still there."

"Okay." There was something more, she sensed. "What aren't you telling me?"

He took her hands. "I don't want to scare you, Em. I just want you to be careful." Left unsaid, he didn't want a repeat of the Dry Port incident. For weeks after, at least one of the three men practically shadowed her if she left the ship, with the exception of her time out with Donna and friends. They didn't smother her, but she felt protected.

* * * *

Her first trip outside the docking facility took place three days after their arrival. Ford volunteered to go with her to the agri-complex.

"Dress warm, sweetie," he said. "It's usually a little on the chilly side here, even in the middle of the day."

The journey to the agri-complex took an hour and two tram transfers. And Emi saw her first non-human species, treaty races who were allowed access to the Mars facilities and even had their own diplomatic domes on the planet.

Many species couldn't safely travel to the Martian surface, even fewer to Earth, because of atmospheric, gravitational, and other concerns. The few that could were biologically similar to humans. Conversely, humans couldn't safely set foot on many of the treaty planets either due to biological or atmospheric reasons. A diverse series of space stations allowed for diplomatic and commercial contacts, where vastly different species could interact in safety and comfort. There were currently forty-two intelligent, sentient treaty races, and fifteen known sentient non-treaty races. Not hostile, but who opted not to mingle with the other races for a number of reasons. There were only three known hostile races, but because of the size and number of treaty races, they were legislatively isolated, with a coalition force policing the boundaries to keep them from causing trouble.

As part of her studies, Emi had learned about the most common treaty races she might encounter. "That's a F'ahrkay?" she whispered to Ford as they sat on the tram. The thin, willowy man sitting ten rows ahead of them was approximately seven feet tall, with a bluish tinge to his pale skin.

"Yeah," he whispered back. "I actually think I've met that guy before. You don't see many of them shore-side. They've got their own orbiting space station."

When they debarked the tram, the F'ahrkay man was nowhere to be seen. Ford took Emi by the hand, following signs in multiple languages until they reached the agri-complex. The half-submerged dome was a self-contained environment, including weather. A variety of species of plants from Earth and elsewhere grew in carefully controlled settings. They had to pass through a decontamination room on the way in to prevent outside pathogens from infiltrating the ecosystem.

"This is amazing!" Emi stopped and stared, looking up at fifty foot tall redwood trees flanking the entrance.

"Genetically modified to survive here," Ford said, following her gaze. "Wait'll you see the produce section."

Familiar selections from bananas to citrus, as well as unfamiliar species from other worlds, were carefully labeled. Interactive signs allowed visitors to pick their language. They also offered a variety of classes, including modified cooking and baking, as well as how to preserve fruits and vegetables grown on-board.

"Can I sign up for these?" Emi asked. She'd been persistently vexed by baking bread and cakes on board once they left Earth. Despite meticulously following recipes, she had only produced three edible baked products. She could cook nearly anything else and it frustrated her.

"We need to ask Aaron," he said, studying the brochure, "but I don't see why not. It won't interfere with our schedule."

They spent five hours touring the complex. On the way back to the ship, they stopped at a commissary and picked up groceries, including fresh meat and vegetables grown on Mars. An isolated, self-contained livestock dome provided fresh beef, pork, poultry, eggs, milk, and farm-raised fish of various species for human Martian residents.

They were almost back to the docking facility when a woman's sing-song voice reached them. "Oh, Foooord!"

"Aw, fuck," he muttered under his breath.

"What?" Emi asked.

He shook his head, a gesture she knew meant he'd tell her later. They stopped and turned to watch a woman jogging toward them. Ford's energy had shifted from relaxed to stressed in just a few heartbeats. Whoever this woman was, she wasn't someone he wanted to see.

The woman was lithe, taller than Emi, almost as tall as Ford, with large breasts and graceful strides, long blonde hair flowing down her back and green, almond-shaped eyes.

Emi despised her on sight.

The woman most likely would have hugged Ford if he hadn't already slipped an arm firmly around Emi's waist. "Hello, Jezeen."

Jezeen pouted. "I thought you'd be happy to see me, I'm happy to see you. It's been a long time."

"Not long enough."

Jezeen grinned. "I heard you guys got the Tamora Bight. Great ship. Big ship. Need another hand?"

His arm tightened around Emi. "Nope. We're full and closed."

A frown passed Jezeen's face as she glanced at Emi. "Who's she?"

"Not that it's any of your business, but this is Dr. Emilia Hypatia, our med officer. Alpha-ranked healer."

One of Jezeen's carefully plucked eyebrows climbed. "Alpha-ranked? Really?"

Emi forced a smile to her lips and stuck out her hand. "Really. Top of my class."

Finally remembering her manners, Jezeen shook hands. "Come on, Ford. Are you guys still holding a grudge?"

"No, we're not holding a grudge, Jezeen. But we sure as hell don't want you anywhere near us or our ship. When we lifted from Earth, there were still several crews there looking for extras. Go talk to someone who gives a shit."

Jezeen lost all pretense of politeness. "Aw, Ford, that was years ago. Aaron's still pissed?"

"Not just Aaron. Look, you had a chance and you blew it. Come on, Emi. Let's get back."

He turned, taking Emi's hand, and they pushed their cart full of supplies toward their gangway, leaving Jezeen with a gaping jaw.

Emi leaned in and whispered, "I want to hear this story."

"You will, sweetie. I'm sure we haven't heard the last of her."

Once they were safely inside the ship, he told the story as they made their way toward the crew area. "She's a real bitch. We had to take her on as crew a few years ago on a long jump."

"Really?" Emi tried to stay cool, but her tone of voice didn't fool Ford.

"Not like that. *Just* as crew. I told you, you're the only woman we've been with like that since Kels. Not for lack of trying on her part, but her and Aaron hated each other. Caph and I wouldn't have any part of her because of that. She tried her damnedest to split us up and run a game, but fortunately we were once up on her. We dumped her ass at a station out in Gamma Six. Told her to find her own damn way back."

"I'm surprised she still wants to get on board with you guys."

"She's got the hots for Caph. Big time."

Emi stopped short, and Ford realized what was wrong. "Don't worry, Emi. It was one-sided, believe me. He hates her, saw right through her."

Jealousy and relief fought for control.

Ford smiled. "Sweetheart, you're one of us, part of us. And we don't want anyone but you." He leaned in and kissed her, and for a minute she forgot all about Jezebel or Jezweed or whatever the frak the skank's name was.

"Okay," Emi gasped when Ford released her.

* * * *

Emi thought Ford might mention the meeting to the other men immediately, but he didn't. He waited until after Aaron had asked them about their day and agreed Emi should take the classes, working it in casually between their shopping trip and a few things he wanted to do before they left.

Emi glanced at Ford and Caph. Both men tensed.

"Jezeen's here?" Aaron asked.

Ford nodded. "Yeah."

Caph put his fork on his plate. "Crap. Well, there goes my appetite." He looked at Aaron. "Permission to never leave the friggin' ship?"

Aaron laughed, shaking his head. "You'll have to face her some time, Caph." He smiled at Emi. "Now *her*, if you wanted to pull your little exhibition stunt for her benefit, we'd be more than happy to play along."

Emi relaxed. These were *her* men. Every ounce of energy from them screamed their love for her and their collective distaste—if not outright disgust—for Jezeen.

"I'll protect you, big guy," Emi teased, bringing a smile to the large man's face.

"I don't want to have to break up a cat fight, sweetheart."

"How about I just shove her out an airlock?"

The men grinned.

* * * *

The next morning, Emi walked with Aaron to a meeting with the port cargo foreman. He was in the process of trying to explain the jump engine to her—again—when a woman's voice carried to them across the facility.

"Aaron!"

He cringed, as did Emi.

Jezeen.

They both turned as she ran toward them, a huge smile on her face. "Aaron! Long time, no see! Did Ford mention I saw him yesterday?"

Aaron tightly gripped Emi's hand, his thumb stroking her. "Yes."

The flicker of a frown crossed Jezeen's face. "Can I talk to you alone for a few minutes? Please?"

He shook his head. "Anything you want to say, you can say here and now. You're not crewing on my ship."

With her pre-emptive strike neutralized, she dropped all pretense of coquettishness. "Please, Aaron? I'm dying to go on a heavy. Get me off of my ship."

"Talk to someone who cares, because I don't. I have all the crew I want." He started to lead Emi away when Jezeen's voice dropped, threatening.

"Look, I didn't file a complaint against you guys for booting me the way you did. I still could."

He shook his head. "Statute of limitations ran out on that, not to mention you were booted for cause. You violated ten different regs, in some cases multiple times. You're lucky I didn't have you tossed in the brig."

She switched to annoyingly whiny. "I need off this rock!"

"I don't owe you anything, Jezeen. Go away," he said over his shoulder, pulling Emi with him. Emi had to take quick strides to keep up with him. He was beyond pissed—enraged would cover it.

Almost.

He muttered under his breath the rest of the way to the cargo foreman's office. Emi knew Aaron needed to blow off steam and to not talk to him. They finished their errand, and he detoured their return.

"Where are we going?"

"Shopping. She'll be waiting to pounce. There's a few more things I want to get for the ship anyway."

Emi walked quietly beside him while he stewed, knowing he needed to deal in his own way. From the way his thumb constantly rubbed her hand, stroking her flesh, he was deep in thought and drawing comfort from her.

They killed a couple of hours in the commercial district before returning to the ship. Ford greeted them with a smirk in the galley. "You're a fucking chicken, Aar."

"What?"

"Oh, the little bitch tried to pay Caph a call earlier. Don't worry, I ran her off."

"Where is he?"

"Hiding in the engine room. I tried to get him to go out and take a walk around and he won't. He's afraid of running into her."

Aaron shook his head. "Why the hell is she so eager to hook up with us all of a sudden? Does she not remember how much we hate her guts?"

Ford's grin told Emi more than his air of pleased satisfaction. "I did a little asking around. She's getting booted from another ship.

That makes three. They're leaving in three weeks, and she's got until then to find another ride or she'll be stuck here."

"Couldn't happen to a nastier woman."

Emi knew she'd missed something. "What's wrong with that?"

"In the Merchants, if you get booted from three ships, you're out, discharged, no benefits, unless you can find a ship that will take you. She could transfer to DSMC if we took her—which we're not, obviously. She'll lose everything she's stored up in terms of retirement. You don't get booted from a vessel without cause. I have yet to meet a captain who's that much of an asshole to boot someone just for spite. You really have to be fucking up or endangering lives or pissing off all your crewmates to get booted."

"Or all of the above?"

Ford nodded. "Exactly."

"Which category did she fall into?"

Ford and Aaron parroted, "All of the above."

Aaron winced.

Emi strolled down to Engineering and found Caph buried halfway inside the main life support circuit panel. She made sure he heard her entrance so she didn't startle him.

"Hey, sweetie. You okay in there?" she called out.

"I'll be done in a minute." He handed out tools and backed out of the access hatch. "You run into the unholy whore again?"

"Jezebel?"

He laughed. "As good a name as any for her, I suppose."

"I hear she's got her sights set on you."

Caph grabbed Emi's arm and pulled her into his lap. "Why the hell would I want table scraps when I've got prime cut filet mignon for every meal, baby?"

She grinned. "Filet mignon, huh?"

"Yeah." His hand slipped under her shirt, gently cupping her breast. "I've got the best right here. I don't need a chip in my head to keep me faithful to you, sweetie. You can lead me anywhere you want, I'll follow you."

Cuddling with him was like snuggling into a large, comfortable chair with a soft quilt. She slipped her hand between his legs and lightly ran her nails up and down his shaft through the fabric, enjoying the feel of him hardening under her fingers.

"Watch out, babe. You're playing with fire there."

His mood had shifted from his slightly mopey attitude to playful tenderness. "Maybe that's what I want." She nibbled the tender spot behind his ear that always made him moan.

In one fluid move he stood, carrying her back up to their cabin. Emi sensed Aaron and Ford were on the bridge, but she felt Caph needed a little alone time with her.

"Go close the door," she whispered into his ear after he set her on their bed.

He did, then quickly stripped and joined her, helping her shed her clothes.

"You're so beautiful," he moaned, his lips exploring her flesh. He started to move lower and she pulled him up.

"No, baby. I want you to do something else for me."

"What?"

She pushed him into a sitting position and climbed into his lap, facing him, her legs around his waist. "What do you think?"

There'd been so few chances to be alone with him, to try again. She wanted this from him in the worst way, something to totally take his mind off Jujubee or whatever her name was.

His hands skimmed down her back, cupping her ass, pulling her tight against him. "Yeah?"

"Yeah." Then they were kissing, and his cock slid comfortably deep inside her the way it always did. She dropped her head to his shoulder and let him cradle her as they started a slow, sensual rocking, their own intimate rhythm.

He took his cues from her, letting her set the pace, letting her use his body. His mind was totally on Emi now—she felt it. Not a trace of stress in his system.

She took her time, and when she felt his cock slide over her clit just right, she managed to duplicate the sensation and adjusted her body accordingly.

He felt it, felt her tensing against him. "That's it, baby. Take your time and do it."

Emi felt like she was alone in the universe with Caph, just her body merged with his, every sensation magnified.

She was so close, hovering on the edge, not quite enough pressure on her clit to bring her over.

"Tell me what you need," he whispered.

Grinding her hips against him in response, she shifted her weight a little and gasped as it felt like the length of his cock stroked down her slick nub. "That!" she gasped. Now that she had the sweet spot she didn't want to risk losing it.

Caph's hands caressed her back. "Let me feel it, sweetie."

So close…so, so close. Only with him, the others so far unable to duplicate this sensation. No, not as intense or easy to achieve, but that made it all the sweeter.

Frantic, thrusting, she panted against his neck, her eyes squeezed shut, trying to tune out the world. Then a gentle coasting, cresting, and she cried out.

"Oh, baby, that's it, I can feel you." His hands slipped to her hips, steadying her, giving him leverage to help him thrust. In just a few strokes he was there with her, and they sank to the bed, spent and sweaty.

Emi cried.

He kissed the top of her head and held her close. "Are you going to cry every time we do that? Because it might give me a complex."

She laughed and lifted her head to look at him. "Maybe after a few years, once I have a chance to get used to being able to do that. These are good tears, Caph."

"As long as you're sure about that."

"I'm sure."

They must have dozed, because she awoke to the feeling of being pleasantly sandwiched between two warm, firm bodies. She sensed without looking that it was Ford napping behind her. Tipping her head, she noticed Caph watching her.

"Nice nap?" he whispered.

"How long?"

"Long enough for Brainiac to discover us."

"I *can* hear you," Ford mumbled.

Emi smiled. "Where's Aaron?"

"He's checking the cargo layout," Ford said.

Emi rolled over and kissed him. "And what are you up to?"

He stiffened against her, making her chuckle.

"I'm up to doing you, sweetie, if you're in the mood."

"That sounds nice."

She didn't stop him when he slid down her body and spread her legs with his hands. "Perfect," he murmured, lowering his mouth to her mound.

Caph pulled her against his chest, holding her. "Do we make you feel good, baby?"

"Uh huh!"

Still sensitive from her session with Caph, it didn't take Ford long to bring her over, relentlessly drawing every last gasp out of her.

"Jesus, that's a beautiful sound," Caph hoarsely whispered.

"Yeah," Ford agreed, moving into position between her legs, lifting them to his shoulders. He went so much deeper this way, touching her in ways and places normally left undisturbed.

Caph moved out of the way. Emi closed her eyes and enjoyed the feeling of Ford filling her when he jumped, then laughed.

"Trying to get me to explode?" he asked.

"Damn straight," Caph growled. She knew he was down there somewhere, but she didn't feel like looking.

Ford stopped thrusting and moaned. "Oh, yeah!"

"What's he doing?" Emi asked, feeling something brush against her backside.

Ford gasped. "He's working his tongue over my balls."

She fought the urge to giggle. Caph certainly did have a talented tongue.

After a minute, Ford thrust again, but they were harder, jerky motions. Emi peeked. He'd closed his eyes, his lower lip caught under his upper teeth, trying to hold back his climax against Caph's persistent mouth.

It was a losing battle. Ford cried out and drove deeper, harder than before, and collapsed on her. She held him against her chest, arms and legs trapping him.

Caph sat up and laughed. "That was fun. Haven't done that in a while."

"You cheated," Ford grumbled. "That's not fair."

"How's it cheating?"

"You made me come too fast."

"Ah, but you came hard, didn't you?"

"Yeah, I did."

Caph stretched out next to them, his arm around Ford's waist, Emi's head tucked into the crook of his arm. "I love doing that to you." He met her eyes. "And I love doing that to you too, baby girl."

No hit of stress from either. Jezapalooza wasn't anywhere in their thoughts.

* * * *

They were in the shower an hour later when Aaron caught up with them. He stepped in, and the other two men finished and left them alone.

"Did you have a nice nap?" he asked.

She loved his playful smirk, the one he seemed to always wear now when around her. They hadn't talked about what happened to him, but his overall outlook had much improved from when she first met him.

And she rarely thought about those three little words anymore. He more than showed her every day how much he loved her.

"Only one thing missing," she whispered, pulling him close.

"Really? And what would that be?"

"You." He stiffened against her, and she backed him into the shower wall, kneeling in front of him.

His fingers gently fisted her hair, his hips rocking against her as she wrapped her fingers around his shaft and licked him.

He moaned.

"You like that?" she asked.

"Yeah. You know I love it, baby."

She took her time slowly going down on him, savoring it, enjoying his reaction. With her other hand she cupped his sac, massaging it and making him groan deep in his throat. His fingers tightened in her hair.

"That's it," he growled. "You know what I love, baby."

Urged on by his deep voice, she continued, laving her tongue over his shaft, feeling him tense, tighten. When he emptied, she grabbed his hips and held him tight until he was totally spent. His hands dropped to her shoulders, leaning on her for support.

"Damn, baby," he gasped. "You put the twins to shame, you know that?"

She grinned. "Oh, I doubt that. Different doesn't mean better."

He pulled her to her feet and held her. "You have no idea how good you are, sweetheart."

* * * *

Emi ventured out with Caph the next day. They'd managed to avoid Jezeen until she spotted them on their way back to the Tamora Bight.

"Caph! Wait!"

He gripped Emi's hand and swore. "What?"

"Did Ford tell you I was looking for you?"

Emi didn't miss the nasty look Jezeen cast her way.

"Yeah. So?" Caph asked.

"Look, can I please talk to you?"

Emi had had enough. Not letting go of Caph's hand, she stepped in front of the large man. "Listen, woman, apparently you aren't good at taking a hint. We are not taking you on as crew. We're a four-pack, and we'll stay a four-pack. They can't stand you, they don't like you. Go run your scam on an unsuspecting ship and get taken on as crew there." She made sure to say it loud, and people from other ships turned to watch and listen.

Jezeen glared at her. "Look, kid, you have no say—"

"I have *every* say. We're a bonded crew. *We.* As in I'm one of them. Back. The *fuck*. Off. Bitch." Emi stepped forward, glaring, and felt Caph's stress levels rise as he worried about a fight between the women.

Jezeen's eyes narrowed. "What the hell do they see in you?"

"They see a woman who loves all of them for who they are and who doesn't play favorites. They see a woman who cares about them, *all* of them. When they look at you, they see an annoying skank who makes their skin crawl. Go to hell. Come on, Caph." She glanced at him long enough to note his amused smile as Emi led him back to the ship.

When they were inside and the hatch was safely closed behind them, he laughed and picked her up, swinging her around. "You were great!"

She felt great. "I was more than happy to stand up to her. I'll be damned if I'll share my boys with anyone, especially not with a skank ho like her."

"Skank ho? Is that a medical term?"

"Yeah, it is now."

The other men laughed at Caph's recounting. He embellished a little, making Emi look even braver than she was, but she didn't correct his version.

Aaron smirked. "Well, maybe she'll leave us alone now."

No such luck. The next morning, the com chirped when Emi was alone on the bridge, the men down in cargo working on load set up.

"Tamora Bight."

The caller hesitated. "This is Captain Jenkins from the Kelso Bay. Is Aaron there?"

"He's down in cargo. This is Dr. Hypatia, the medical officer. What can I do for you, captain?"

"I need to talk to him about a crew transfer."

Emi's gut tightened. "Is this about that Jezeen woman?"

Another hesitation. "Yes."

"Well, I can tell you his answer is a resounding no. We're a bonded crew, captain, and we're not taking on any extras."

Yet another hesitation. "Ah. I didn't know that." A woman started to protest in the background, then suddenly cut off like she was shushed.

Emi pushed the advantage. "The captain, the officers, and I already informed her that we were bonded crew and closed to new members. She will have to find another ride, because the Tamora Bight is full. What part of no doesn't she understand, because Aaron, Ford, Caph and myself have all told her no. She has no chance of crewing with us."

"Thank you, Doctor. I'm sorry I bothered you. Kelso Bay out."

Grinning ear to ear, she cut off the com link and ran down to cargo to pass the message.

The men laughed. "Damn, she just doesn't take a hint, does she?" Ford said, shaking his head.

"She's gotta be desperate if she's that bad off. Must have run through all the other crews," Emi said.

Aaron smirked. "She's got a bad rep. Troublemaker. Finally looks like she hit a wall."

* * * *

Ford or Caph went with Emi to her classes. They spotted Jezeen from a distance a few times, accosting crew from other ships in her desperation to switch rides. Jezeen didn't approach them again, but she did shoot Emi murderous glares on more than one occasion.

The classes paid off, and Emi managed to produce edible baked goods. Not perfect, but better, and she learned how to modify the oven and recipes to counteract the effects of space and reduced-G. She picked up a few extra seedling plants, modified beans that would flourish in the hydro lab and give them an alternate protein source. She also learned how to can and freeze-dry vegetables, giving them options besides the pre-packaged, processed food.

Aaron personally took Emi to her driving lesson on the rover. She was both thrilled and terrified to be motoring on the surface of Mars. She bounced over hills on the outdoor track set up for this, laughing as she learned how to negotiate tricky terrain and how to use the built-in leveling system if she flipped it.

After several hours, Aaron felt confident enough in her skills to declare her safe on it, and they returned to the ship. Never in her life would she have imagined she'd be doing something like this.

As their time on Mars drew to a close, Emi checked their food inventory and stocked up on last-minute fresh items. They would be en route for months before they stopped at a military station to replenish supplies. They had one last crew dinner out before starting their lift countdown the next morning.

The lift procedure was faster and simpler than on Earth, due to decreased gravity, lack of atmosphere, and no large metropolitan areas nearby. It only took two hours to move out of the docking facility and three hours to lift. The front plates were closed, and as Mars slipped away from them in the vid screens, Emi felt an odd thrill. Mars wasn't home by any stretch, but it was firm ground. She now understood some of the men's excitement to be underway again.

She felt it.

They switched back to a twenty-four hour cycle and set a course for their first stop. They would jump to a nearby solar system, a trip that would take three days. Boiled down to basics she could understand, the jump engine allowed them to cover vast distances in a short time, but it took a lot of energy to run. They only used it when the time and energy and supply usage of travelling with the normal engines would outweigh using the jump engine.

The Tamora Bight performed flawlessly. After a week in space, Emi lost track of time again. One evening, she joined Aaron on the bridge when he had night watch. She spent alone time with each of them, albeit not in bed, during bridge watches. It kept them from being lonely, and while she felt she knew them fairly well already, it gave them time to lower their emotional defenses around her.

He patted his lap, and she gladly curled up against him. She met a previously unfilled need for each of the men, but they did for her, too. Caph was her playful buddy; Ford was her intellectual partner; Aaron was her quiet strength and steady hand.

"How are you feeling, sweetie?" he asked, his arms comfortably setting around her.

"I'm okay. Better than I thought I'd be."

"No regrets?"

"Absolutely not. Well, maybe one."

"What's that?"

"That I didn't have a chance to give Jezehussy the same kind of dry dock show we gave the guys in New Phoenix."

Aaron's laugh warmed her heart. "I told you, I wouldn't have minded that."

Chapter Sixteen

The first month flew by. If anything, it was almost boring. Not being with her boys, because that was never dull or a chore. She jogged through the ship with Ford, worked out in the exercise room with Caph, and practiced her self-defense techniques with Aaron. They played poker—often strip poker—most nights after dinner. She also learned more about the ship, getting frequent pop quizzes from the men about different functions.

The only one surprised when she answered correctly was Emi.

After completing a rapid-fire round of life support-related questions, Caph grinned. "By jove, I think she's got it."

"Must be osmosis, because it sure as hell doesn't feel like I'm an expert."

He hugged her. "Honey, we don't expect you to know the entire ship, but you know a hell of a lot more than you did before. By the time we get back to Earth, you'll know this crate as well as we do."

"I wouldn't bet on that." The jump drive and grav plate systems still stymied her.

* * * *

Their first stop after leaving Mars was a military outpost at the outer edge of the solar system they were scheduled to explore. They dropped off a shipment for the outpost, picked up some of their own supplies, and Aaron took her with him to a meeting with the base commander.

For the first time, Emi could admit to a raging case of nerves, her brief interaction with the ISNC grunts coming back to her. Smiles were in short supply, and the general overall mood of the base was serious, businesslike.

Thank the gods I didn't pick the Kendall Kant!

Aaron misinterpreted her edginess. "Relax, sweetie," he whispered, his thumb stroking her hand. It was an unconscious tic he had, and he gained as much comfort from the gesture as she did. "Everyone here is chipped. You're safe."

"That's not what I'm nervous about."

The base commander was polite, but efficient. "Captain Lucio, Dr. Hypatia." He handed Aaron a computer cartridge. "Your mission downloads, Captain. We received them yesterday from the DSMC."

Emi felt something from the commander, a flash of…pity?

"How long have you been in the ISNC, Commander Rawley?" she asked. His name was familiar, but she couldn't place it.

His eyes flicked to Aaron and back to her. "Sixteen years."

Rawley was a man used to hiding his emotions and keeping a poker face firmly in place. "Do you enjoy your work?"

He nodded. "Mostly. It's like any other job, Doctor. Sometimes there's good things, sometimes there's bad."

A shadow crossed his mind, and at almost the same time a dark thought flitted through Aaron's. And she knew.

Rawley was involved, somehow, with the events on the Wayfarer Margo.

They chatted for a few minutes, discussing the security situation of the area they were heading to—fortunately calm—and both men's tension levels gradually ratcheted up until she almost couldn't stand it.

Aaron stood and shook hands. "Nice seeing you again, Rawley."

Rawley nodded and shook hands with her. "You too. Doctor."

Aaron took her hand, his thumb stroking hers as they walked. "Did you know he'd be here?" she asked.

He stopped short, looking at her, genuine surprise on his face.

"I *am* an empath," she reminded him.

He brought her hand to his lips and kissed it. Then they continued their walk. "I don't think about that," he said. "Your skills. I keep forgetting."

"Was he on the Margo?"

Aaron's face tightened, but he nodded. "Yeah. He transferred over to the ISNC."

She left it at that, her question answered. Eventually Aaron relaxed, and later sought her out in the galley, wrapping his arms around her waist as she made them lunch.

He kissed the back of her neck. "Thank you," he murmured against her skin.

"For what?"

"For being you. For picking us." He turned her to face him, his brown eyes searching hers. "Thank you, Em. From the bottom of my heart."

"You don't have to thank me, Aaron. I love you, *all* of you."

He smiled and touched his forehead to hers, his eyes closing, the worst of his tension now draining from him. "Me too, babe."

He couldn't say it, but it was okay. She knew the last person he'd said it to had died in his arms, and he still hurt from those wounds. Maybe his soul would always ache.

But he *did* love her.

"So when do we start working on your head?" she asked with a smile.

"You already are, babe. Every day with you, I feel better," he whispered against her flesh.

She closed her eyes and basked in his warmth, his body enveloping hers. One of the few things she didn't like on board was the temperature. Not in the crew area, but elsewhere, it was always on the cool side to conserve energy. She nearly always felt chilly. The men easily tolerated it, but for her comfort they kept the crew area and bridge slightly warmer.

"Are you happy with us?" he asked. "Seriously."

"Aaron, you guys are stuck with me for life," she assured him.

He squeezed her tightly, nearly desperately. "Good. I couldn't stand losing you, babe. You or the twins."

* * * *

The next night was Emi's turn at watch. Around three a.m. she felt Aaron's approach before he reached the bridge.

"What are you doing up?" she asked.

He composed his thoughts. "You do know how I feel about you, right?" he softly asked.

She smiled and nodded. "Of course I do."

"I wanted to make sure you knew. I know I'm not good about saying it—"

"Aaron," she softly interrupted him, "you don't have to say it as long as you show me."

He studied her face. "Have I been showing you enough?"

"Yes, you have. Come here."

She put her arms around his waist and rested her face against his firm stomach. "I love you, Aar," she said. "And I know you love me and the twins. I understand why it's hard for you to talk about it. As long as you keep showing me how you feel, I'm okay with that."

"Really?"

"Yes, really." She looked into his face. "Don't ever shut us out, that's all I ask. We all love you and want to help you heal, whatever needs to happen."

He stroked her hair and rubbed her shoulders. "How did I get so lucky?"

"You've got it backwards. I'm the lucky one, times three."

He took her hand. "Stand up, baby."

She did. He sat, then pulled her into his lap and she comfortably curled up against him.

"Is this showing you?" he softly asked.

Emi slipped her arms around him. "Absolutely."

* * * *

Aaron was healing, slowly but surely. All the men were, but Aaron's wounds ran especially deep. She suspected many of them were thickly scabbed over and in need of debriding. In subtle ways she worked with all of them, indirectly, with her empath skills as well as good old psychology, combined with the most effective mental medicine of all.

Love.

She loosely scheduled alone time with each man every day, even if only an hour, although they might not have realized she did. Several times a month she tried to spend as much of a full day with one of them as she could. It helped.

It was during one of these alone times that Emi was on the bridge with Ford. They'd been talking when his attention suddenly drifted from their conversation as he stared at the command console. He quickly checked several settings.

"Shit!" Ford yelled from the command chair.

Emi flinched, startled, and turned in her seat. "What? What's wrong?"

He shook his head, his face grim. *No time for questions*, that look said. His fingers flew over the console and he punched the com. "Aaron, to the bridge. Now."

Emi got up and looked over Ford's shoulder. He was working too fast for her to make any sense of what he did, but from the blinking red warnings on one screen, she imagined it wasn't good.

He was stressed, but it was more disgust and irritation than fear, so that reassured her whatever the problem was, it wasn't life-threatening.

She heard Aaron's pounding footsteps before he ran onto the

bridge. "What's wrong?"

Ford pointed at the console. "Jump engine relay's burned out."

"Aw, shit." Ford slid out of the command chair and Aaron took his place. "Let me guess."

"I bet you do," Ford said.

Caph jogged onto the bridge. "What's wrong?"

"We lost the jump relay."

"Crap."

Emi didn't want to interrupt, but she couldn't stand not knowing. "What's wrong?"

Ford grimaced. "One of the spare parts we don't carry is the jump engine relay. They normally don't go bad, and it's not considered a critical or life-support part. But without it, we can't jump."

"Where do we get one?"

"I don't know. We'll have to figure it out."

Caph slid into his seat and looked it up. She watched as his entire body language changed. He tensed, defeated. "Tay-Dax'n. Four days away at normal speed."

Aaron sat back and shook his head. "No. We'll put in an order for one and ask them to deliver it. How long?"

Caph looked it up. "At least three months, probably six."

Emi held up a hand. "Whoa, wait a minute. Why can't we get it at this Tay-whatever planet?"

Caph shook his head. "Tay-Dax'n. And no." He looked at Aaron and Ford. "I'm voting no."

Aaron agreed. "No. Ford?"

"No."

Emi seethed at not getting a say in the matter. "You guys don't get to vote on something like this without me hearing the whole story. What the fuck?"

Aaron set his jaw. "We aren't going to Tay-Dax'n, and that's final."

"No, Aaron. You don't get to pull captain rank crap on me like that. What's up with this planet?"

The twins remained silent, knowing better than to challenge their captain.

"Em," Aaron said, "it's a Class 2-A treaty race. Do you know what that means?"

She thought back to her lessons. "No. Enlighten me."

"It means free trade, but we have to abide—fully—by their customs while dealing with them."

"And that tells me nothing, Aar."

He took a deep breath. "They've got a dress code that's not like ours. We would have to abide by it."

"What, man skirts? Plaid with polka dots? Horizontal stripes? Quit beating around the fucking bush and tell me, dammit!"

Ford took over. "They have very specific views on women and their role in their society. While they're considered goddesses, in effect they are property of their men. They are not abused. In fact, it is illegal to touch or even talk to a woman unless you ask her permission first. They have the lowest incident of assaults and crimes against women anywhere."

Crossing her arms in front of her, she directed her ire at Ford. "You guys are being a bunch of pussies, you know that?"

"I'm getting there, Emi." Ford glanced at the other men. "Women are worshipped, literally. And their dress code tends to favor showing off the female form."

She snickered. "You're afraid of looking at a few naked women? I won't get jealous, I promise."

The men shook their heads, and she knew she hadn't heard the whole story yet.

"Emi, you would have to walk around dressed like them. They allow for very sheer skirt-type garments called t'apaurs, but women don't wear any other clothes." He couldn't meet her gaze any longer. "They also wear collars identifying who their man is."

"Fine. I'll stay on the ship."

Ford let out a deep sigh. "You can't. When a non-local ship arrives, even just at a docking station, the entire crew must meet with the controlling magistrate. Dressed the way the locals dress. The men dress enough like human men. But the women…"

It finally sank in. "I'd have to walk around pretty much naked and with a collar on, that's what you're saying?"

The men nodded.

Aaron sat back in his seat and scrubbed his face with his hands. "Now do you see why we all voted no?"

They were genuinely worried for her. It both touched and pissed her off.

"So you're saying I don't get a vote in this?"

"What?" the men parroted.

"Me. Vote. Don't I get one?"

She'd managed to shock Ford into silence, a rare occurrence indeed. Caph spoke first. "And how would you vote?"

"It's stupid to hang around wasting that much time when we can have the flipping part in a few days, all because you guys don't want other guys seeing me naked. Hell, I run around the crew area nearly naked half the time, and you aren't complaining about that."

Aaron frowned. "It's not that. Em. We aren't going to put you through something like that."

"Something like what? All the other women are like that, right?"

The men nodded.

"So what's the problem? You said it's safe. Get me a freaking collar and let's do this."

She'd stunned them all into silence.

"You're *not* serious?" Caph asked.

"Fucking A I'm serious. We've got a job to do, boys. I'm willing to take one for the team, so to speak."

Incredulous, the men stared at her.

"I vote we get the part from Tay-Dax'n." She raised her hand. "All in favor, boys?"

Caph, then Ford reluctantly raised their hands. She waited, and Aaron finally nodded. "All right. I don't like making you do this."

"You aren't making me do anything. I appreciate your concern, really. It means a lot to me that you care that much, but it's okay." She winked. "I'd be willing to bet I keep all y'all's interest up while we're there."

The men laughed.

* * * *

Despite her bravado, Emi was scared shitless and thanked the gods the boys weren't empaths. They docked and made arrangements for the part while Ford went out shopping with a special preliminary debarkation pass from the local magistrate. The silver collar he brought back was engraved with beautiful, intricate filigree and her name as well as the men's names. He'd taken her measurements before going out, and when he put it on her, it fit perfectly.

The t'apaur was dark blue, nearly sheer, and loosely flowed from her hips. She looked at herself in the mirror then spun for Ford's approval.

"Well? How do I look?"

He grinned. "I'm not looking forward to strangers seeing you like this, but I'll damn sure enjoy the view. I tried to find the darkest color I could—I figured it'd give you a little extra cover."

"It *is* safe, right?"

"Oh, absolutely. They've got a weird society that works for them. Women aren't oppressed, they're free to come and go as they please, work, whatever. It's just a weird dynamic. The irony, I suppose, is women lead the men around by their...well, like you lead us, sweetheart." He smiled. "But out of the men's appreciation for their women came the urge to protect them while wanting to show them off. They feel no need for modesty, because they take great pride in their bodies. Just don't be shocked when you get your view of the population."

"Why? Am I a porker by comparison?" She'd lost a few pounds during training, and some of her pre-launch plumpness had converted to muscle. The men constantly nagged at her not to "get skinny" as they said, because they loved her the way she was, full thighs and all.

He grinned. "You'll see. It's safe to say that to the three of us, believe me, you have no competition among their women."

Ford and Emi met up with Caph and Aaron at the hatch.

"You don't have to do this, Em," Aaron quietly said. "We can cancel the order and leave."

"Don't be silly." She kissed him. "I appreciate it, I really do. Let's get this over with so I can get back here and put some clothes on. It's cold." She was barefoot, and the cold floor wasn't helping the waves of gooseflesh that crawled over her skin. Her nipples were nearly painfully pebbled in the cool air.

Caph held up a shawl. "Once we meet with the controlling magistrate, he can give special permission for you to put this on because you're chilly. His guards will escort us back here so there's no trouble. They'll be happy that we observed their customs, and you won't have to leave the ship again while we're here."

"Anything else I need to know?"

Aaron reddened. "You have to walk in front of us. We can't touch you in public, can't hold hands, that kind of stuff."

Okay, that was unexpected. She'd counted on at least being able to sandwich herself between two of the men for warmth and comfort. "Oh. Okay." Emi took a deep breath. "Let's do it."

The air outside the ship felt uncomfortably chilly. They met with the official greeting magistrate at the end of the gangway. He was a short, squat man, built like a fire plug if he was to be described on Earth, rotund and with a pale complexion. She glanced around. The few other men she saw looked similar in appearance.

He noted Emi's dress—or lack thereof—and looked pleased, but not overly interested. "Captain Lucio, welcome to Tay-Dax'n."

Aaron introduced them all. The magistrate shook hands with the men and bowed to Emi. She glanced at Ford. He bowed his head, mouthing, "Thank you."

She tipped her head. "Thank you."

The magistrate smiled. "Please, follow me. The controlling magistrate is awaiting you."

She glanced at Ford again. He motioned for her to follow first. She did, and as they exited the facility she saw more people, including women.

The Tay-Dax'n women were built much like their men, only with breasts.

And they were covered with large amounts of body hair.

Emi fought to control her amused smile. While she wouldn't win any beauty contests here, she felt an inordinate amount of relief and amusement that her boys' eyes would be only for her.

Her self-consciousness soon slipped away as she tried to step into the role of anthropological observer. Each woman seemed to have an invisible buffer around her—no men ever stepped inside that neutral zone around a woman, even the women they appeared to be with. Young girls wore sheer t'apaurs that covered their entire body while most of the older women did not, and only women dared get close to or touch another woman. Their collars all ranged from plain leather—most likely denoting lower income—to extremely ornate. Ford had apparently spent some bucks on hers.

That instilled her with a surprisingly odd mix of comfort and pride.

Men steered clear of Emi, few even casting a glance her way. She was an oddity of height in this world—most of the other women were much shorter than her, but she was also much thinner by their standards.

And a lot less hairy.

Aaron and the twins trailed behind as closely as they could by local decorum, and she felt rather than heard them let out an audible sigh of relief when they reached the controlling magistrate's office.

The man stood when they entered and repeated the welcome they'd had with the greeting magistrate. Then he asked, "Captain, may I speak to Dr. Hypatia?"

"By all means."

He turned to Emi, focusing his eyes at her feet. "Doctor, we appreciate you adhering to our customs, but I imagine you are rather chilly, are you not?"

"Yes, I am. Very."

"If you'd like, I see one of your men has brought you something appropriate. Please feel free to wear it if you need to. We understand not all races can tolerate our chilly conditions the way we can. The gesture alone is more than enough to satisfy us of your honorable intentions."

"Thank you."

Caph immediately handed her the shawl and she wrapped it tightly around her.

"My guard unit will escort you back to your ship once we finish so that there will be no complaints. Again, I must say I admire you for this. Most of the treaty races we deal with refuse to dock here if they have female crew. I will be sure to send my appreciation and regards to the DSMC about your character, Captain."

"Thank you, but I'll be honest, Dr. Hypatia is the one who insisted we dock. We didn't want to make her uncomfortable."

"Extraordinary. You are an amazing woman, Doctor. You are all welcomed to conduct your business and move freely about the station as you need. Dr. Hypatia, I understand if you'd feel more comfortable staying inside your ship."

She nodded. "Thank you."

"Please enjoy your stay. Thank you for your time."

The guard briefly spoke to Aaron, and they all returned to the ship after being issued passes. Now with the shawl wrapped around her, Emi noticed strange looks her way, a few frowns, mostly from other women. On their way to the magistrate's office, barely a glance had been cast their way, but with the shawl around her it was like she drew attention to herself. Emi suspected if they didn't have the official guards with them, local law enforcement would have been called on them for violating the dress code.

When they reached the hatch, Aaron sent Caph in with Emi and left again with Ford to go get the part. Safely behind the door, Caph scooped her into his arms and she started shivering.

"You okay, babe?" He carried her down the main corridor.

She clung to him. "No," she chattered, "I'm fucking freezing!"

He hurried to their crew quarters and turned up the thermostat in their cabin, slipping under the covers with her until she stopped shivering. Part of it was the sudden stress relief, she knew, but she'd been fucking cold.

"I'm not nearly as furry as I need to be to survive here." She laughed.

He hugged her close. "Thank the gods, honey." He realized she was still wearing the collar. "Why don't you turn around, and I'll take that off you?"

She playfully smiled. "I don't know. I kind of like it."

"You're a riot, kiddo," he snickered, unhooking the complex clasp and carefully removing it from her neck. "Hey, anytime you want to play slave, we're up for it."

"Ha ha."

He laughed and patted her on the rump. "I'll go make you some coffee. Why don't you put something warm on."

"Maybe I'd like you to stay and keep warming me up."

He kissed her on the nose. "I'd love that, but I need to get back up to the bridge and go over the systems schematics for replacing that relay when the others get back." He hesitated, then leaned in close, one hand brushing between her legs. "Later, I promise, I will let you use my body any way you see fit."

"Now who's the tease?"

* * * *

Ford and Aaron returned an hour later with the relay. Emi was bundled in sweats and sneakers. When Ford and Caph set off for engineering to replace the part, Aaron grabbed her arm.

"Thank you, Em."

She shrugged. "Hey, we're crew. If positions were reversed…" Suddenly, she felt there was no good way to finish that sentence, not with knowing what she knew about Aaron's past. "Look, it was a little embarrassing, it was freaking cold, but I'd do it again in a heartbeat. It's not like I had to walk down the center of Main Street in New Phoenix dressed like that. Although that would be a lot warmer than it is here."

He nuzzled her neck, his lips warm against her flesh. "Em, you're an amazing woman."

"Yeah, just remember that when I use this to guilt trip you guys into doing stuff for me later," she quipped.

* * * *

It took them three hours to replace and test the relay. They picked up a spare to be on the safe side and were on their way again the next day. As they backed the Tamora Bight out of the docking berth, Emi shook her head. "Next time, let's break down near a planet where the guys have to run around naked, okay?"

The men laughed. "I can't promise that," Aaron said, "but we'll run around naked for you whenever you want."

"Not the same, but that's a deal I'll take."

Chapter Seventeen

They arrived at their first planet, dubbed XP-3 by the DSMC, three days later. Emi stared in wonder as the vid screens showed the purple and orange planet beneath them. Twice the size of Earth, it had a similar climate, atmosphere, and gravity, but more studies were needed before a detailed pre-settlement team would be dispatched.

One of Emi's jobs was to man the scanners on the drones sent to explore the planet's surface. The water appeared purple, taking up approximately half of the planet's surface, and the orange land mass was due to the overall color of the vegetation on the surface. Instead of Earth's greens, oranges, reds, and umber tones defined most of the local plants.

Animal species abounded, many quadrupedal like on Earth, but looking like nothing they'd ever seen before. There weren't many reptiles, at least not large ones, and the temperatures, even at the equator, were slightly cooler than Earth averages.

They spent three weeks orbiting the planet, making detailed maps, studying different areas, gathering readings of water, polar ice, and air in various regions.

"Why aren't we using the rover here?"

Aaron shook his head. "No orders. We can only use it on planets where we're the tertiary exploration, meaning they've already done what we've done here and deemed it safe enough to explore. Don't worry, you'll have a few chances to go four-wheeling," he teased with a playful grin.

Working with the men was far from a chore. One time, the boys had to walk around naked for three days after losing a particularly aggressive game of strip poker to Emi.

She loved playing poker and suspected they might have lost that game on purpose.

Another time, she ended up cooking dinner for a week when she lost. That one she did lose on purpose, because she had grown tired of Caph's soup entrees, not that she would ever admit it to him.

Disaster struck one morning when Ford was on watch. She awoke before Aaron and Caph, pulled on a pair of sweats, and went to the galley to start coffee.

The Java Max wouldn't run.

"Nooo!" she screamed, nearly panicked. Aaron and Caph ran into the galley, both scared and still naked, at the sound of her desperate wails.

"What? What is it?" Aaron asked.

Near tears, Emi slapped at the side of the coffee machine. "I can't get it to work! It won't work!"

Caph bit back his laughter while Aaron pulled her away from the coffee machine. They'd learned early on not to get between her and her first cup of coffee in the morning under risk of serious bodily injury.

"It's not funny, Caph!" she yelled, fuming. "What are we going to do?"

He lost his battle to stay silent and roared with laughter. "Sweetie, it *is* funny. You're the lady who thought nothing about parading around naked on a strange space station, and you're about to have a nervous breakdown over the coffee machine?"

He wasn't as dedicated a java drinker as she was. She shoved him, hard.

"It's not funny!" she screamed. Emi wheeled on Aaron, who was bent over it. "Fix it! You have to fix it!"

"I will, sweetie, just give me a minute. Calm down, Em."

Ford, drawn by her anguished cries, ran into the galley. "What's wrong? What's the matter?"

Caph clamped his lips closed, trying to quiet his laughter.

Emi cried. Maybe it wasn't just coffee, maybe it was a tangible link to a normal life being taken away from her that had unnerved her, a wrinkle in her familiar routine that helped keep her sane and focused. Until now, she could almost imagine being able to walk outside and get what she wanted from New Phoenix. Living in the ship in space wasn't much different than living in the ship in dry dock, as long as she didn't look at the bridge vid screens.

She burst into tears and headed for the hydro lab, her other source of peace and comfort. The large room was now a virtual jungle, overflowing with fresh fruits and vegetables. She sat on the floor between two of the tanks and looked up, the ceiling nearly obscured by climbing squash and bean vines trellising on wires she'd run all over.

Ford found her twenty minutes later, a steaming cup of coffee in his hand. He sat next to her and she cried, relieved, as he handed it to her.

"You fixed it!"

"Sweetie, it wasn't broken. If you hadn't run off like that, you'd have known. I cleaned it last night and forgot to plug it back in."

Embarrassment flowed through her. Ford's amused smile set her off into another bout of tears.

"I feel like I'm losing my mind," she admitted. "I thought I was handling this so well. I don't understand."

"I think you need a couple days off. We all do from time to time—it's normal. We'll change the watch schedule and let you get some rest." He stroked her cheek. "You spend all your time trying to shrink our heads, baby girl, but the truth is, you need some TLC too."

She sipped her coffee and settled against his firm shoulder. "How stupid am I? I mean, I thought crap, no more coffee for years, and I panicked."

"I would have panicked too, except for one thing."

"What?"

He kissed the nape of her neck. "We have another Java Max down in the cargo hold, and plenty of spare parts for them both. If you think I'm going without coffee, you're fucking nuts."

Emi froze, then burst out laughing. Ford joined her, and eventually she calmed down enough to let him lead her back to the galley. Caph sat at the table, eating.

"I scrambled you some eggs, sweetie."

"Thank you."

Ford made her sit while he fixed a plate for her. "We did a little talking. We agreed you and Caph should spend the day together. Tomorrow it can be me and you, and then the day after you and Aar. Is that okay with you?"

Emi nodded. "Thank you," she said quietly.

Caph reached across the table and touched her hand. "Hey, babe, it's okay. We all have meltdowns occasionally. It means you're normal, not that you're cracking up. If someone's totally calm all the time, that's when you worry about them."

"So what are we doing today?" she asked.

He smiled. "Sim room."

* * * *

He'd even turned up the temperature a little. Not uncomfortably so, but she didn't feel the slightest bit chilly when she stretched out on the blanket he spread on the floor.

"Where are we going today?" As if she couldn't guess.

"You'll see." He programmed the room. The walls disappeared, changing to their private oasis by the stream. He knelt beside her on the blanket. "Roll over, sweetie. You need a backrub."

Her sweats made her hot. She stripped off her shirt and rolled onto her stomach, moaning with satisfaction as he straddled her body, his strong hands working every ounce of stress out of her muscles. They could have been there ten minutes or ten hours, she didn't know.

Didn't care.

When he eventually worked his way south she raised her hips as he slipped her sweatpants and underwear off her legs, leaving her comfortably naked on the blanket. And still he didn't make any sexual overtures, his fingers kneading her legs and feet, nearly putting her to sleep again.

Emi thought he would try to make love to her, but he didn't. He stretched out next to her, pulling her against his side, his arm around her.

"You feel better, babe?"

"Yeah. Mellow."

He laughed. "Good, because you were pretty stressed."

"Don't you want to do anything?"

He shrugged. "Talk. Nap."

Emi playfully poked him. "Not what I meant." He was still dressed in a T-shirt and shorts.

"We've got all day, babe." And they took it. Talking, napping, relaxing. Being with the men was so comfortable, she'd long since gotten past feeling self-conscious if they were dressed and she wasn't.

"They won't come in here with us?" she asked.

"No. We wanted you to have some down time. If you want some alone-alone time, we'll be happy to give you that, too."

"No. I spent more than enough years alone-alone to last me a lifetime." She rolled on top of him, feeling him harden through his shorts. "What I want right now is you." She kissed him, and he wasted no time rolling her onto her back and ridding himself of his clothes. With the simulated scene around them, the sounds and even the temperature, it was easy to pretend they were back in New Phoenix at their picnic.

Caph took his time experimenting with positions, finding that with one of her legs hooked around his, his strokes rubbed her clit just right. From the change in her moans, he knew he had her.

"Is that good for you, baby?"

"Yeah," she whispered, working her hips against his.

This was her special connection with Caph, her gentle giant, so to speak, his every move, every breath speaking of his dedication to her.

Emi laid back and enjoyed it, the feeling of his turgid cock slick with her juices hitting just the right spot with every stroke.

"I love you so much, Emi," he breathed, brushing his lips against hers. "I love that I can do this for you."

She tangled her hands in his shaggy hair, pulled his face to hers, her tongue stroking in time with his cock.

It caught her by surprise, like being tossed off her feet by an ocean wave. She cried out against him as her muscles spasmed, trying to keep him inside her.

He lifted her thighs and fucked her, fast and hard, trying to climax with her and just barely making it. Still sheathed deep inside her he rolled to his side as she softly wept against him.

"Shh, it's okay," he whispered. This still unnerved him, she knew, that something that felt so good could make her cry.

Emi drifted to sleep with the feel of his fingers brushing along her spine, soothing her, comforting her.

* * * *

Her day with Ford started out sleeping late, then curling up on the large sofa in the rec room and watching several old movies, talking, snuggled under a blanket and playfully petting.

They did a lot of talking, Ford somehow seeing deep inside her in a way the other two men didn't. "Feeling better?" he asked as his fingers playfully slipped inside her sweats.

Emi shifted position. "I have a feeling you're going to make sure I feel better."

His finger dipped inside her, then trailed a slow, teasing circle around her clit. "Absolutely," he softly growled in her ear.

Ford knew what buttons to push, physically and emotionally, to bring her to the edge of release and keep her there. He slipped two fingers into her, and she moaned with disappointment when he stilled his hands.

"Don't rush me, sweetheart." He nipped her earlobe, making her arch her back and press her body against his. "I want to spend all day keeping you begging for it."

Her soft gasp of disappointment made him laugh. "You love it, and you know it. You can't lie to me, baby."

No, she couldn't. He knew her too well that way.

He shifted position on the couch and pulled her sweats off. She kicked them out of the way and felt him shed his shorts, his stiff cock throbbing against her cheeks.

The movie played on without them noticing. His free arm circled her, his fingers gently plucking at her nipples, back and forth, just hard enough to make her sex tingle around the fingers he had comfortably buried there.

Emi rocked her hips against him. "Please," she gasped.

"I will, but not yet."

Nudging against him, she tried to coax him into replacing his fingers with his cock, but he wouldn't. Then his hand settled over her right breast, gently massaging it, his thumb rubbing her rock-hard nipple, keeping it pebbled beneath his finger.

Torture. The sweetest torture in the known universe. The slightest movement of her hips or his hand brushed against her clit in a tantalizing way, but without enough pressure to get her off. After an hour of this he took a little mercy on her.

"Do you trust me, sweetheart?"

"Yes," she gasped. Anything, she wanted him to do anything to bring her relief.

He pulled his hands away, leaving her agonizingly empty, making her moan. He chuckled. "Don't worry, I'll be taking care of that for you."

He pushed her onto her stomach. She closed her eyes, wiggling her ass at him, anything to have his touch against her flesh again. Then she felt a familiar, cool wetness against her puckered rim. She froze.

"You okay, sweetie?"

"Yes," Emi whispered.

"You sure?"

She nodded. "Please don't stop."

He placed his cock against her dark hole and slowly pressed forward, giving her time to adjust. When he was fully inside her, he carefully rolled to his side again, holding still, returning his hands to their previous positions.

Emi gasped. What would it be like if it was one of the other men inside her instead of Ford's fingers? That was something she'd thought about but not tried, still a little too chicken to ask for that in real life.

"You okay, sweetie?" he murmured in her ear as he took a slow stroke inside her.

"Yes!"

"You like this?"

She pressed against him, turning her head so she could kiss him.

He took his time, reading her body, never letting her get close enough to release to send her over the edge. He tormented her, switching between slow strokes of his fingers in her slick sex and slow thrusts in her ass, alternately playing with her nipples. She lost all track of time in his arms, knowing he could do this to her all day. And he would, if she didn't come first.

"One of these days, baby," he whispered, "I would love to take you like this while you're fucking one of the others." He punctuated the words with another deep thrust. "I'd love to feel their cock sliding into you, feel them having you at the same time.

Emi whimpered, beyond rational thought.

He withdrew his hand, making her moan with disappointment.

He laughed, sucking his fingers. "Dammit, you taste so good, baby. That's something else I love. I enjoy going down on you while one of them's fucking you, baby. I love making you scream."

He made her scream, all right.

With a hand on her hip he took several strokes into her, his shaft never softening. This wasn't something she did all the time with them, but it was always easiest and felt most natural with Ford for some reason.

"What's the matter?" he whispered against her neck.

She wiggled her hips against him in response, making him laugh.

"Aw, did you want my hand back there?"

"Uh huh."

Slowly, teasing, he slipped two fingers into her, sheathing them deep inside her and she sighed. Still no release, but the feeling was amazing.

She rocked her hips, but he pulled her tight against him, holding her captive.

"No, babe. You're mine for right now, and I'm having fun. Is that okay with you?"

She groaned, but didn't protest. Spending all day with Ford like this was definitely not something to complain about.

"Unless..." He didn't finish.

"Unless what?" she gasped.

Seductive lips pressed against the nape of her neck, in the sensitive spot that always made her shiver. "Unless you want me to call Aaron in here to help us play a little." He slowly fucked her with his fingers, and she knew what he wanted, that he did *really* want it.

"Okay."

He froze. "Really?"

"Only if it's what you want. This is your day alone with me."

He throbbed inside her ass. "Oh, damn, baby, you mean it? I've been fantasizing about this."

She couldn't help but smile. "Then let's take care of that, because if I don't come soon, someone's going to get hurt." Emi knew Aaron was in the galley and Caph was on the bridge. She called out to him. "Hey, Captain, got a minute?"

"Hold on," he called back.

Ford snickered against her shoulder. Thank the gods the sofa was huge, more than big enough for the three of them.

Aaron walked in, pausing in the doorway. "What's up?"

She stuck her arm out from under the blanket and hooked her thumb at Ford. "Him. And he's got an indecent proposal for you."

Amused but curious, Aaron walked over. "What?"

Emi pulled him down to her and kissed him. "Drop your pants and we'll show you." She pulled the blanket back, and it didn't take him long to catch on. He was stiff by the time his pants hit the floor. Ford moved his hand out of the way as Aaron carefully nudged into position, his cock pressing at her wet entrance.

"You okay, Em?" Aaron asked. She nodded, kissing him.

He slowly slipped into her wet sex, drawing moans from all three. Having both men inside her stretched her in an erotic way, and Ford shifted position, allowing Aaron to get a better angle for thrusting.

"Jesus," Ford gasped. "That's better than I ever imagined!"

Emi laid back and let them take her. She had to remember to breathe. Both of Ford's hands stroked her nipples, sending shockwaves through her.

Aaron stopped and slipped a hand between their bodies, his thumb rubbing her clit. "How long has he been torturing you, baby?"

All she could do was nod, and the men laughed. It was good, sooo good, having them both. Why had she waited to do this?

Her world ended outside of what they did to her, their arms and lips and cocks owning her body, deciding when—if—she'd climax. They took their time, stopping frequently to cool down, not wanting their release to come too soon.

"You're so tight, sweetheart," Aaron whispered, his lips parting hers.

Ford moaned in agreement.

She hovered on the edge, Aaron not letting her come. When she tried to rock her hips against them, he thrust deep and held her, impaled on their shafts. "No, baby girl," he whispered, "we're not through with you yet."

She couldn't take much more of this. Her body screamed for release, every touch of their flesh against hers trying to push her over the edge. "Please make me come!"

"What was that?" Ford asked, teasing. "What did you want?"

"Please," she begged. "Fuck me! Make me come!"

"Do you think she wants it bad enough, Aar?"

He shook his head, smiling. "I don't think so." His long, slow strokes were well-timed with Ford's; as one man stroked in, the other withdrew, keeping her on the edge.

"Aw, she's been so good, maybe we should let her come," Ford teased.

Emi whimpered again, helpless against the combined strength of their bodies controlling her.

Aaron hesitated, then leaned over and kissed Ford. "Thank you for this. For letting me cut into your time." He kissed her. "And you."

"Shut up and fuck me!"

The men laughed. "She sounds pretty adamant there, Aaron," Ford quipped. "I dunno. What do you think?"

Aaron sighed and stroked her clit again, thrusting as he did. "I think we should give her what she wants. She does take good care of us." With the pad of his thumb circling her clit, he brushed his lips against hers. "Come for us, Em. Show us what we do to you—"

It hit her like a searing hot tidal wave, raking through her body and tearing a passionate scream from her lips, her body squeezing both cocks inside her, milking them, the pressure intensifying the strength of her climax.

"That's it," Ford said, his hands sliding down to her hips, giving him better leverage. "Give it all to us."

Beyond reason, beyond control, she tried to thrust against them and finally gave up, letting them set the pace.

"Look at me," Aaron whispered.

She did, losing herself in his eyes.

"Watch me, watch what you do to me."

She held his shoulders while Ford grunted behind her, "I'm close, man."

Her eyes locked onto Aaron's. He took another stroke, and both men cried out at the same time, plunging deep into her, taking her.

Emi tangled her fingers in Aaron's hair and pulled his lips to hers as he breathed her name. Then in a collective sigh, they relaxed, spent, content.

When they'd caught their breath, they carefully untangled legs and arms and soft cocks from each other. Emi winced a little, and Aaron noticed.

"Are you okay?"

She nodded. "I'll be walking bow-legged for a few days, I think. But it was worth it." She turned to Ford. "Ready for a shower?"

"Yeah."

Aaron joined them, and then Emi curled in bed for a few minutes, meaning to take a short nap. When she awoke two hours later, Ford was smiling at her.

"How do you feel?"

Quick inventory. "Actually, not as bad as I thought I would." She wasn't a bit sore. How the men ever managed that, she had no clue. It never failed to baffle her.

"Good. Dinner's almost ready. Want me to bring it in?"

"Where's the others?"

"Aaron's taking night watch tonight. He said he'd eat on the bridge."

"I feel bad Caph got left out."

"Don't worry, sweetheart. He can have extra cuddle time with you tonight."

"How about the three of us eat in here then?"

That's what they did, and she snuggled between the twins as they watched a movie. The next thing she knew, it was morning and Aaron was bringing her coffee.

"Jeez, how long did I sleep?" She rarely awoke at night and could count on both hands with fingers to spare how many bad dreams she'd had since hooking up with the boys.

His playful smirk warmed her. "Not that long. You were exhausted. Not just playing yesterday, but accumulated stress. And frankly, since I had watch last night, I could use a nap. So how about we just stay in bed today?"

"Do you really think I'm going to say no to that?"

"I didn't think you would."

Chapter Eighteen

Emi sat in the command chair, her legs drawn up under her, reading a book on her hand-held console. It was nearly two a.m. in their daily cycle. The boys were all asleep after their poker game, leaving her on watch.

The blinking indicator caught her attention a split-second before the alert beep.

She sat up, her heart racing. She'd never had a real-life notification during a watch before. This felt bad, very bad. With shaking fingers, she touched the screen, and a message box popped up.

Sensor indicates sentient signature.

Fuck. What the hell did that *mean?*

She couldn't think. Then another message appeared.

Sensor reading, signature closing fast.

She punched the com panel, straight to the cabin. "Aaron? Guys?"

Aaron's sleepy voice. "What's wrong, hon?"

"Can you come up here? There's something on the sensors I don't understand."

He was immediately awake. "I'll be right there."

She'd no sooner sat back than a klaxon sounded and the whole screen flashed red.

Aaron ran onto the bridge a moment later, in boxers and pulling on his shirt, barefoot, wide awake now. She moved out of the command chair and he slid into it.

"Fuck!"

"What is it?"

He shook his head. She knew that meant both that he didn't know and to hold off on the questions.

The twins ran onto the bridge, Caph carrying his shirt, Ford carrying his shorts, both trying to dress.

"What is it?" Caph asked, sliding into his chair, alert and in crew mode. Ford went to the weapons panel and activated it, all business.

"Large vessel," Aaron said. "Full power to defenses, back off secondary systems."

"Roger," Caph said, his fingers flying over his panel.

Emi froze, despite the literally hundreds of hours in simulations. She watched, panicked, as Aaron barked orders at the twins and they responded immediately with acknowledgements or requested information.

Aaron glanced at her. His voice softened, calmed, the same voice he used with her that night at the Dry Port. "Em, take the secondary weapons controls from Ford."

She nodded, sliding into the chair and activating the panel as feeling slowly returned to her numb limbs.

Just a simulation, she chanted in her mind. *Just a simulation. This is just a sim, stay calm. Just a sim.*

It wasn't a sim, but maybe if she thought that hard enough, it would keep her focused.

Whatever it was, as soon as it picked them up on their sensors, it changed course and headed right for them. It was big and would intercept them in an hour at current speed. It wasn't carrying an ID beacon, meaning it was unidentified or possibly hostile.

How Aaron maintained his calm, she didn't know. "Can we jump, Ford?" he asked.

Ford shook his head. "I need three hours warm-up from current sleep mode. I shut it down to save the extra energy since we weren't close to a solar source. We jump with it cold, it'll burn out the circuit board trying to backwash the energy."

"Can we out-run it?"

"It's doing L-6," Caph said. "The fastest this crate will go outside of jump mode is L-5. We can run, but it'll catch us, and we don't have anywhere to run to. We don't have the energy to run L-5 and weapons and defenses and life support and warm up the jump engine at the same time."

Aaron activated the com. "Unidentified vessel, this is DSMC Exploration Vessel Tamora Bight hailing, over."

Silence. After two minutes, Aaron tried again, recording the message to auto-hail over a wide variety of frequencies, hoping to snag a valid one. Twenty minutes later, the ship was still closing with no response.

The tension on the bridge thickened, suffocating. Aaron looked at Emi, and in the same calm, soothing tone said, "Go to the cabin, get dressed, and bring us full uniforms." He tossed her a key card. "Then I want you to go to the arms locker, get us each—including you—a side arm, and bring us extra plasma energy cartridges for them, okay?"

She nodded and sprinted to the cabin, her hands fumbling her belt as she dressed, trying to find everyone's clothes and not grab the wrong ones or forget anything. Emi raced back to the bridge and dumped them on the floor. Before she could leave again, Aaron snagged her arm and kissed her, distracting her the way he always did, even under these circumstances.

"Em," he whispered, "it's okay. Just a precaution. You're doing great."

She nodded but felt anything but great. She bolted for the weapons locker and had to try three times to get the key card in the lock before it opened. Her fingers didn't want to hook the holster clasp to her belt, and she nearly burst into tears trying to get it right.

Taking a deep breath, she imagined Aaron's calm voice. The boys weren't panicking—neither would she.

She raced back to the bridge. She'd been gone maybe five minutes, but they were all fully dressed and at their stations. She handed out the side arms and extra cartridges and returned to her seat.

Then a tell-tale beep sounded. The men froze.

A low voice growled through the com, sounding like it was running through the translator circuits. "Vessel Tamora Bight, this is Granz executive vessel. You will maintain course and prepare to be boarded."

Aaron tapped the com. "Granz executive vessel, we are a DSMC exploration vessel, not a military vessel. Under interstellar treaty—"

"We are not a treaty race. Your crew will not be harmed." The com link went dead while Emi fought a wave of panic.

Aaron was tense, as were the twins, but they hid it well. "Em," Aaron said, "look them up, see if there's anything on them. Caph, what do you have?"

He shook his head. "Their sensor is overriding ours, or their defense shields. Energy pattern nothing like I've seen, can't penetrate it. All I know is they're a big fucking box, bigger than us by four times."

Nerves and adrenaline sent Emi's fingers flying over the computer, trying every possible spelling she could think of and coming up with nothing.

"Look up non-treaty species, cross-reference with this sector," Aaron calmly suggested.

She did, then a notation popped up: *Unknown species, intelligent race, restricted contact, DNC-2 standing orders.*

She sent the notation to Aaron's console. His face tightened. "Okay, hon. Thanks."

"What? What does it mean?"

He'd sent it to the twins' consoles, and Ford spoke. "Do Not Contact."

"What does the two mean?" she asked.

Caph answered, his face hard. "If someone's taken prisoner, no one's coming after you."

Just a sim…just a sim…

The vessel slowed as it approached. Another klaxon went off. "Tractor beam," Ford said, his fingers manipulating settings, trying to prevent life support overloads. "Way too strong to fight it."

Aaron nodded. "Then don't. Power down the engines to ready-neutral, let's not burn them up."

Just a sim…just a sim…

The com signaled again. "Captain, our diplomatic emissaries will appear on your bridge. In three…two…one."

Before Emi had time to register they'd said "diplomatic," the air shimmered behind her, like heat waves off the New Phoenix pavement. Two large, humanoid figures appeared. The air glowed faintly yellow around them, and from the way her hair felt like it was standing on end she suspected they had an energy barrier protecting them. Emi thought transporter technology like that was the realm of futuristic stories, a favorite topic for writers for hundreds of years, not something any race really possessed.

Both were huge, nearly eight feet tall. They could almost pass for human except for their size, the way their black eyes were set much wider apart than a normal human, and their flat noses. They wore matching flowing blue tunics and didn't appear to hold any weapons. Then again, if you could materialize inside another ship through their defense shields, you probably didn't need weapons.

The taller one turned to face Aaron. "Are you the captain?" Apparently the ship's computer was still translating.

Aaron stood. "Yes."

"Our sensors show four crew total. This is your crew?"

"Yes."

The alien's black eyes settled on Emi. An uncomfortable mental chill swept through her. She wanted to move closer to either of the twins but suspected a movement like that might be misinterpreted.

The second alien still had not spoken. The first alien looked at the twins, then back to Aaron. "Disarm. You will be transported to our ship to speak with our executive."

Executive. That can't be too bad, right? Just a sim...just a sim.

Aaron nodded, but his eyes focused on Emi. She felt him trying to send calming thoughts to her, sensing she was close to panic. If he was calm, she had to stay calm.

The twins and Aaron disarmed, laying their holsters in their seats. Emi tried, but she fumbled the catch on the buckle and couldn't get it. The harder she tried, the more upset she got until she was nearly in tears.

The alien apparently sensed it. "Captain, you may assist your crew member."

Aaron walked around the aliens and placed his hands over hers, waiting for her to look up and meet his eyes. He touched his forehead to hers.

"It's okay," he whispered, then smoothly released the catch and placed her holster on her seat. He turned, holding her hand, his thumb stroking hers.

"Gather here." The alien pointed at the floor in front of them. All four moved to comply. When they were standing where indicated, Emi felt Aaron's fingers tighten around hers, his thumb pressing into her palm, trying to distract her. Next to her, Ford caught her other hand. Behind her, Caph placed his hands on her waist, pressing close.

The air shimmered, shifted, and they stood on the alien vessel.

It was chilly, nearly uncomfortably so. "Follow us." The aliens started down a corridor. Behind her, Caph gently nudged her forward when he realized she was too scared to move.

As one, the four trailed after the aliens.

Okay, so they didn't have weapons trained on them. That was good, right?

Just a sim....Just a sim. It wasn't working, but it was that or she was going to scream and succumb to the hysterics threatening to take her over.

They stopped at a closed doorway, and a low tone sounded. After a brief moment, another tone sounded in response, and the door slid open. Inside stood another alien, even larger than the first two. Naked.

And if their physiology was similar to a human, he was male. Emi was shaking, shivering, her teeth chattering in the chilly air and from the stress taking her over. From the size of the alien's...appendage, either he was *really* large when he was aroused, or they liked it cold. She prayed he wasn't looking for a little loving either, because he would rip a human apart.

Head naked alien dude wasted no time. "What is your purpose?"

Aaron subtly stepped in front of Emi without releasing her hand, sandwiching her between him and Caph. "We are a research vessel."

"You are armed."

"Only for defense, not attack."

The alien nodded. "You are humans?"

"Yes."

Naked alien dude stepped forward, but Aaron didn't flinch. Emi watched from over his shoulder.

"What is your relationship?" The alien pointed at them, circling his hand, indicating all of them. Now she realized he had six fingers on each hand, and six toes.

Bet their decimal system is whacked...

She struggled to choke back the hysterical laughter. If she started, she knew damn well she wouldn't stop.

Emi had no idea how Aaron kept his voice so strong and firm. "I am the captain of the Tamora Bight. This is my crew, my first officer, mate, and medical officer."

The alien looked at Emi. "She is your mate?"

"She is our medical officer. We call our third in command the mate."

The alien nodded. "Ah, I see. She is *not* your mate, then?"

"She is not my second officer, no."

"I meant your mate. Your...*female.*"

Aaron tensed. "We are bonded crew. We are partners together."

The alien's eyes looked at each of them in turn, then lighted on

Aaron again. "You are not a family unit? Spouses?"

Emi felt tension build in the men. This couldn't be good.

"No," Aaron said. "We are designated as bonded crew by treaty—"

"But you are not...married?"

Now Aaron's voice tightened. "No."

"So you are *not* spouses?"

"No."

The naked alien turned and muttered something in a clicking, chirpy language to the alien who spoke to them on their ship, then walked behind a long, heavy purple curtain dividing the room in half.

Okay, that wasn't so bad—

"Our executive says one of you will stay here, he doesn't care which one. The rest of you are free to go."

Okay, not good.

Aaron shook his head. "We all leave."

"Captain, either one of you stay, or all of you die. There is no exception. You are not spouses. We would not separate you if you were spouses, but since you are merely crew, one of you stays."

Aaron's voice was tight. "Why?"

The alien shrugged. "Our executive is bored. He wants a new toy. Whoever stays will...service our executive."

Okay, very bad.

Aaron tensed. "I will *not* leave one of my crew."

"Either one of you voluntarily stays behind with us and services our executive, or all of you die. You will have five minutes to give us your decision." He stepped back to the other alien in the blue tunic and talked to him in their native language in low, clicking tones.

"You said you wouldn't harm our crew!"

The alien looked over "We won't, if one of you willingly stays and submits."

"That will harm our crew."

The alien shrugged. "I don't see how, it's just...sex, but you have five minutes to choose."

Aaron stepped back, forcing Emi and the twins to move. He left her standing there and pulled Ford and Caph a few feet away, huddling with them for a moment. Whether it was their nerves or the weird energy in the ship or what, she couldn't read what was going on, couldn't hear them.

Caph said something, sharp, and Aaron shook his head. Ford's voice reached her, but she couldn't tell what he was saying, only that he was arguing with Aaron.

The last thing she made out before they broke their huddle was Aaron's firm, "...that's an order, officer. Do it. You're my first, that means you're in command."

Aaron turned to her and took her hands, looked into her eyes. "I love you, Em," he whispered, then leaned in and kissed her.

Stunned, she tried to process what was happening. Caph and Ford suddenly flanked her, their hands resting on her arms.

Aaron met her eyes. "I will always love you, babe. You take care of these two guys for me, okay? Promise? Keep them out of trouble?"

She nodded, numb. Surely he wasn't saying what she thought he was saying?

He released her hands and kissed Ford, whispered something to him. Ford nodded and whispered something back, tears in his eyes.

Then Aaron kissed Caph and whispered something in his ear. He looked at Aaron and finally nodded, his face sad. Aaron quickly stepped away from them. Before Emi could stop him, Ford and Caph grabbed her arms and held her.

Realizing what was happening, she screamed, "No! Aaron, you can't do this!"

He turned and smiled, but it was full of sadness and regret. "It's okay, Em," he said softly.

"No, it's not—"

"Emi, *please*," Caph pleaded in her ear. "Don't make this any harder on him than it already is."

She crumpled in their arms, sobbing as Aaron walked away from them, heading toward the curtain and disappearing behind it.

"It'll kill him," she whispered in a tortured voice. "He's volunteered. The chip will go off and kill him if the alien doesn't."

"He's our captain," Ford said, his voice thick with emotion. "He's given us his order. I know it sucks, but no matter what, the bottom line is he's our captain first."

"We've got to save him," she begged.

"Emi, we can't, sweetheart. One of us has to stay behind, and we will *not* sacrifice you. He's ordered us to go. I hate it as much as you do, but he's given us his orders." Tears ran down Ford's cheeks, and she knew how final this was, no chance to go back and change anything.

No chance to tell Aaron one more time she loved him.

She cried, her heart breaking. She wanted to stay—she couldn't stand the thought of losing any of her men. She'd gladly stay and die if it meant they would live.

Ford and Caph forced her from the room, half-carrying, half-dragging her as she screamed and struggled against them to get to Aaron. A low tone sounded as they reached the doorway. They all looked up as an intercom cut on.

"Simulation complete," a soft female voice spoke.

They froze. Ford started to say, "What the fu—"

There was sudden, deafening silence, followed by a moment of blackness. Then a light invaded Emi's eyes and she realized she was laying down, the technician from the New Phoenix DSMC brain scan center bent over her.

"Dr. Hypatia?" He looked at someone. "She's awake."

A male voice from somewhere else said, "They all are."

Confused, Emi struggled to sit up, wobbled, disoriented, and the technician helped steady her.

"It's okay, Doctor. That feeling will go away in a few minutes as the sedative wears off."

Emi looked around and realized she was dressed exactly as she'd been the day she first went for the interview at the DSMC. "What's going on? Where am I? Where's Aaron? Where's the twins?" She wiped at her face and realized she'd been crying.

"The simulation is over." Dr. Graymard walked into her field of vision. "I'm sorry, Emi, but this was necessary. We can't throw you into space together for five years without seeing how you would handle realistic situations. I apologize for the deception, but the initial simulations are always more accurate if the subjects aren't told about it up front."

"They weren't real?" Part of her was slowly starting to accept that Aaron wouldn't die, but part of her was already grieving for her boys, her new family. Her friends, her lovers.

Her crew.

"Oh, they were real. They were in the simulation with you."

Grief quickly swung over to anger. "They were using me?"

"No!" Graymard quickly said. "They didn't know it was a simulation either. The other two crews you met at first you really did meet—they were all tied in. As you rejected them, they were pulled from the simulation and their experience altered so they thought they really met and were rejected by you. That way, the next time they're scanned they won't know it was a simulation. The next step is real-life training with your crew to ensure compatibility. We can't let subjects know it's a simulation ahead of time or it might invalidate the results. It's okay for training, but for the initial scans it has to be a surprise."

"How long have I been here?" She remembered much of what happened, but it was swirling, starting to lose clarity, like a vivid dream flowing away at dawn.

Dr. Graymard looked at his watch. "Barely two hours. That's why your sense of time in the simulation frequently seemed skewed, as were your senses of taste and smell, and why you rarely felt pain. We obviously had to speed it up to get through as much as possible.

Congratulations, you made it much further than any crew has ever made it. Successfully, I might add. Most of the time we have to stop the simulation earlier."

Emi stood, the strength returning to her legs. She heard familiar voices from across the room and turned to look. Aaron, Caph, and Ford were sitting up in their scanner beds, looking as confused and stunned as she felt.

Unable to help it, she screamed when she saw them. She stumbled over to them and fell into Aaron's arms, sobbing tears of relief as he held her, nearly crushing her in his desperate embrace.

"It's okay, Em," he hoarsely whispered, stroking her hair. "I'm okay, babe."

Caph and Ford also put their arms around them. "Dude, that was rough," Ford said.

Aaron glared at him. "No shit. You're telling me?"

Emi sat back and looked at him, touching him to ensure he was really there and okay. The others, too. "It didn't happen. None of it happened," she said, awe-struck.

Graymard had followed her. "No, but you were all in the simulation together, went through it together. As far as we can tell, you'll be a perfectly matched—"

He couldn't continue, because Emi launched herself at him, screaming, decking him. "You son of a bitch! I thought he was going to die!"

The men pulled her back, Aaron catching her around the waist and dragging her into his lap. "Hey honey, try thinking you were the one gonna die." He turned her to face him and kissed her, and that last little bit of what was missing slammed home. He smelled like oranges and cinnamon and tasted like apple cider.

Sobbing with relief, she pulled him close again as they formed their group hug. Their bodies pressed firmly against her, enveloping her with their warmth.

Graymard laughed and rubbed his jaw. "Well, Emi. Do you want to sign with this crew?"

She looked into Aaron's deep brown eyes and smiled. "Damn fucking straight I do. These are *my* boys."

"That's my girl," Aaron whispered, kissing her again.

"Hey, what about us?" Ford playfully griped.

She turned to him and laughed. "Give me some sugar, baby."

He kissed her, long and sweet, and she felt the familiar thrill run through her. He smelled faintly of cologne, a warm, musky scent she absolutely adored.

"Ahem." Caph smiled, and she fell against him.

"There's my buddy."

"Thought you'd forgot me."

"Never." His kiss was even better in real life, tantalizingly seductive and lighting fires inside her. He had a natural, almost sweet scent, and his kiss reminded her of their afternoon spent alone making love by the small stream.

Something that hadn't happened in real life, but she felt was a part of her memory.

The technician escorted them to a recovery room to fully shake the effects of the sedative they'd been given. Ford pulled her into his lap and wrapped his arms around her.

"Damn, I'm glad you're not an illusion. They woke us up, and after I realized Aaron was okay, for a minute there I wanted to cry when I thought you weren't real."

"Join the club." She looked at her hand, which felt quite bare without the familiar ring on it. "I don't know what I'd do without you guys."

Caph sat on the bed next to them and held her hand. "What would I do without you to keep me in line?"

Aaron stood in front of them, smiling, his color looking better now that he realized he wasn't going to die as an alien's sex toy. "You realize we're just as bad in real life, right?" His smile could melt the coldest heart. She knew she was deeply in love with this man who, technically, she'd only just met. All of them.

Caph and Ford pulled him in close. Emi turned, slipping her arms around Aaron's waist. "You were going to die for us," she whispered, her face pressed against his firm abs.

"I can't lose my crew."

"We can't lose you."

Ford's voice sounded strained. "Jesus, don't you ever scare us like that again, Aar."

Aaron buried his face in her hair. "Well, let's just hope we don't ever have to go through anything like that again."

"You were really gonna die for us," Caph said. "Man, I felt horrible I cheated at that last poker hand..." He stopped. "Well, I can't say last night because we've only been here a couple of hours." He laughed roughly. "Damn. So none of the good stuff happened either, huh?"

Aaron's eyes held Emi's. "No, but we can get started on that as soon as we can get out of this place."

She nodded. "Yeah."

"Ooh," Ford cooed. "I get to pop her cherry ass again."

She blushed and laughed as his hand snuck up her shirt, pulling her tight against his chest.

Aaron stroked her cheek. "You think you might like that? Not many women get to do that twice."

She eagerly nodded. "You'd better believe it, mister."

Caph snickered. "I think it's safe to say captain gets first dibs."

Ford sighed. "Yeah, I can't argue with you there. It's the least we can do."

Chapter Nineteen

Emi still needed a chip in real life. They waited impatiently as they were synced before being given permission to leave.

Laughing, they practically tripped over each other rushing to the dry dock facility where the Tamora Bight was undergoing retrofits. Even though she'd never been there in real life, Emi felt she was home. They left a trail of discarded clothing from the main hatch to the cabin. By the time they all tumbled into bed, she had her arms wrapped around Aaron's neck and pulled him on top of her.

"Permission to come aboard, Captain?" she asked, her voice husky.

"Permission to come wherever the hell you want, baby girl."

He kissed her, and she felt the familiar reaction take her over, only this time in full blinding color with taste and scents and touch. His lips felt hot and moist against her flesh as he worked his way down her body. His deep, rumbling chuckle sent her heart fluttering as he caressed her lower belly with his tongue.

She hooked her arms around Caph and Ford's necks, pulling them to her chest. They were more than happy to oblige. Each man latched on to a nipple, gently suckling them into the hot, moist heat of their mouths. Her content sigh drew a soft groan from all three men.

"That's my boys," she whispered.

Aaron finally settled his lips where she really wanted them, between her legs. As his tongue laved her, the real experience even better than simulation, she threw her head back and moaned.

"That is so. Fucking. Good."

The captain lifted his head for only a moment. "It's about to get a lot better, baby girl. Remember, now we know what you love already."

"Shut up and do it, dammit."

All three men laughed while Aaron returned to his task. When he pushed two thick fingers inside her and added slow, steady strokes, it was more than enough to push her over the edge.

"I love you," she whispered when she could speak again, her eyes boring into Aaron's.

He smiled, and it touched every corner of his face. "I love you too, baby girl. You have no idea."

The twins lifted their heads and at the same time said, "Hey."

Emi laughed. "I love you—" she kissed Caph. "And I love you—" she kissed Ford.

"I love you, too," they parroted.

She laughed again. "Okay, *that* part was always a little freaky. My mismatched twins."

The two men each slipped an arm under her thighs, and as Aaron sat up, they gently spread her legs wide for him. She crooked her finger at Aaron and he was hard and ready as he slipped inside her, both groaning as he sank the full length of his cock deep into her. He was every bit as large as he'd been in the simulation. She suspected tomorrow morning she would be pleasantly sore after her night of fun with all three men.

Emi wrapped her arms around him. "Get busy, Cap. There's a line." He thrust hard, the slick walls of her cunt greedily trying to take him deeper. "Oh, wow!" she breathed.

He held still. "Better than the simulation?" he asked.

"Yeah. You?"

She loved his smile and hoped now she could see it all the time. "Yeah. Oh yeah." He thrust again, and Emi closed her eyes and threw her head back. As good and as real as it felt in the simulator, it couldn't compete with the actual man—men. Every stroke took him to her very depths, and as he picked up the pace she felt his balls gently slap against her ass.

"Don't you dare stop," she gasped.

He slowed down. "I'm going to have to stop sometime," he teased, and when she looked he was still smiling. "You think I'm going to stop before I have a chance to come inside you, baby girl, you're crazy."

"I want all three of you inside me." She looked at the twins, tangling her fingers in their hair, enjoying the way their teeth gently raked against her nipples. "I want my men to fuck me good."

The men groaned as one, and Aaron took a hard, deep stroke. "Damn, baby, you keep talking like that, I'm gonna come right now."

"You'd better, because I want you three to take turns fucking me all night long. I want to wake up tomorrow morning barely able to walk—"

"Oh, man!" Aaron's last, deepest thrust shook all of them. He closed his eyes, breathing hard, his body trembling.

Emi wouldn't let him go and kept her legs wrapped around him. "You okay, Captain?" she teased.

He laughed and kissed her. "I'm better than I've been in a long, long time, sweetheart."

Aaron and Caph traded places. The large man pulled her up from the bed and into his lap. "Hi there, sweetheart." His playful smile melted her the way it had in the simulation.

His thick cock rubbed against her slit, teasing her. "Looks like you're happy to see me, buddy."

Caph lifted her onto his shaft, both of them moaning with pleasure as he buried his cock deep inside her. "That would be a definite yes," he hoarsely whispered in her ear, wrapping his arms tightly around her.

She knew that while it wouldn't happen this time, in real life she'd be able to duplicate her experiences with him. Emi relaxed against him, letting him set the tempo while Aaron and Ford surrounded them. She dropped her head to his broad shoulder, laying a hand against his cheek.

He was so big, outside and in, a heart as large as his body. He nuzzled his face in her hair, whispering her name. She could sit there with him like that all day and hoped that, like in the simulator, she'd get that very chance.

Ford pressed close behind her. She felt his hand slip between their bodies. "Let's get another one out of you, baby girl."

As his skilled fingers stroked her sensitive clit, Caph moaned. "Jesus, she's so tight, that feels so good, Ford."

Emi closed her eyes and relaxed, giving her body to her men. She sensed Aaron move behind Caph, his arms around them both. "Come for us, Emi," he whispered. "Squeeze his cock, baby."

There was no way she could resist them if she tried. Then Caph hit her G-spot at the same time Ford's fingers stroked her perfectly, and she cried out, squirming against the large man's body.

With his hands on her hips he pressed down on her, driving his shaft inside her, coming with her. Ford and Aaron held them as they recovered, kissing them both before Caph gently lowered her to the bed.

She crooked her finger at Ford. "Come here."

He smiled. "I think you need a minute or two to catch your breath, babe."

Emi grabbed him, kissing him hard, driving her tongue into his mouth, and he quit resisting. She turned around and guided his cock into her from behind, enjoying his hungry growl as he sank home balls deep inside her.

A few days ago, she never would have imagined anything like this happening to her. Now she took charge, pulling Ford's arm around her waist and nudging him, getting him to roll over onto his side.

"What are you doing?" he asked, chuckling.

Emi tipped her head back and kissed him. "One more." Stretched out against Ford, she crooked her finger at Caph and he knew what she wanted. He dove between her legs as Ford slowly fucked her, using his tongue on her while Aaron held her leg.

"Jesus," Ford gasped. "That's great!"

Emi closed her eyes again, enjoying the decadent sensation of Caph's talented tongue swirling around her clit and Ford's balls.

"Don't you make me come too fast," Ford scolded, making Caph chuckle.

She reached down and buried her hand in Caph's soft, shaggy hair. "Don't worry, baby. If he does, you can be first in line next time."

Aaron spoke from behind them. "Dammit," he growled, "that is so fucking sexy. How's it feel, baby girl?"

"Amazing."

Ford flexed his hips against her, hitting a different spot inside her at the bottom of his stroke. "You feel so good, Emi."

"I know what would make you feel better," she gasped, trying to hold back her release despite Caph's eager efforts.

"What's that?"

"Having Aaron in your ass."

All three men moaned. Ford squirmed against her. "You really okay with that?"

"Fuck yes! In fact, you three better be ready to give me a damn good show later."

Aaron grabbed the lube. Ford held still while he nudged into position.

She felt Ford's cock twitch inside her, even stiffer than before, if possible.

"Dammit! That's so fucking good," Ford said.

Emi knew they'd have to get out of bed at some point, but she wished she could freeze the moment in time. "All right, boys," she sighed. "Make me scream loud enough the whole dry dock can hear how good you are."

Caph slowed his tongue, switching to light flicks across her clit that made her jump. Ford's hands cupped her breasts, rolling her nipples in his fingers.

"I won't last long," Aaron said.

She pulled Caph's face tight against her. "Do it, baby."

He suckled her swollen nub, gently biting down. She screamed as white-hot sensations exploded inside her.

Ford sucked in a breath. "Fuck, yes!" he said, taking another hard thrust, and she knew he was there.

Aaron followed, and they all lay there breathing heavily, the tangy scent of their passion hanging in the air.

Caph shifted position, kissing her. "Great. Now I'm horny again," he quipped.

"Come here then," she said without opening her eyes, reaching for his shaft.

Ford and Aaron didn't move, too fascinated by the sight of her swallowing Caph's dick. Emi carefully squeezed his sac, making him moan and quickly bringing him off. When his hot juices hit the back of her throat she swallowed every drop, not releasing him until she knew he was done.

He collapsed to the bed next to them. "Wow," he whispered.

Emi snuggled between them. "Give me a few minutes to catch my breath and we can go for round two."

The men laughed. "We're not dreaming this time, right?" Ford asked. "This isn't another sim session, is it? Please tell me it's not."

Emi shifted position and winced, already feeling the effects of having three large cocks fuck her in quick succession. "We're not dreaming this time."

* * * *

They were given two weeks off as vacation before their real group training started. They would have a minimum of six months training, both real-life and simulation, preparing them for their journey. Much of it was remedial for Emi because she retained a lot of the information she received in the initial simulator session.

She had a private talk with Ford and confirmed that while it happened in the sim, the discussion they'd had at the Botanical Gardens was still valid. And that yes, even though it was only a two-hour sim session, Aaron was a much-changed man.

For the better.

While Emi wasn't required to live at the ship, she moved in the next day. The boys went with her to help her pack. When Aaron asked if she wanted her own cabin, she gently smacked his shoulder.

"What, you think I'm crazy?" she asked, grinning.

"I don't know. Maybe. You signed on with us." His playful laugh as he dodged her swats warmed her heart.

They were at Emi's dorm apartment, gathering the last of her belongings, when Daniel showed up. He stopped short when he saw the three men with her.

"Hi, Emilia." He licked his lips nervously. "Can I talk to you for a moment?"

She didn't look up from the box she was packing. "No."

Daniel obviously didn't expect this from her. Until now, she'd usually let him talk to her. "Um, please?"

She crossed her arms. "If you insist, spill it." Even though she knew it'd only been two days since she last saw him, to her it felt like nearly a year. It would take all four of them a little while to reconcile reality with what they went through in the simulator.

Daniel looked at the three men, who now stood protectively behind her, drawn up to their full height, arms crossed, unfriendly glares on their faces. Emi didn't need to look to know Aaron stood closest to her, nearly touching.

"Who are these guys?" Daniel asked.

"That's none of your business. Is that what you came to ask me? You lost all rights to ask me those kinds of questions when you were screwing Trixie or whatever the Hades her name was. I dumped you."

"I want another chance."

"Too late."

"Can we please talk in private?"

She stepped back against Aaron, who put his arm protectively around her waist. "Whatever you want to say to me, Daniel, you say in front of them." Caph and Ford stepped forward, flanking them.

Daniel glared at the other men. "I heard you were applying for the DSMC. Is that true?"

Emi silently swore at Donna. She must have told one of their friends about it. The grapevine made sure it got back to Daniel.

"I've signed on for a five-year mission. This is my captain and my crew."

Daniel eyed them. At just four inches taller than Emi, even Ford, the shortest of the three men, was taller than Daniel and definitely beefier. "So what about us?" Daniel asked.

That was it. She'd had it. "Look, asshole, I dumped you three weeks ago because you cheated on me. Funny how two days later, when I found out I was top of my class, you were crawling back to me. Wouldn't have anything to do with wanting someone to help pay off your fucking student loans because you knew I could get a damn good job, is it?"

He reddened, and she knew she'd hit it on the nose. Daniel was a dump-er, not a dump-ee. He hadn't really expected Emi not to take him back. Her refusal to let him return to her life was now also a personal challenge for him.

"What's happened to you? You've changed. I thought we had something. I want you to marry me. She didn't mean anything to me, I swear."

She bitterly laughed. She'd changed, all right. "Yeah, that makes me feel a *lot* better. Asshole, read my lips—you *cheated* on me, you lying sack of shit. I'd still be with your worthless ass if you hadn't, so you did me a favor." She met Aaron's possessive gaze. "If you hadn't been a jerk, I wouldn't have met these guys." She glared at Daniel. "And you'd better believe they aren't about to cheat on me."

The twins chimed in. "Fucking got *that* right."

Aaron wanted his shot at Daniel. He let go of Emi and stepped forward, nearly six inches taller than Daniel. "We know how to treat a lady right, *kid*. I suggest in the future you learn how to keep your pants zipped." He stepped forward again. Daniel was forced to step back or get stepped on. Daniel finally took the hint and backed out of the doorway.

"You're going to regret this, Emilia. You don't know what you're losing."

"Uh, that would be a lying, cheating, sack of shit ex-boyfriend I'm losing, right? Toodles!" She waggled her fingers at him. Aaron shut the door in his face and the men burst out laughing.

Aaron turned and pulled Emi into his arms. "What an asshole. I guess I should have told him thank you, though."

She put her arms around his neck and felt the twins press close. "*So* not worth the aggravation."

They heard another knock on the door. Emi groaned. "Hades, what now!" Aaron opened the door. Donna stood there, looking confused.

"I just passed Daniel in the hall. Looks like he's pretty pissed." She eyed the three men.

"Yeah, we just threw him out. Come on in." Emi introduced the men.

"Wow." Donna looked at the men, smiling. "Want another crew member?" Donna graduated with a Beta healer ranking, no empath or psych training, but still a very skilled surgeon.

Emi grinned. "Sorry, it's a four-crew ship, and I don't share well. I know there's at least two more ships needing a med officer. One of them were military guys, really built." Donna didn't care about personalities—she liked her guys stacked. She was also slim and trim, a better "physical specimen" than Emi.

"Really?" Donna asked, curious.

"Mm hmm. You should apply. You can always decide not to sign on if you don't like them."

Caph slipped his arms around Emi's waist and kissed the back of her neck. "You ready to go, Emi? Looks like we've got everything."

She patted his arm. "Yep. I have a storage locker we need to clean out, that's not too far away."

Donna couldn't take her eyes off Ford. "Wow. When you told me yesterday morning you were going for an interview, you weren't even sure you wanted to sign on."

Emi shrugged. "A lot happened since then." *Boy, had it!* "I met these guys." She stepped away from Caph and hugged her friend. "I'll see you when we get back. I'll send you notes from the road."

"Stay safe." Donna stepped aside as the men finished loading the transport cart with Emi's things for the final trip to the truck.

An hour later they were back at the ship, stowing her belongings in the storage room she'd staked out for herself near sick bay. Aaron looked inside as they stacked the last load for her.

"You know, it's weird how this is mostly déjà vu," he said.

She grinned. "Tell me about it. No regrets, right?"

He smiled. "No regrets."

Emi snapped her fingers. "Man, almost forgot."

"What?" the twins asked.

"I've got to give you your crew physicals!"

The men laughed. Aaron pulled her to him, his hands sliding down to her ass. He kissed her behind the ear and whispered, "Feel free to give me the same treatment you gave the twins."

She raised her eyebrow, hopeful. "Really?"

His playful smirk melted her. "Really. If I can't trust my ship's med officer, who can I trust?"

Chapter Twenty

Graymard sent Emi a report about their time in the simulation. Crews didn't have to make it all the way through the scenarios to be paired, but where and how they failed determined where extra preparation or even repairing was necessary. The "required" simulation usually ended at the Tay-Dax'n scenario, which many crews failed to complete. But they'd done so well and progressed so quickly, Graymard told the techs to keep them in and see how far they played it out. Not only had they made it further in the simulation than any other crew, they scored the highest in the individual situations. The report included summaries of what each situation was designed to evaluate.

In a confidential aside to Emi, Graymard apologized for the Dry Port scenario and explained they were evaluating the Angor Bay's crew before deciding whether or not to accept them into the DSMC. They would not have been allowed to sexually assault her, even in the simulator—they would have been removed from the simulation before that happened—but what the two men did automatically disqualified them from consideration for service, even though they faced punishment in the simulation to keep it realistic for her and the boys.

The Dry Port was not a normal scenario she would have been placed in, but the unintended benefit was it gave them extra data not only about the men's devotion to her, but her ability to follow command orders and place her trust in her commanding officer despite her personal feelings to the contrary. It was also an unexpected but vital test for Aaron, to see if he could accept and have confidence in a "weaker" crew member he worried about, allowing her the ability to learn and grow and prove herself despite his obvious fears over her welfare.

"We had to gauge his trust and confidence in you and your abilities," Graymard wrote, "as surely as we had to gauge your trust in him and in his."

* * * *

They spent a good chunk of their two weeks off in bed at the hillside resort in New Phoenix. The boys recreated their dream days with her. The only difference was that for the nights alone, they got a second room next door, and they all had breakfast together each morning. Otherwise, they spent every day—and night—together.

They also re-enacted Ford's claiming of her virginity, so to speak. She was nervous at first, but as his gentle fingers massaged her virgin rim and pressed for entrance, she relaxed and enjoyed the strange, new sensation. Aaron and Caph kept her busy and distracted. When Ford pushed his cock past the first resistance, she took a deep breath, and the slight burning as he stretched her soon transformed to pleasure under their hands.

She looked over her shoulder at him and wiggled her ass. "What are you waiting for?" she asked, smiling.

With his hands on her hips he carefully thrust into her, letting her get used to him. So this part wasn't exactly like it'd been in the simulator, but in many ways it was better. She tasted the last remnants of champagne on Aaron's lips, and Caph's breath hinted at the chocolate mousse he'd had for dessert. Their skin felt warm and responsive, their collective musky male scent intoxicating to her senses. The simulation explained why she had always felt like she had a stuffy nose and could barely taste or smell anything. In real life she savored every scent and taste and feel of their bodies, from the salty tang of their juices as she went down on them, to the rough stubble on their cheeks at the end of the day.

Caph's skilled fingers coaxed her toward her climax. This time, she pressed her lips against Aaron's neck and didn't bite down, her body going limp in their arms as Ford quickly followed her. With his arm around her waist, he kissed her shoulder, holding her until she recovered.

"You okay, baby?" he asked, concerned.

They carefully untangled. Emi turned, wrapping her arms around him. "Yeah, real good," she assured him, kissing him. She'd be pleasantly sore tomorrow, as she had been nearly every morning since their real time together started. Just in a different way this time.

It only slammed home the fact that these men were hers and weren't a dream this time—they weren't sim images that could disappear.

They were hers.

And she was theirs.

* * * *

Four days before they were required to report for duty, Emi rolled onto her side and propped herself on one elbow, looking deep into Aaron's eyes.

"How do I get made a permanent part of this crew?"

He smiled, amused. "You already are. We sure as hell aren't getting rid of you." They'd already signed the paperwork making her a bonded partner.

Caph had been dozing at the far end of the bed. "Who's getting rid of someone?"

Ford nudged him with his foot. "Shut up, Sleepy. We're having a moment."

Caph sat up. "What?"

Emi's eyes never wavered from Aaron. "That's not what I mean."

His eyes searched her face. After a long moment, he said, "Are you asking what I think you're asking?"

"I was hoping you'd do the asking."

Caph was wide awake now and quickly grasped the situation. Aaron looked at Caph, who nodded, then Ford, who also nodded. Aaron sat up and held her hands. "Would you do us three jerks the honor of becoming our wife?"

"You're not jerks. And yes, I would love it."

He pulled her into his arms and kissed her deeply as Caph and Ford crowded close.

"Holy crap, we're gettin' married!" Caph crowed.

Ford rolled his eyes. "You're just now getting that?"

"I was asleep. Would have been nice you'd woke me up."

Emi couldn't resist Aaron's deep brown eyes. "Well, if we'd been married in the simulation, the Granz wouldn't have taken any of us."

"Thank the gods there is no such race."

"Yeah, but at least if we ever run across one like that again, maybe we can all get out with our asses intact." She smiled and looked at the other two men. "You okay with making this legally permanent in all ways, boys?"

They nodded.

"Fuckin' A," Ford whispered.

"Damn straight," Caph said.

"Wait a minute," Aaron interrupted. "You're not doing this just because of the simulation, right?"

"Hell no. I want to make sure when we get back from the mission that they can't try some horseshit to separate us. You'll be stuck with me forever."

Ford took her from Aaron and kissed her, lowering her to the bed. "We're not 'stuck' with you, lady. You're the best freaking thing to ever happen to us. As much as I wanted to deck Graymard for putting us through hell in the simulator, once I had time to get my head around it, I had to admit it was a pretty smart thing to do."

Caph stretched out next to them, capturing her lips. "Yeah, and now we don't even have to teach you how to play poker."

She gently poked him in the arm. "You don't get to cheat. No dealing from the bottom of the deck anymore."

"Aw, sweetie, you'll keep me in line, won't you?"

"Better believe it."

* * * *

They showered and dressed and found the same jewelry store they'd visited in the simulator, only this time the three men put their heads together while Emi browsed. The men narrowed the choices down to a few rings they all liked and let her pick. They refused to let her see price tags.

Then she had an idea. "I want to get something else." She mentally calculated the money in her bank account and knew there was more than enough.

"What?" the men asked. Aaron wasn't wincing as much when he joined the twins in their parrot act.

She smiled and led them to another display. "If I'm wearing your ring, y'all are going to wear them too." They picked a set of matching bands, three for the boys, one for her.

Dr. Graymard had the authority to perform the ceremony. Emi invited Donna and a few other friends. The next day, she officially became the men's wife, and their plural marriage was made official.

Emi talked to Graymard alone a few hours later. "You knew I'd sign with them, didn't you?"

He shrugged, carefully concealing his thoughts from her. "I hoped."

"You knew I wouldn't pick the Kendall Kant or the Braynow Gaston. One extreme to the other."

Graymard smiled. "You had a psych minor, and you're an empath. What better choice for those men?" He met her eyes. "They did have nine refusals before you. That part was true. No one stopped to look at the men as individuals, to see who they were. The other candidates were focused on making a choice they could live with. You were more interested in how you could heal them."

"Would you really have pulled them from mission duty if they hadn't found a match?"

"No, but it would have taken time to find someone willing to go out with them basically as a lone person. No one wants to be devoid of partnership that long." He studied her face. "I think it's safe to say you've found a certain amount of healing with them, too."

She couldn't deny that but didn't want to talk about it. Then she felt something from him that surprised her. "How long have you known them?"

"I was one of Aaron's doctors."

Stunned into silence, Emi stared at him.

Graymard continued. "When I was given this assignment a few years ago, I immediately started trying to get Aaron and the twins to sign on with the DSMC. It took a while, but I finally convinced them to join us. When your information request came through and I looked up your background, I knew you'd be a perfect match for them. And them for you."

"You played me?"

"You're complaining?"

She studied him, then shook her head, smiling. "No. I can't complain about this. But you're a sneaky asshole, aren't you?"

"I've been called a lot worse than that, Emi, but I won't apologize for how this worked out."

"So what's next?"

"We put you through real training."

* * * *

Even going through it in the initial sim and the months of training didn't prepare Emi for the real-life emotions and anxiety as the

Tamora Bight slowly crawled out of the dry dock facility on the back of the hover lifts. The men flanked her on the bridge as she watched through the front ports, Aaron's hands lightly resting on her shoulders.

"You all right, sweetie?" he asked.

She nodded. "Yeah. I think it's safe to say I'm better than I've been in years." She looked at him, then at Ford and Caph. A wide, content smile crossed her face. "Boys, let's get the hell off this rock."

THE END

WWW.TYMBERDALTON.COM

Siren's #1 Bestseller
LOVE SLAVE FOR TWO

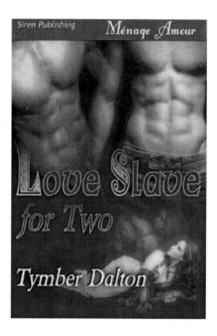

ADULT EXCERPT

Thomas stepped behind her while Tyler took her hands. "You were breathtaking tonight," he whispered. "Truly, absolutely marvelous. Did you have a good time?"

"Yes, Master, I had a good time."

"You don't have to play any longer if you don't wish to."

She squeezed his hands. "But I *do* wish."

"Go ahead, Tom. Take it off."

Thomas touched the collar. She yanked her hands free from Tyler's and clamped them to the back of her neck, preventing Thomas from getting to the buckle. Both men froze.

She finally worked up the nerve. "I promised my masters twenty-four hours of my time. It hasn't been twenty-four hours yet."

Thomas spoke near her ear. "Sweetie, we don't expect you to—"

"Please." She met Tyler's eyes. "You promised you'd take care of my every need tonight," she whispered, struggling not to cry at the thought of sleeping alone. She admitted it. She wasn't strong enough to do this. She needed them, would beg and plead if she had to. Fuck, groveling looked like a damn good option, if necessary. "My masters promised their little slave. You told me to trust you. I trust you both of you."

Tyler's gaze never wavered. He took her hands again. "Nevvie," he whispered, "we have a confession to make."

Confused, she didn't reply.

He continued. "Thomas and I are not gay, love. We're bisexual."

As his words sank in she looked at Thomas. He nodded. "That's right, sugar." One corner of his mouth curled in a playful smile. "As if you couldn't guess."

Tyler spoke, recapturing her eyes as she struggled to absorb this new information. "We have been attracted to you since the first day we met you. We were afraid to tell you for fear of making you uncomfortable."

Dare she hope? "You're not teasing?"

Both men shook their heads.

"You're not gay?"

Again they shook their heads.

She stared into Tyler's eyes then looked at Tom for a long agonizing moment before deciding to step off the cliff, praying they caught her. She put an arm around Tyler's neck, her other hand finding Thomas and pulling him against her back.

The men put their arms around her and she looked into Tyler's eyes. "Will my masters take care of my every need tonight?"

"We promised you anything," Tyler whispered. "We meant it."

Thomas ran his lips along the nape of her neck, making her shiver. He placed his lips to her ear and whispered, "Any need our sweet little slave has."

She closed her eyes. "If I want to say no to anything?"

"Absolutely," Tyler assured her.

"I've never…you know…in my ass. I'm not ready to do that."

Tyler pressed against her, pushing her into Thomas. She felt their hard erections. "We will never force you to do anything, sweetheart. Ever. If we wish to do that, we always have each other."

She wiggled her hips, making the men groan.

She could have both her sweet love gods tonight and they wanted *her!*

This was too good to be true. What was the downside? "What happens in the morning?" she whispered. "After this. What next?"

Tyler stroked her cheek. "We are at your beck and call, love. We will do whatever you want. Perhaps you didn't understand. When we've told you we love you, we meant it the same way you did."

Her heart pounded in her chest. Thomas had worked his way across her shoulders to her other ear and was still nibbling.

Tyler spoke again. "We love you. It broke our hearts when Alex attacked you. We will never hurt you, sweetheart. We want you to be a part of our life in all ways."

Nevvie couldn't catch her breath. "In all ways?"

Tyler nodded. "In *all* ways. We don't mean a night or a weekend. For as long as you'll have us, but it must be both of us." The men froze, and she realized they waited for her to speak.

"Yes. Please."

Every muscle tensed, her skin on fire from the heat of their bodies and Thomas' lips on her flesh. She kissed Tyler and heard his hungry moan, his tongue and hers dancing, exploring. Thomas wrapped his arms around both of them and gently nipped her neck.

Forget throbbing, her sex ached from need and desire. Tyler broke their kiss and slowly worked his way down her body with his lips while Thomas held her against his chest. She closed her eyes as she tipped her head back and Tom's lips found hers, eagerly devouring her with hungry, possessive need.

Tyler removed her sandals, then slid her costume bottom off and caressed her legs. He held her hips and she felt his hot breath against her wet slit. Her knees trembled. If Thomas wasn't holding her, she'd collapse. Then Tyler's tongue, soft and gentle, a light tease from the top of her folds down as far as he could reach.

"Ohhh!" she whimpered, sucking harder on Thomas' tongue, spreading her legs for Tyler.

"Did you like that, little slave?" Tyler whispered.

She made a sound she hoped they knew meant, "*Hell* yes!"

"She's beautiful," Tyler whispered, one finger carefully spreading her. She loudly moaned into Tom's mouth as Tyler's words set her on fire. "You should feel her, Thomas. She's very, very wet."

Thomas broke their kiss. "Why don't you give our little slave a reward right now, Tyler? She was so good tonight. Then she'll be able to focus on what else she wants to do."

"Hmm. That's a good idea." Tyler licked her again. She shivered, every nerve in her body screaming for release. Thomas held her tightly as Tyler set to work, running his tongue up and down her clit to her pussy, where he slowly worked two fingers into her.

No longer capable of coherent speech, Nevvie threw her head back against Tom's shoulder, closed her eyes, and moaned. Tyler's lips and tongue scorched her, branding her as theirs. She gave in to the pleasure, desperately in need of release.

Nothing had ever felt this good, this right. Tyler drew tight circles with his tongue around her clit, then gently wrapped his lips around it, lightly sucking. As her climax rocked her she screamed, grabbing his hair and grinding her hips in time with his motions as he kept her coming and coming for what felt like hours.

When her knees finally failed her, Thomas scooped her into his arms. Tyler stood and leaned in, kissing Thomas.

Thomas moaned. "Damn, she tastes good!"

Tyler licked his lips and touched his lover's cheek. "You'll get your turn soon enough." He unsnapped the leash. "Do you want your collar off or on, sweetheart?"

"On."

She was recovering from the sensation, her body covered by a fine sheen of moisture as Thomas gently laid her on their bed. Tyler kissed her. She wrapped her arms around his neck, throwing a leg around him.

He laughed. "Did you like that, my sweet little slave?"

"Yes, Master."

Thomas stretched out on her other side and slid his hand under her top, gently massaging her breast. "I think our little slave should get completely naked."

Tyler helped remove her top. The men gasped, each bending to take a breast in their mouth, running their tongues around her nipples and drawing soft mewing sounds from her. She put an arm around each head, clasping them to her, tangling her fingers in their hair, praying this wasn't a dream. Or if it *was* a dream that she never woke up. Their mouths on her soon had her pussy aching again, throbbing, begging for relief.

Both men were still dressed. Thomas lifted his head from her left breast. "I want to taste you next, little slave."

All she could do was nod. Tyler took her left breast in his hand, gently rolling her nipple between his fingers while still suckling her right. Thomas kissed down her belly and shifted position to lay between her legs, driving his tongue into her throbbing sex, fucking her with it.

She arched her back and spread her legs wider, giving him full access. This couldn't be happening! Then he slipped two fingers into her and nibbled on her clit, and as she felt the build-up to her next climax she sobbed with need. His touch was different than Tyler's, and still so hot and perfect it wasn't long before she cried out as the next wave hit, leaving her shaking and trembling on the bed.

Tyler took her into his arms and kissed her as she gasped for air. "Did our little slave like that?"

She nodded.

"Would our little slave like us to fuck her?"

"Yes!"

Then Tyler bent to her ear and softly whispered, "Have you been taking the Pill?"

She nodded.

He nuzzled her ear, his voice low. "Tom and I haven't been with anyone else since we've been together. We're clean, but if you wish, we will use condoms."

He wouldn't lie to her. "No." If there was no risk she wanted to feel her men, wanted them to totally possess her.

"Very good, sweetheart." He cradled her against his chest. She reached behind her and wrapped her arms around his neck, kissing him. Thomas sat up and looked at Tyler.

"Go ahead, Thomas. I think we have a very ready slave who's dying to feel us inside her."

Thomas stood and slowly unbuttoned his shirt. "Sugar, I'm going to enjoy this so much," he whispered. She shivered in Tyler's arms as he held her.

"Our Thomas has a wonderful cock," Tyler murmured in her ear. "Believe me, love, he knows how to use it. I can't wait for you to feel it."

She'd seen Thomas bare-chested plenty of times, but knowing his bare chest was about to be pressed against her bare chest intensified her aching need. Lean muscles rippled as he dropped his shirt to the floor. Sparse, curly hair dusted his chest and a thin line of dark hair started under his navel and disappeared beneath his waistband. How many times had she fantasized what he looked like down there?

Thomas opened his pants and as he slid them down, his hard cock sprang free. She moaned. Christ, he was beautiful!

He spread her thighs, kneeling between them, rubbing his swollen head between her legs from her clit to her ready entrance and back. "Do you want to feel me inside you?"

She nodded, clinging to Tyler. "Yes, Master, I want to feel you inside me."

He placed his large head against her and leaned forward, his hands on the bed on either side of her.

Tyler nibbled on her neck. "Do you want him to fuck you, sweetheart?"

"Please fuck me, Master!"

He pushed in a little, and both groaned. "Jesus, Nevvie, you're so tight! God Tyler, she's wet and she's so tight, damn!" He slid a little further, not wanting to hurt her, taking his time. Thomas kissed Tyler, then her, sliding in more. "Damn, she's so hot, Ty."

"Fuck her well, Thomas," Tyler said, slipping a hand between her legs, his fingers playing with her clit. "She's been very good tonight."

"Do that again, Ty. Her whole pussy throbbed when you did that."

Tyler kissed her neck while he stroked her clit. "Do you like that?"

"Uh huh!" She didn't care what they did to her. Between Tyler's mouth and hands and her extremely full pussy, she was beyond reason. She'd never been with someone as large as Thomas before, and he stretched her in an incredibly erotic way.

Thomas gave one last, gentle thrust. "Jesus, I'm all the way in. I won't last long, not as tight as she is. See if you can make her come again, Ty." He gently massaged her breasts, rolling her rock-hard nipples in his fingers as Tyler kissed and licked her neck and played with her clit.

"Come for me Nev," Tyler whispered in her ear. "Come for me, my sweet, beautiful angel. Show us what we do to you."

She cried out, sobbing, arching against Tyler, her fingers digging into the back of his neck. Thomas started thrusting, trying to come with her. She was beyond trying to thrust back, unable to do little more than lay there and enjoy it.

He gave a final, hard, deep stroke. "Oh, God, baby!"

He fell forward, throbbing inside her, collapsing on her with his head between her breasts. She wrapped her arms and legs around him. Nevvie kissed Tyler, deeply, longingly. Even overwhelmed she knew she wanted him inside her, too.

Soon.

Panting, Thomas kissed her between her breasts and pushed up. "I didn't hurt you, did I?"

She broke her kiss with Tyler and smiled. "No, you didn't hurt me, Master."

"Oh, baby girl, you are amazing!" Thomas pulled her to him, hugging her. "We love you, Nevvie. Really and truly."

"I love both of you, too," she said.

Tyler nibbled the back of her neck, tracing her spine down to her hips with his tongue, making her shiver.

Thomas whispered in her ear, "I think it's time Master Tyler gets to sample you, darlin'."

Love Slave for Two
is available at
www.sirenpublishing.com/tymberdalton

ABOUT THE AUTHOR

Tymber Dalton lives in southwest Florida with her husband (aka "The World's Best Husband™") and son. She loves her family, writing, coffee, dark chocolate, music, a good book, hockey, and her dogs (even when they try to drink her coffee and steal her chocolate).

When she's not dodging hurricanes or writing she can be found doing line edits or reading or thinking up something else to write. She's a multi-published writer in several genres and loves to hear from readers. Please feel free to drop by her website to keep abreast of the latest news, views, snarkage, and releases.

Please visit Tymber at
www.tymberdalton.com
myspace.com/tymberdalton

Siren Publishing, Inc.
www.SirenPublishing.com